To Arno Olsen
Very valued friend
With Best Wi
Bert L

MW01235116

A Matter of Precedents

Berl Falbaum

Proctor Publications

Proctor Publications
P.O. Box 2498
Ann Arbor, MI 48106
(800) 343–3034

Publisher's Cataloging in Publication
(Provided by Quality Books, Inc.)

Falbaum, Berl, 1938–
A matter of precedents / Berl Falbaum. -- 1st ed.
p. cm.
Preassigned LCCN: 98-65519
ISBN: 1-882792-65-3

1. Employers' liability--Fiction. 2. Asbestos--Carcinogenicity--Fiction.
3. Industrial hygiene--Fiction.
I. Title.

PS3556.A42M38 1998 813'.54
QBI98-450

ALSO BY BERL FALBAUM

Just For Fun
The Anchor, Leo & Friends
The Definitive Guide to Organizational Backstabbing

ACKNOWLEDGMENTS

I have been blessed with a loving family, loyal and supportive friends and relationships with exceptionally talented professionals, all of whom helped me with this project.

• Detroit area attorneys Don Loria and Margaret Holman provided valuable advice and did so very generously.

• Maurice Kelman, a retired Wayne State University law professor and an acknowledged expert on constitutional law, has not only given me his friendship over many years but provided me with his clear thinking and keen editing on this manuscript.

• Jack Koblin, a retired attorney, took the time to help and I am grateful for his contributions and for the development of our recent friendship.

• Javan Kienzle, whose husband, Bill, has left his mark on the literary world with his mystery novels, took time off from editing her husband's work to give me the benefit of her immense talents.

• Michael B. Serling, an attorney who has dedicated his professional life to assisting workers who, as a result of industrial negligence, contracted cancer after exposure to asbestos (the subject which is the basis for this novel), was more than generous with his time and expertise. He provided vital public records and pointed me to important sources. Similarly, his associate, Eric Abramson, a recent graduate from the Detroit College of Law, was extremely helpful in assisting me with research that answered many of my technical, legal and medical questions.

• Ann BeVier, a copyreader whose skills and talent should be available to every writer, gave me immeasurable assistance with her editing. I am also grateful because she and her husband, Bill, joined our family when her son, Peter, married my daughter, Julie. I hope to take advantage of her professionalism more often.

• Frank Martin, a longtime and valued friend who served Detroit area newspapers for almost four decades as an uncompromising perfectionist, provided invaluable insights as well as perceptive – and admittedly, at times – painful critiques.

• A special word to Bill Haney, a Renaissance man, who has given me the benefit of his incisive thinking for more than two decades. He assisted me in publishing my first two books and I could not have completed those projects or this attempt at fiction without his help.

• Kyle Scott, of the publishing firm, Momentum Books, was never too busy to lend good counsel and make vital recommendations for improvements.

• Dr. John M. Malone, Jr., vice president of academic affairs at the Detroit Medical Center, an oncologist, was very kind in explaining and simplifying the complexities of the rare asbestos-related cancer, mesothelioma.

• A special thanks to a Detroit area woman who shared with me the painful story of her husband who died of mesothelioma. With tremendous courage, she explained the horrendous ordeal and helped me understand how this disease ravages the body as well as the toll it takes on families. I would like to thank her by name publicly but, even more, I want to respect her request for privacy.

• I want to express my appreciation to the principals at Proctor Publications whose recommendations throughout the editing process were more than insightful. Hazel Proctor, Don Proctor and Sarah Newland, patient and understanding of the idiosyncracies of this writer, were always helpful and I am delighted that I had the benefit of their strategic advice.

Then there is my wife, Phyllis, a teacher's teacher who has made immeasurable contributions to the fourth-grade children in her classroom. She has given them once-in-a-lifetime learning experiences and many continually stay in touch with her years later, recognizing the unique experience they had enjoyed.

I have recognized my good fortune as well. She is one of the best editors who ever gave me feedback. And she left her mark on this work as well. But, of course, there is more and, frankly, I don't know how to express my admiration and respect for her. I have marveled, for four decades, at her uncanny psychological makeup. She always knows just what to say, what to do, no matter how tense the circumstances or even if she is suffering with problems of her own. She has a unique gift and it was given to me.

As to errors and other weaknesses in this book, I am tempted to point the finger at my counselors. Suffice it to say that the blame for mistakes and other shortcomings in this novel are no one's fault but mine.

–b.f.

For my wife, Phyllis,
and daughters, Julie and Amy,
who have endured my foibles and given more love
than a man could ask for.

And for my extended family which has been a constant source of support:
My mother-in-law, Yetta Zager; my brothers-in-law and sisters-in-law,
Paul and Elaine Goldsmith and Dr. Bernard and Debbie Zager.
My gratitude to them for taking me into their lives.

A Matter
of Precedents

ONE

"Paul, you can get dressed now."

"Thanks, Doc."

"When you're ready," said Dr. Julius Sobel, "come to my office and we'll talk. And bring Angie in from the waiting room."

Paul Ferguson slipped off of the examination table, took his clothes from the hook behind the door and dressed. Never comfortable with the dynamics of a medical environment, he felt very ill at ease. He never liked physical examinations or the entire dynamics of a medical facility and their implications. In hospitals, when visiting sick relatives or friends, he would fulfill his obligations and, desperately trying not to be rude, leave as quickly as he could. He would stay at the bedside for only a few minutes and then wait in the hall for his friends.

He agreed to see his doctor only because of Angie, his wife of 35 years, a warm, caring woman. When he complained continually about a shortness of breath for several months, she started nagging him to see Sobel. A few weeks before making an appointment, he suddenly found himself unable to breathe while watching television at home. His wife called 911 and he was rushed to emergency at the local hospital. He was diagnosed with pneumonia and given antibiotics. He improved in the following weeks, but still suffered from breathing problems. He finally agreed to make a doctor's appointment, giving in to his wife's demands not so much to please her, but because he started to worry as well. Of course, Ferguson did not reveal his own anxiety to her although, as a smoker for many years, he was aware of its dangers. However, it was a habit that he was never able to break. But then, he had never really tried.

He felt better now – now that his examination was over. Despite his own worries, he told himself repeatedly that his breathing problems were probably caused by some kind of flu virus. After all, Sobel did not seem worried.

But Sobel was concerned. Ferguson did not notice the hesitancy in Sobel's voice when he told him to get dressed. Nor did he reflect on the implications of the doctor sending him to undergo a needle biopsy or the admonition that "we'll talk." Neither did he wonder why Sobel had asked him to return to the office but with his wife.

Ferguson finished dressing, opened the door to his room and headed for the doctor's office. He knocked on Sobel's office door, which was open, and waited to be invited in.

"Paul, come on in."

Ferguson sat on a small couch in the office.

"Man, am I glad that's over," Ferguson said. "You sure poked in more holes than I thought I had. No offense, Doc. Sorry, didn't mean to take up your time. Let me tell you, I didn't like them pushing that needle in my chest. So, what's the scoop?"

"Is Angie here?"

"She wanted to come with me but I told her to stay home," Ferguson replied. "I said this was no big deal. Had to fight her a little bit but I told her I could handle this."

Sobel did not like the fact that Ferguson had won the dispute with his wife. He had hoped that Angie Ferguson would accompany her husband. Given her absence, Sobel was revamping his strategy on how to break the news to Ferguson.

Ferguson waited, still not recognizing the gravity of the situation, until he impatiently asked Sobel, "So, come on, Doc, give me the bottom line."

Sobel, seeing no alternative, began.

"Paul, this is never easy. It's especially difficult because I've been your doctor for years. I've cared for Angie and the children."

"What is it, Doc?" Ferguson inquired, finally beginning to understand that what was coming might be serious.

"Paul," Sobel said, trying to display as much sympathy as possible, "you have mesothelioma."

Ferguson, almost stuttering, asked, "I have what? What's that?"

Sobel used the medical name for the disease to buy time, as an ice breaker. He realized that Ferguson might not comprehend medical terminology.

"Paul," he said. "Paul, in simple terms, you have lung cancer."

Sobel looked down at his desk. He tapped on a writing pad. He looked at Ferguson, then turned away.

Ferguson, at first, stared at Sobel. Then he looked at the ceiling. He turned his head from side to side. He coughed into his cupped hand.

"The big C?" he finally asked.

"Yes, Paul, you have lung cancer. Specifically, as I said, mesothelioma, which is caused by exposure to asbestos."

Ferguson was visibly puzzled. He furrowed his brow, indicating confusion.

Sobel, recognizing Ferguson's bewilderment, explained.

"Paul, for many years, you inhaled small asbestos fibers into your lungs and these little fibers have caused this cancer."

Ferguson, with little beads of sweat appearing on his forehead, listened with increasing agitation.

"The process of causing cancer takes years, but there's little doubt about what has happened to you and others at the plant."

Ferguson, his heartbeat increasing, said, "I'm not very good at these things. I'm not sure I understand. But what difference does it make."

Then he added that perhaps the disease "got worse since I didn't have it checked out when I first started feeling bad and kept coughing. Angie kept pushing me but I didn't listen."

Sobel did not want to make Ferguson feel guilty, thus he reassured him, "I doubt that, Paul. Don't think about that now."

The doctor added, "The symptoms from the cancer are shortness of breath and some pain in your chest. I assume you've had both."

"Yeah, but it wasn't so bad."

Sobel was reluctant to continue the conversation. He knew Ferguson's limitations; that's why he had asked Angie Ferguson to join her husband. He tried to make Ferguson feel better. "Paul, this is very complex. So don't worry about the scientific explanation now. At another time, I'll explain the disease to you and Angie. I also have a lot of literature on the subject."

"Yeah, I need to know more about this thing. But what I want to know is what happens next? Do I have an operation? You know what I mean?"

Sobel ran his hand through his hair.

"Paul, I'm not sure what we can do in your case. I..."

"What do you mean?" Ferguson asked.

"You remember the X rays I took the last time you were here? About a month ago? They showed some very suspicious spots on your lung and that's why I sent you for the needle biopsy. Unfortunately, the specialists and I are in agreement. The pathology reports are very clear. Of course, you can – and should – get another opinion."

"Doc, I still don't know what you're saying," he said. "I'm not gonna die, am I? I'm not gonna die. That's right, isn't it?" he asked with a nervous laugh.

"Paul," said Sobel, as he worked up his own courage. "Our best estimate is that you have six months to a year."

"Six months to a year to what? To live?"

Sobel simply nodded slowly but deliberately.

The words echoed in Ferguson's head. He impulsively reached for his cigarettes in his shirt pocket. He lit a cigarette, took a puff, then recognized the tragic irony of his smoking at this time. He looked for an ashtray. There was none, but Sobel, noticing Ferguson's discomfort, quickly told him it was all right to smoke.

"So I am gonna die, right? Six months to a year. You're sure?"

"As I said Paul, you might consult with another doctor. That would be a good idea."

"But you said you already asked the others, the specialists."

"Yes, and I think, unfortunately, that the conclusion is correct. These doctors are experts and they know much more about this issue than I do."

Ferguson took a puff of his cigarette, unconsciously flipping ashes on the floor. Without being aware of his actions, he stood up and paced quickly around the office.

He suddenly stopped and faced Sobel, almost demanding, "What now?"

Sobel tried to comfort Ferguson. "This is not the best time to discuss that, Paul. Go home. Talk to Angie. Take a few days and we'll talk again. You need to process this."

"What's to process?" Ferguson asked rhetorically. But after a few seconds, he added, "Yeah, I guess you're right. Tell me, Doc, why me? How did I get this? Why me? I never hurt no one."

Sobel shrugged his shoulders.

"I can't answer that, Paul. It's a question many people ask me. But the cause, I believe, is simple to explain. You had a period of extensive exposure to asbestos at Thompson Brakes. Smoking did not help, although it's not the cause in this case. I've treated others from your plant who contracted mesothelioma or other cancers from breathing in asbestos. It's obvious to me and to the other doctors I consulted that the company, over the years, was remiss in not providing air filtering and overall health protection against the dangers of asbestos. But, as I said, this isn't the time. Come back with Angie and we'll talk some more. Paul, leave your car here. I'll take you home. I'm leaving soon and we could talk in the car. You can pick it up later."

Sobel knew that Ferguson might not be able to digest the implications of everything he was telling him. A little time in the car with him might comfort Ferguson and give him an opportunity to ask questions. Sobel would wait for Angie before offering a more detailed explanation.

"No, thanks. It's okay. I think I'd like to drive by myself."

Ferguson got up and walked out of the office. Then he turned and, instinctively, said, "Thanks."

Yeah, Doc, he thought, thanks, thanks a lot.

TWO

In Sobel's parking lot, Ferguson sat quietly behind the steering wheel of his car for several minutes. His mind filled with questions. Will I suffer? How much pain will I have? How much can I take? How long will I be able to work? God, what will happen to Angie? Will she marry again? If so, how long after I'm gone?

Then he turned to financial questions. What does the union contract provide? Do I have life insurance? Wait a minute. I don't have any. I didn't sign up. Shit, they warned me about that. He had many questions but no answers. He was angry with himself for his shortsightedness.

He lit a cigarette and then angrily tossed it along with the entire pack out the window. Then, just as impulsively, he recognized the futility of his action. Too late for that, he thought. He got out of his car, picked up the cigarettes and lit another one.

As he started the car to drive home, tears welled up in his eyes, but he worked to suppress them. He always considered crying a sign of weakness and even the big C was not going to defeat his masculinity.

He began to reminisce about his life. It had been okay. Nothing special, but also no big tragedies – until now. He grew up in a lower-income family. His father, an assembly line foreman, and his mother, raised his two brothers and him.

All the children had graduated from high school but none attended college. He went to work as a maintenance man for Thompson Brakes immediately after his graduation from high school. He helped clean up the plant, mostly mopping the floors of dirt and asbestos dust created in the manufacture of brakes.

He spent almost 30 years on the floor of the plant in different jobs sweeping, cleaning machinery, painting and even, at times, helping the mechanics repair parts. He liked that because it required more skill and gave him a sense of pride.

Through the years, he received a number of promotions but never moved into a management position. Now, at 64 and after a total of 46 years with the company, he had a desk job, checking delivery invoices.

As he thought about the many issues he would need to confront, he concluded he could and would continue to work at his desk job until... But maybe he should just quit and go on a vacation with Angie.

A last fling, he thought. No, better save the money for her. She'll need it.

Suddenly, he realized he had driven past his usual turn. He looked around and spotted a bar. He parked his car, walked in and sat on a stool at the end of the bar, purposely avoiding several other customers. He was not in the mood to make small talk about sports or politics.

"Give me a shot and a beer," he told the bartender.

He had not had a boilermaker in years. But today...

He lit another cigarette and stared at the smoke as he held the cigarette before his eyes. He followed the smoke as it rose to the ceiling.

Six months to a year, he thought. Could be he's wrong. They've been wrong before. Maybe the reports got mixed up. Could happen. It's happened before.

Maybe he should give Sobel a call to recheck the records. He started toward the phone to call his doctor but stopped.

Quit kidding yourself, he thought. He said he checked and double checked with two other guys. He's been good to us all these years. Nice guy, didn't charge us too much. At times, he looked at the kids for nothing, especially when I was laid off. He would've said if he wasn't sure. It's cancer all right.

He rubbed his chest as if to massage the cancer. Funny, it doesn't hurt a lot. Thought it was a muscle. Doc's right. Lot to talk about later.

He saw the bartender looking at him. "One more time."

Halfway through his second beer, the others came into his consciousness: Joe Smiley, George Warshawski, Tom Saunders and Bob Preston. He thought of a few more whose names he could not recall but who also died of cancer. He had gone to the funerals but he never remembered hearing the word *mesothelioma.*

He did remember talk at union meetings. There were those who insisted Thompson Brakes was at fault. He did not understand the issues or the arguments and never participated in the discussions. He wondered whether the others died of the same illness. Most of them smoked.

Hell, just about everyone smokes in the plant, he thought.

He sat there a long time, staring at his drink and the ashtray spilling over with cigarette butts and ashes. Perhaps he should visit their families and get some information. Would that be the right thing to do? Angie would know. Yes, Angie would guide him through this. She always seemed to know what to do.

He stared at himself in the mirror behind the bar, trying to digest and process the devastating diagnosis he had just received. Your life sure has changed in the last hour, he told his reflection. What the hell do you do now? You strong enough to handle this? Guess you have no choice.

He finally looked away and picked up a discarded newspaper on the vacant stool beside him. He never read the paper, not even the sports section, but he picked it up and scanned the pages absentmindedly, not really digesting what he was reading. He stopped turning the pages abruptly when a headline in the obituary section caught his eye. "Michael Callahan, community leader in Irish community, dies at 57." He read the first few paragraphs, looked back into the mirror and wondered, What will they write about you, if anything? What will they say at the funeral? You really haven't done anything. Worked at Thompson Brakes. That's probably it.

His thoughts were interrupted by a burly man in his 30s who tapped him on the shoulder. "Want to shoot a game of eight ball?"

"No, thanks," Ferguson answered. "No, not now."

"Come on, one game."

Ferguson started to refuse again but changed his mind, thinking the game might take his mind off his troubles.

"Okay, one game."

The younger man put two quarters in the pool table's coin slot and racked the balls. "You break."

Ferguson chalked up the cue stick, took aim, but as he shot, the stick glanced off the cue ball, which barely broke the rack.

"Hit the damn thing. You ain't gonna beat me like that."

Ferguson's pool partner broke the balls, sinking a couple. He then sunk one more before missing.

Trying hard to think about the game but periodically reflecting on Sobel's diagnosis, Ferguson missed the next shot completely.

He threw the stick on the table. "Some other time. Sorry, I'm not up to it."

"Five bucks," his pool partner said.

"What?"

"House rules. We play for five bucks. You owe me."

"Another time," Ferguson said, trying to walk away from the man.

"I said you owe me five bucks, old man." He grabbed Ferguson by the shirt.

Ferguson's lower chin trembled, not out of fear of a beating but from the pressure of all he had experienced that day. As he looked into the man's eyes, he relented, reaching into his back pocket and taking out his wallet as the man released him. He gave the man five singles without saying a word.

"If you come back here, don't fuck with me again," the man warned. "I'll break you in two. Rules are rules."

Ignoring the man, Ferguson realized it was time. It was time to go. It was time to tell Angie.

He ordered a final boilermaker, drank the whiskey, washed it down quickly with the beer and walked out of the bar. He got into his car, started the motor and began to drive.

At a red light, his mind drifted again. How would he tell her? Should he have Sobel do it? No, that would not be right. I'm her husband.

The light had turned green but he did not notice. The driver of the car behind him honked. Ferguson turned around just in time to see the car swerve around him and, as it passed, the driver gave him the finger and sped away. Ferguson reacted by shouting profanities, but as quickly as he had turned to anger, he eased the pressure on himself, relaxing, and with a sardonic smile on his face, he thought, I have bigger problems.

THREE

Reluctantly, Angie Ferguson had given in to her husband's wish not to accompany him to Sobel's office. She recognized that he could not be persuaded to change his mind and she did not pursue the argument.

Waiting alone in the house for her husband's report, she tried desperately to make the time pass. She was terribly worried as her mind drifted to a review of her life with her husband. Still attractive as she approached 60, she had no complaints about her marriage to Paul Ferguson. Of course, they had their fights, but overall, Paul Ferguson was a good man. He provided for her and their two children. They took annual vacations – nothing fancy – usually to places like Cedar Point and Disney World. Since the kids left the Ferguson home, Angie and her husband would often rent a cottage and sit on the beach for a week.

Angie was brighter than her husband and long ago came to grips with the fact that she would lead a simple life, with few luxuries or money for any little extras. But she recognized that while Ferguson was a man of less than average intelligence – a man who loved his sports and beer – he was a good, kind man. He loved her in his own way; he never told her, but she knew.

She had pestered her husband to see Sobel for several reasons. She did not like the sound of his cough. He complained of a pulled muscle in his chest and she noticed that he would try to catch his breath even when he did not exert himself very much. But more importantly, several of Ferguson's colleagues at the plant had died of cancer and she remembered that they had experienced similar symptoms before their deaths.

Angie considered that either her husband never recognized the similarities or purposely ignored them. Whatever the reason, after the emergency incident in their home, she demanded he visit Sobel.

Angie, who had a college degree, also had seen references in newspapers to the relationship between smoking and exposure to asbestos which, experts quoted in the papers said, caused cancer. She never discussed this with Ferguson, knowing it would be useless. He would belittle the experts, saying there was no proof. He would add he couldn't quit smoking and he certainly would not quit his job. Thus, she avoided an argument she knew would lead nowhere. But she worried and, from time to time, she would stare at her husband as if she were giving him a medical examination.

The sound of the car on the driveway interrupted her thoughts at the kitchen sink. After drying her hands with a towel, she walked to the front door. She took a deep breath, opened the door and prepared to meet her husband with the smile that had welcomed him home for more than three decades.

"Hi, how's it going?" she asked.

She noticed that he had his head down as he walked toward the house. He ignored her greeting and avoided eye contact.

"I said," she repeated teasingly, "how's it going?" She tried to ease what was an awkward moment.

"Hi," he said in almost a whisper, kissing her on the cheek, which she recognized as totally out of character since he seldom, if ever, displayed affection. She knew immediately.

"So, what did Dr. Sobel say?"

He sat on the couch, rubbing his chest and wringing his hands.

"He said…"

She watched him closely and lovingly as he looked around the room. "He said…," he tried again.

Angie Ferguson waited patiently as she began to tremble a little bit. She suppressed the tears welling up in her eyes as he had done in the doctor's office earlier.

They both sat in silence for a few seconds. It was a terribly long silence.

"He said...he said I have...I have...cancer."

A hot flash shot through her body. She turned pale and felt momentarily faint. She was stunned but not surprised. She had hoped against hope and, although she had tried to prepare herself, the news struck her as if she had had no suspicions.

Finally, she asked, "Mesothelioma?"

He did not hear her question. Nor did he hear her use the medical term or ask how she knew the name of the illness.

As he finished the word *cancer*, he broke down in uncontrollable sobbing.

First, she just touched him softly on the shoulder, gently patting him. He had never cried before, at least not in front of her.

She took him in her arms. At other times, she knew he would have rejected this comforting. He would not consider it manly. But now, as she offered him her deepest compassion, he collapsed in her arms. He did not protest.

"It will be all right, Paul," she lied. "It will be all right."

She held him close and, as he cried unashamedly, she did not hear him mumble into her bosom, "Six months."

FOUR

While Angie Ferguson was trying to console her husband and working desperately to control her emotions, George C.L. Simmons, Jr. presided over a meeting to discuss his annual address to employees at corporate headquarters in Detroit. The occasion would be a major one for Simmons, the chairman and chief executive officer of Thompson Brakes, Inc., one of the nation's leading manufacturers of brakes. He was determined to make the most of this meeting with employees. For the first time, the speech, always a major event at Thompson Brakes, would be carried live via satellite to the corporation's divisions throughout the U.S.

Simmons was joined at the meeting by his chief financial officer, Robert Jameson; his legal counsel, Alfred Hawthorne; the vice president of human resources, Judy Robertson; and his speechwriter and media spokesman, Tim Kaufman, vice president for corporate communications.

"Tim," said Simmons, "I want this speech to be a barn-burner. I want it to be upbeat, warm, compassionate. When I'm done, I want all of our employees to feel proud that they work at Thompson Brakes. You get the picture?"

"Yes, sure," said Kaufman, who dreaded these sessions which, as far as he was concerned, were always the same. He had heard these instructions at every meeting since he began writing speeches for Simmons five years earlier. Never a new idea, thought or concept, whether the speech was for employees or other audiences.

Simmons, 63, was not a very intelligent man. He had worked at

Thompson Brakes in various executive capacities for 33 years. A little luck along with some politics took him to the top job. But he had few outstanding management skills.

The CEO was absolutely incapable of thinking on his feet. Indeed, he even carried in his wallet prepared statements on sensitive subjects written by company attorneys should he be approached by news reporters about these issues. For instance, one on how to respond to rumors involving Thompson Brakes, read: "We, at Thompson Brakes, do not – we never have – comment on rumors. We don't believe it is in the interests of anyone to do so. Thank you very much." Simmons would have difficulty commenting without a statement in his pocket.

He also was not a particularly good manager. His financial advisors misled him frequently and he did not have the ability to analyze their reports or uncover misrepresentations. Similarly, his other executives took advantage of his lack of sophistication.

Thus, over the years, the company performed marginally. Thompson Brakes was profitable in some years, lost money in many. It never enjoyed any consistency in its performance.

Thompson Brakes' investment community, although not rebellious, was overall unhappy with the financial results. But Simmons had managed to pacify them with messages of hope.

Simmons had worked hard at being admitted to the country's special corporate "in" group – those elite executives in America who, by virtue of their power and personality, captured major attention – in corporate America. These CEOs would meet periodically to discuss business issues and were the ones approached by the media for their predictions on future economic trends and major political events.

But Simmons' CEO colleagues recognized his shallowness and did not admit him to their inner circle. The refusal to welcome him into the power base of corporate America frustrated Simmons and contributed to his inferiority complex, which he tried to overcome with a dictatorial approach to management.

When Simmons briefed Kaufman on the proposed content of the company's annual report and other financial communications, he would give

Kaufman material collected from documents of other companies, telling his writer to simply plagiarize these thoughts. Incapable of intellectual creativity, he was not remiss in stealing ideas from others and he even naively thought that he might get credit for ingenuity.

"Nothing wrong with plagiarism," Simmons would instruct Kaufman. "No need to reinvent the wheel."

Whether the purloined thoughts were relevant to Thompson Brakes seemed to make no difference.

"Look at this, Tim," Simmons would say. "It's really well-stated."

Recognizing the futility of explaining the dishonesty involved, Kaufman did not protest these instructions. He would take the material but rewrite the language, trying hard to make it relevant to Thompson Brakes. Kaufman, a former newspaperman, had almost become contemptuous of Simmons because he lacked any ethical or moral foundation. But he also felt a little sorry for him given his intellectual shallowness.

Simmons' instructions to Kaufman when he assigned him to prepare a speech were even more bizarre. He would give Kaufman material from various speeches he collected, circling the ideas he wanted to steal.

"You know," Kaufman told his colleagues in the PR department, "it doesn't matter whether the material represents the philosophy of Karl Marx or Ronald Reagan. The man has no philosophical base."

But as with the material for financial communications, Kaufman did not fight Simmons' directions. He did the best he could under the circumstances, working with what he was given. He tried hard to have the speech read smoothly and inserted some originality.

"I want them cheering in the aisles," said Simmons, who always assigned Kaufman to plant clackers in the audience when he delivered his speeches. Having seen the President of the United States interrupted by applause in messages to Congress, Simmons wanted similar recognition. He would have Kaufman anoint 10 to 15 clackers, who applauded almost every sentence, sometimes to the point of embarrassment.

Simmons constantly needed reinforcement and reassurance. He once accumulated costs of $30,000 on a photograph of himself that accompanied the letter to shareholders when he delayed the printing of the annual report at the very last minute. Just before the report was to go to press, Simmons decided he did not like his picture in the report. He held up the press run while he flew to New York to sit for a new portrait in the most expensive photo studio in the city. Then the film had to be flown to the printer on the West Coast. When Simmons saw the proofs, he still did not like them and ordered air-brush touch-ups on the final, chosen photograph.

He was also very self-conscious about his height – five-feet, seven inches tall – and symbolism was very important to him. At meetings with his board of directors, he would sneak into the conference room before the start of each session and swivel his chair up to assure that his head was an inch or two above the other directors.

Similarly, as he sat behind his desk in this meeting, his head was above all his officers as they discussed the upcoming speech.

"So, what do we need to cover?" Simmons asked the group.

"Well, I'll prepare some financial figures for Tim," said Jameson.

"Good idea," said Simmons, acknowledging Jameson.

"I'll get him figures on the increases in employment, promotions from within, new plants, and our benefits program," said Robertson.

"Excellent," beamed Simmons. "What else?"

"Maybe you can dictate some notes for me on the outlook for the next three, five or ten years, George," Kaufman suggested. "I'd like your view of the company's future. Some in-depth stuff, you know."

"Of course, good idea. Consider it done," Simmons replied. "Come on, fellows, you must have some other ideas. This has to be a memorable day."

"How about production figures?" Jameson inquired.

"I'll call Dave Anderson to get those to Tim," Simmons said. "The figures are good. Shows I appreciate their work."

"Judy, has our safety record been good?" Kaufman asked.

"Yes, but you know, there are so many rumors about that asbestos thing," she replied.

An uneasiness crept into the meeting when Robertson mentioned asbestos.

"Fuck," Simmons shouted angrily. "I'm getting really pissed off that we can't put that to bed. We got rid of asbestos in making brakes and it's history. I'm sick and tired of liberal troublemakers trying to blame us for something that happened 30 or 40 years ago."

"Absolutely," agreed Hawthorne. "There's no proof that the exposure to asbestos caused cancer nor that we were remiss in protecting employees."

"But the rumors are prevalent and maybe we should say something," Robertson said, this time more tentatively. "The media keep writing about it. If we say something, maybe it will go away."

"No way," Hawthorne said. "It's bullshit and, as George said, we want to be upbeat."

Kaufman listened to the exchange, but anticipated that Robertson would lose her appeal. He respected her for trying but he also knew that Simmons would overrule her on this subject.

As for Hawthorne, Kaufman despised the man. He was the ultimate sycophant with absolutely no intuitive intelligence, not even in the law. His success at Thompson Brakes was the result of Hawthorne catering to Simmons. He managed to carry out his legal duties by getting approval from Simmons to hire a very prestigious law firm to be of counsel. Hawthorne called the firm on almost every matter. When he gave his advice on legal matters, it was based on what he was told by the law firm, Kramer, Wilkinson and Thomas. Under questioning, lacking depth, Hawthorne frequently was unable to explain the reasoning. But Simmons either did not mind or he did not grasp Hawthorne's shallowness.

Hawthorne's wife, Betty, known as the "conniving bitch" around corporate gossip circles, helped her husband's career by ingratiating herself with Simmons' wife. At corporate functions, Betty Hawthorne would not leave the side of Patricia Simmons. She spent hours with the chairman's wife, but neither Simmons nor his wife seemed to notice the not-so-subtle kowtowing. What was worse, Betty Hawthorne spread the most horrendous and unseemly gossip about Simmons and his wife in the community. The duplicity earned her the nickname.

Indeed, the gossip circles could not understand Simmons' support of Hawthorne. They concluded, somewhat viciously, that either Simmons had "something going" with his protégé or his protégé had some "dirty pictures" on Simmons.

But the truth was that Simmons had few managerial skills and was unable to appoint competent executives. The average tenure of senior executives at Thompson Brakes was about 18 months. Then the board would order Simmons, who had hired these people, to fire them.

Hawthorne knew that Simmons feared devastating financial consequences if there were a major public discussion on the asbestos issue. A public dialogue on the relationship between exposure to asbestos and cancer could and probably would depress the company's stock value.

"We can't risk a public discussion on asbestos," the lawyer admonished. "Can you imagine what it would do to our stock price? The media wouldn't go away. They would have a field day."

"Al is right," the chairman said. "It would be too risky."

Then Simmons addressed Kaufman. "You're the expert. Why is this starting all over again? Why is this in the papers again? I thought it was done with years ago."

Thompson Brakes had escaped press coverage in the 1970s and 1980s when asbestos manufacturers, such as Johns-Manville, were the target of major stories as public officials probed the cancer-causing health issues related to the use of asbestos. Company executives had expected some coverage but were grateful that the focus was on others. Since asbestos had not been used in manufacturing in recent years, they had assumed the issue was dead.

But they were wrong. Fatalities among Thompson Brakes employees from cancer caused by exposure to asbestos 30 to 40 years earlier and the union's successful efforts in calling public attention to the issue had put the company in the headlines.

"The issues are very different today," Kaufman said, explaining the press coverage. "Now, there have been some deaths that the union blames on asbestos used in brakes. So, it's newsworthy. They have taken their case to the media, making some strong charges and using the press with some sophistication."

"Bullshit charges," scorned Hawthorne. "It happened a long time ago. It's old stuff and I don't see the point."

"It may be bullshit to us, Al," Kaufman replied, "but the media are buying into it. You can't deny it's a good story and we're going to have to deal with it."

"We ought to sue them for libel, for defaming our company," Hawthorne continued. "We shouldn't let them get away with this."

A sarcastic smile crept over Kaufman's face. "That should get the story out of the paper. That's a helluva strategy. *All* of the papers would be interested in that."

With Hawthorne fuming at Kaufman's sarcasm, Simmons berated the two.

"Cut this shit out. We may have to deal with this issue eventually, but not in this speech," he told Kaufman. "No asbestos, no fucking discussion of cancer. Nothing that will pour cold water on an upbeat occasion."

Kaufman did not argue; he knew the battle was lost.

"So, Tim, do you have enough?" Simmons asked.

"Yes, I think so."

Simmons stood up, signaling that the meeting was over.

"Remember, a little about our financial performance, some stuff on human resource programs, our production achievements and, yeah, something from me about the future. Tim, I'll send you the material I have collected from other speeches. Upbeat, upbeat, upbeat.

"And remember, Tim, no mention of asbestos. Rumors or no rumors. I'm not going to let them ruin this day. Screw them all."

FIVE

"Is Dr. Sobel in, please?" Angie Ferguson asked the nurse answering the telephone.

"He's with a patient now. May I take a message?"

"Yes, please ask him to call Angie Ferguson."

"Mrs. Ferguson," the nurse replied. "Please hang on. I'll see if he can talk to you."

The nurse, instructed by Sobel to alert him if Angie Ferguson called, as he expected she would, put the telephone on hold. She walked to an examining room, knocked on the door and said, "Doctor, Mrs. Ferguson is on line two."

"Ask her to wait. I'll take it in a minute."

"Mrs. Ferguson, the doctor will be on the phone soon. Please stay on the line."

Angie Ferguson waited anxiously. She had not asked her husband one question after he recovered from his breakdown. She knew it would have been too painful for him – and her – and she also knew he did not have the aptitude to fully discuss all of the medical, emotional and personal issues involved.

"Hello, Angie," Sobel said. "Let me say, Angie, I'm very sorry. I'm glad you called."

"Doctor, I really hate to bother you, but I'd like to see you for a few minutes."

"Absolutely. I wanted to talk with both of you when Paul was here. I'll have my nurse schedule an appointment."

"Yes, Paul did not want me to come with him. Do you have time today?"

"I'll make time. Wait on the line, my nurse will take care of it."

Angie waited another few minutes before she heard a voice say, "How is 3:30 this afternoon?"

"Fine, thank you."

For the next few hours, Angie Ferguson worked to keep herself occupied. She washed clothes, tried to read, watched a few soap operas, but she could not concentrate on anything.

As painful as she knew the doctor's visit would be, she was glad when the time came to leave for the appointment. Preoccupied, she almost knocked over garbage cans as she backed the car out of the driveway and headed to the doctor's office. She was so distracted, she did not notice several neighbors walking on the sidewalk waving to her. At times, she drove very slowly, not wanting to arrive at her destination. Then, changing her mind, she stepped on the accelerator to get it over with.

She parked in the doctor's office lot, walked in and printed her name on the sign-in sheet.

She picked up a magazine, turning the pages aimlessly until a nurse told her, "Mrs. Ferguson, the doctor will see you now."

She got up and followed the nurse to Sobel's office. "Please sit down. He'll be right here."

Angie Ferguson sat down, opened her purse, took out a handkerchief, blew her nose and waited, fearful of the news she was about to hear.

"Hello, Angie. It's good...," he caught himself. Yes, he liked her but under the circumstances "it's good to see you" did not seem appropriate.

He sat down behind his desk and, as with Paul Ferguson, struggled to deliver the news.

"Angie, let me begin and then I'll try and answer any questions. I'm sure Paul told you he has lung cancer," said Sobel, suddenly realizing that discussing Paul Ferguson's illness the second time was a little easier. "He has lung cancer, a cancer called..."

"Mesothelioma?" she asked.

"Yes, how do you know?"

"Well, I've read the papers about the others. That's why I forced him to see you. He kept saying it was a stubborn cold but I didn't believe it. It sounded different."

Sobel explained to her the major symptoms: pain and shortness of breath.

He continued. "In my opinion, the cause is exposure to asbestos. Paul worked at Thompson Brakes, which used asbestos in making brakes for decades before changing to different materials. I think you know – since you urged him to see me – the manifestations…"

"While I've read about it, I really don't understand it."

"Let me try to explain."

Sobel opened a file drawer, removed some X rays and pinned them under an X-ray light on his wall.

"These are Paul's X rays," Sobel explained. "See these blotchy white areas? They prompted me to have Paul get the biopsy. That's where the cancer has spread. This kind of cancer is very rare except among people who have been exposed to asbestos. But you can't diagnose mesothelioma from the X rays, which is why, as I said, we did the needle biopsy."

He paused and looked at her to see if she understood. He noticed her swallowing several times and trying to control her emotions. He asked her if he should continue.

"Please."

"Asbestos fibers get into a person in one of two ways: breathing or swallowing. Of course, in Paul's case, it was breathing. Our body protects itself against what we breathe in. Our respiratory system filters out much with tiny hairs called cilia. But the fibers from asbestos are different. They get around the system because they are long and very sharp. They can bypass the cilia and work their way into the chest, abdominal cavities and lungs. And that's what happened to Paul and the others."

Strange, Angie thought, the blotchy areas don't seem so terrible. "I guess I understand. But this happened so long ago. Paul has not been exposed for years."

"That's exactly the point. It takes that long to cause this cancer. I'm sure you noticed that most of the men who died did so 30 or 40 years after their exposure. How long has Paul worked there?"

"More than 45 years."

"That's a long time, of course. And I suspect for many years he was on the floor of the plant where asbestos exposure was the worst."

"What do we do?" she asked, her voice quivering.

"Do?"

"Yes, do?" she asked, somewhat irritated. "What kind of treatment will he receive? Will you operate or will he take drugs?"

Sobel immediately concluded that Paul Ferguson had not told his wife the outlook.

"Paul didn't tell you?"

"All he said was that he had cancer. You know Paul. Then he broke down and we didn't talk anymore. He fell asleep and I thought that was good."

Sobel was hesitant. He did not want to tell Angie Ferguson that her husband would die in six months to a year.

"Angie, I'm not sure it's my role to tell you because..."

"Please," she almost implored. "I'll never get a full understanding unless you tell me. I need my questions answered."

Sobel thought for a minute. First, he had to tell Paul Ferguson, and now, his wife. It was painful for him but he also knew, given the circumstances, he had no choice.

"Angie, there is nothing we can do."

"What do you mean?" But she knew exactly what he meant.

"Angie, Paul...Paul has six months to a year. I'm sorry, very sorry. Mesothelioma is, I'm sorry to say, always fatal."

Angie felt a chill run through her body. The reaction was similar to the one she experienced when her husband told her the news. Tears welled up in her eyes, but this time she let them come. She knew before the words were spoken. She knew when she watched her husband display symptoms she had noticed in his coworkers. She knew, yet Sobel's words caused her head to ache, her heart to beat rapidly.

"Are you certain about this, about Paul?"

"Yes, I'm sorry to say. As I told Paul, I consulted with two specialists. The cancer has spread. But as I also told Paul, you might want to get another opinion. I would recommend that just so you don't have any doubts."

"What about radiation, chemotherapy?"

"I'm afraid they won't help in this case."

Angie sat, fumbling with her handkerchief. Tears continued to roll down her cheeks.

"You're also sure that this asbestos caused the cancer?"

"Angie, there's a substantial body of evidence – medical research that indicates that there's a direct correlation between this kind of cancer and exposure to asbestos.

"As you know, I treated many of Paul's coworkers and they died of this disease and other forms of cancer caused by asbestos. That, of course, could be coincidence. It could be but, in my opinion, it isn't. There are very thorough studies that prove the point. At least, prove it to me. Moreover, the correlation is even stronger when the individual is a smoker, as Paul is and has been for many years.

"Thompson Brakes and others like them in this business did absolutely nothing years ago in terms of ventilation or face masks to protect their workers from breathing in asbestos dust. I'm sure you know people in paint and chemical plants contract other diseases because of exposure to other dangerous substances. In this case, it's asbestos."

Angie had read a little about what Sobel described.

"It's terrible what they did, just terrible."

"Yes, it is," he replied. "I think Paul's union tried for years to get Thompson Brakes to do something, but failed. Now, of course, they don't use asbestos anymore because research led to the development of new materials. But I think the union is still trying to get Thompson Brakes to take responsibility and assume some financial obligations. You might go talk to the union."

"Yes, I'll do that. Right now, I can't think about it."

Sobel regretted mentioning financial concerns. It was insensitive, although he wanted to be helpful.

"Doctor, what do I do for Paul now? I mean, I just can't sit and wait. What can I do for him? For us?"

"When the time comes, I'll prescribe some medicine for pain. Beyond that, I think you need to talk with your children and Paul."

Angie Ferguson's eyes were very red, her face puffed.

"This isn't fair. He's a good man. He worked hard all his life. He gave everything to that company. Hardly ever missed work. Never complained. It just isn't fair."

She stood up to leave. "Thank you, Doctor. I'm sorry to have called on such short notice."

"Please, Angie. Anytime. Again, I'm very sorry."

"I know. You've been very kind. Thank you."

As she left, Sobel was sure he heard Angie mutter under her breath, "the bastards."

SIX

"Business is better than ever," Kaufman wrote. "Our new brake pads containing semi-metallic materials are cheaper to produce than those we manufactured previously. They are stronger and offer better stopping power. As a company always on the leading edge of technology and one that wants to be responsive to the environmental and health concerns of society, we worked hard to develop these pads. And you can be proud of what you achieved."

Kaufman wanted to violate Simmons' instructions not to mention asbestos. He believed that if Simmons addressed the issue, he could defuse it; that would be a proactive public relations strategy. He also thought Simmons had an obligation to say something. Most importantly, he was beginning to feel some discomfort about the way the company was handling the controversy and he was developing doubts on the company's position that it was not responsible for causing any of the various cancers afflicting employees.

Rather than insert copy on asbestos in the speech, he wrote a separate memo to Simmons, recommending he "reconsider" the decision not to mention the subject. The memo, two pages long, outlined the public relations value in being upfront on the issue. He had the speech draft delivered to Simmons and several executives, but his memo was sent only to the chairman.

Overall, the speech was what he considered "pro forma." A few statistics on financial results, a few numbers on increased employment, a listing of key promotions from within and other major developments discussed in his meeting with Simmons and the other officers.

These facts were packaged around such phrases as "we are a team," "this is the best work force in the industry," "our employees – you – are second to none," "management is indebted to you for your loyalty, dedication and hard work," and concluding with the all-purpose "we are optimistic about the future."

Kaufman had written such speeches using this language countless times. Except for some special reference to the audience addressed, the language never differed whether the message went to employees, suppliers ("you provide us with price-competitive, high-quality products") or shareholders ("we will continue to work to maximize shareholder value").

He believed if he were to collect annual reports and other investor communications from other public companies and erase the names of the companies and products they manufactured or services they offered, he would not be able to differentiate the companies because the language was the same. The Simmonses and Hawthornes of America, with absolutely no creative talents or imagination, would reduce all writing to a formula and common denominator and, even worse, not recognize the banality of their own words and how they lacked any credibility.

Whenever he wrote a speech, Kaufman always looked at two cartoons taped on his wall. In one, a CEO tells the speechwriter, "Write me a warm, pithy speech that bears my unmistakable mark of brilliance." The other cartoon has an executive reading a draft speech while asking an assistant, "This is one of the best speeches I ever made. Who wrote it?"

Along with these two on speechwriting, he had taped a third cartoon to his wall that reflected Kaufman's amazement at the total obedience to Simmons and other corporate chairmen in America. It said, "Nietzsche was wrong. God is not dead; he goes by the title chairman of the board."

The cartoons always brought a smile to Kaufman's face and he had no compunction about taping them to the wall of his office for all to see.

Kaufman sent the speech draft along and waited for a call to attend the traditional review meeting. He detested these conferences, particularly when serious issues were at stake. He abhorred the fact that most executives, when making recommendations for language changes, were more concerned about their political interests than the nuances of the issues.

For this occasion, given that the event required little substance – it was more pomp and ceremony – he decided to assume a docile posture and not fight changes even when they might be ludicrous. What's the difference between "we are a team" and "we are one family" or "we are optimistic about the future" and, as he anticipated it being changed to, "we are very optimistic about the future"?

He had become quite cynical about writing speeches for corporate executives and the dynamics of the exercise. In his drafts, he even offered Simmons and the other executives choices in adjectives to describe, for instance, the company's earnings. He had written, "our financial results have been (good, very good, excellent)." There existed no specific guidelines for these judgments other than the political considerations of the moment. Endless hours were spent by the hierarchy of the company – lawyers, bankers and writers – to "refine" language that was designed, Kaufman concluded, to camouflage the truth.

He also considered speechwriting a symbol of the unethical behavior and hypocrisy of such organizations as Thompson Brakes. While he would not admit it to anyone, those reading speeches written by others, particularly if the speech contained new political, social or economic concepts, were, in fact, committing plagiarism; they were stealing.

Kaufman had no problem with their reading what he called "formula" speeches such as those given at award banquets, promotions of employees or similar presentations. But when the speech reflected original thinking, he was bothered that those he served were not troubled by the violation of ethics.

They would not sign their names to a painting they commissioned, he often thought while writing a major speech. But then, maybe they would.

As he was rereading his draft speech, the phone rang.

"Tim, Mr. Simmons would like you to attend the review meeting on his speech at 3 p.m.," said Susan Gray, Simmons' secretary.

"I'll be there, Susan. Thanks."

"Tim," she said. "Before you hang up, Mr. Simmons asked me to tell you 'no' on your memo. He also said for you not to bring it up at the review meeting. Does that message make sense to you?"

"Indeed, it does, Susan. I understand. And thanks."

Kaufman was disappointed, but he felt good about giving Simmons his advice nevertheless. Kaufman had lived up to what he believed was his professional obligation, whether Simmons accepted his suggestions or not.

At 2:55 p.m., Kaufman left his office and headed for the chairman's executive suite. He took the elevator up to the 20th floor and, as always, was upset at the surroundings. Thick rugs, expensive paintings, fancy draperies and furniture. In short, all the trappings of the corporate inner sanctum. He viewed these surroundings as evidence of the institution's double standard, not just that of Thompson Brakes but other major corporations. He reflected on how his speeches often addressed the need to cut expenses, speeches delivered by the very people who wallowed in luxury with fancy offices, chauffeurs, helicopters and corporate jets, not embarrassed by their hypocrisy.

As he approached Susan Gray's desk, she told him to go right in.

"They're expecting you," she said.

"Thanks," he replied, knocking at the door before entering.

Simmons sat at the end of a long, shiny, mahogany conference table with Hawthorne at his right. Jameson sat to Simmons' left with Robertson next to him.

"Sit down, Tim, and we'll begin," said Simmons. "This shouldn't take long. Tim, this is a good start, good job. Let's start on page one. Tim, you keep the master copy."

"Will do."

"Well, let me start," said Simmons. "Tim, get me a joke. Break up the tension. Need some humor."

Kaufman purposely did not offer any humor because Simmons did not have the talent to deliver jokes. Yet, each time, he would ask for humor.

"I'll get you one," he replied.

Hawthorne offered a change from "I am very pleased to be with you again" to "I am delighted." He also changed "during the last fiscal year" to "in the fiscal year ending December 31."

"Good," replied Simmons.

Kaufman did not fight any of the changes. Some dealt with correcting numbers, others with meaningless word changes, all of them minor.

Whenever Kaufman experienced this "editing process," he always thought about Lyndon Johnson's White House Press secretary, Bill Moyers, who observed that before being involved in government he "had the most precious thing a journalist can have, which is the freedom to follow one's intuition without having to write a memorandum and explain it to a committee or work it through a bureaucratic decision."

As with the cartoons on speechwriting, Kaufman had the quote taped on his wall.

"Last page," said Simmons. "Anything else?"

No one offered any additional edits. Kaufman was surprised but also very satisfied. The changes recommended were all very minimal.

They had proceeded through the speech rather rapidly. Although it was routine, Kaufman had expected the meeting to last much longer.

"It's a wrap," said Simmons. "Tim, make the changes, get a new draft to us tomorrow. I'll have Susan retype it in the format I like. Thanks everyone. If we need another meeting I'll call, but I think we're all set. See you at the meeting a week from today. Tim, don't worry. I'll practice reading the speech."

"I'm sure you will. If you need me, call."

"And don't forget the joke," Simmons shouted as Kaufman was leaving the office. "A good one, a thigh-slapper."

He walked back to his department and ran into a colleague, Howard Taylor, who asked, "How'd it go? Anything on asbestos?"

"Things went smoothly. They decided against asbestos."

"That ain't good PR."

"I know, but we tried. That's all we can do. Between you and me, sooner or later he's going to have to address it."

Kaufman did not know at the time how prophetic he was in his observation.

SEVEN

A week after she talked to Dr. Sobel, at about the same time Simmons was waiting to go to his employee meeting, Angie Ferguson walked into the office of the local union president, Steve Marks. She had had no discussions with her husband since seeing Sobel nor had she followed up until now.

Paul Ferguson continued to work, but overall he was moody and depressed. He did not talk much when he was home and at work he tried to maintain a business-as-usual attitude. He did not want to discuss his illness with anyone.

Thus, Angie Ferguson was left to deal with her husband's fatal disease alone. She had not shared the information with their two children; she needed to process all the information.

As distasteful as she considered her next act, she decided to check with the union regarding medical and life insurance.

"Steve," she said, "I appreciate your seeing me."

"No problem. What can I do for you? I saw Paul earlier. He looked sad. Didn't say anything to me. What's up?"

"Steve, I still don't know how to say this. It's been a week since we found out..."

"No, damn it," Marks stated angrily, anticipating Angie's news. "Mesothelioma? Something else?"

"Mesothelioma," she answered and started to cry.

"Sons of bitches," Marks said, pounding the desk. "Angie, I'm so sorry. Damn, I'm so fucking mad! Sorry, Angie."

"It's all right. We found out about a week ago. I didn't know where to turn. You're the first one I've talked to about this. I haven't even discussed it with my family. Steve, I don't know what to do, what to ask, where to go from here."

Marks helped her out. He had gone through the experience several times in the last few years with the spouses and relatives of other members of his union. Experience made the discussions a little easier, but it did not mitigate the pain.

"I've got some answers because, as you know, this isn't the first time. They're not all good answers."

Marks explained to her that her husband might be eligible for worker's compensation and some medical benefits. Financial assistance would be minimal and not cover all the expenses, which would increase as Ferguson got worse.

"The bastards have fought us even on worker's comp," Marks added. "They fight every demand."

He then went to a drawer and removed Ferguson's file, reviewing it quickly.

"Looking at this, Angie," he said, "I don't think Paul has any life insurance. My notes indicate I warned him about that from time to time."

"My God, Steve, what am I going to do?"

Marks walked from behind the desk and bent over, giving her a gentle hug. He had witnessed the despair, the pain and the grief too many times. He was angry and bitter after witnessing the deaths of so many of his union's members. He really was touched but he also realized that Thompson Brakes' uncompromising policies were hurting him politically and damaging his union presidency. His members had expected him to force some concessions from Thompson Brakes.

"Angie, I've got an idea, but I need your help. More specifically, I need Paul's help."

"If we can help, if it'll help my family, I mean, we'll try."

Marks knew that what he was about to recommend smacked of exploitation, but he had tried everything else. For years, he had done all he could to persuade Thompson Brakes to meet its obligations. He told them they had violated laws and been immoral in not providing protection for workers from asbestos dust. Each year, it became increasingly clear, he pointed out, that the correlation between deaths from various cancers and those exposed to asbestos was unusually high. He wanted management to create a fund to finance the medical costs of Thompson Brakes' workers with cancer as well as provide benefits for the survivors. He was prepared to negotiate the size of the fund.

He was willing to give the company the benefit of the doubt by publicly acknowledging that Thompson Brakes may not have known about the risks of asbestos from the 1940s to the late 1960s. While he believed the company was aware of the dangers even in those years, he would not, as a matter of compromise and political concession, say so publicly if the company was prepared to offer financial reparations.

But Thompson Brakes had not been willing to do so, and Marks felt he could no longer let the company off the hook. He was adamant that the company's responsibility dated back at least 40 years because he was confident the facts had been known, particularly after the creation of OSHA, the government agency formed in 1972. The scientific evidence was ample beginning in those years, he continually told the company. If he tried to offer excuses for Thompson Brakes after 1970, his own credibility would suffer.

Despite his constant pressure, Thompson Brakes would not budge. Management held fast, denying any responsibility because, as Marks was told by union attorneys, the company did not want to set precedents that might make them subject to lawsuits. Marks was aghast that Thompson Brakes was not moved by the toll of human suffering. The company worried, the union lawyers maintained, about the potential costs to Thompson Brakes if it were to cave in to his demands.

"Angie, for years we've tried to get Thompson Brakes to meet its responsibilities. Everyone, including the company, knows that it caused this cancer in Paul and all the others who died. But they refuse to acknowledge that or provide any financial relief for wives and other survivors. Now we have a chance to apply some public pressure."

She did not understand what he had in mind, where he was going with his argument, but her curiousity was aroused.

"I'd like to call a press conference with Paul as the center of attention, stating as clearly as possible that Paul's cancer and that of his colleagues was caused by asbestos exposure. I want to hand out his medical records, his X rays and the scientific data we have collected. From time to time, we've received some coverage on our charges but this is the first time we have a live...," he quickly caught himself. "We have someone who has the disease to make our case more dramatic. Do I like using Paul and you like this? No, I don't, Angie. But this may do it. This may put enough pressure on those bastards that they'll have to do something."

He explained that he wanted to file a class action suit, in Ferguson's name, on behalf of all the workers who had suffered from mesothelioma and other cancers and their survivors, and create a fund to pay medical costs for future victims while providing for their families.

"We have been reluctant to sue, but our attorneys have argued that we have a good case if we charge the company with what is called an intentional tort, Angie," he said. "That means they did what they did on purpose. Or put another way, we have a good chance of proving that they knew the dangers but did nothing to warn Paul and others."

Realizing he was confusing her with the legal arguments, he added, "The lawyers tell us employees can't sue their employers unless they prove they knew the facts and did nothing. That's what we want to do."

Angie's first reaction was negative. She and her husband were quiet, private people. They kept pretty much to themselves. It would be out of character for them to step into such a public controversy.

"I don't know, Steve," she said, shaking her head. She was terribly distraught.

"Angie, we don't have to make the decision today. But let me explain further. I'll be right at Paul's side. I'll help him with what to say. I'll brief him as thoroughly as I can before we have the press conference. And I'll assign one of our PR people to him so he'll have help when calls come from the press." He could see that he was not convincing her. He played his trump card.

"Angie, if you don't do it for yourself, do it for all the other widows in town. Do it for those who lost their husbands and are trying to make ends meet. Do it for those who have yet to discover they have mesothelioma or another cancer. Do it to make them pay."

Marks did not like what he was doing. He felt bad making her feel guilty. But he knew this was the best opportunity he had and he was going to do all he could to make sure Angie Ferguson would, at least, give his idea serious consideration. He was confident that if he convinced her, she could and would persuade her husband.

"Damn it, Angie, they shouldn't get away with killing people."

"Yes, you're right," she said. "Everything you've said makes sense, but you know Paul and me. Paul didn't even like giving a toast at our daughter's wedding. Now you want him to stand up before the world."

"Angie, I know, but as I said, I'll help. Our people will help. Angie, it's our only chance."

Marks was shrewd. He had earned his union presidency primarily because of his power at negotiations – not his organizational skills. He knew he was having an impact.

"Think about it, Angie. I'll call you in a few days and you, Paul and I'll talk some more."

Angie stood up to leave. "All right, we will. I'll talk to Paul. I'm not sure what he'll say, but I'll talk to him."

"Good, Angie. Take care of yourself. Talk to you soon."

When Angie Ferguson left, Steve Marks clapped his hands in joy. He was very excited about the possibilities. This was the chance he had waited for. He did not want to lose this opportunity; he did not even want to think about Angie and Paul Ferguson possibly turning him down.

EIGHT

As Angie Ferguson left Marks' office, George C.L. Simmons, Jr. was just offstage in the company's auditorium waiting to be introduced.

"And now, ladies and gentlemen," said Alfred Hawthorne, "it gives me great pleasure to introduce to you the man who makes it all happen. He's our mentor, our leader, the one who creates jobs, who promotes our people, who gives to the community. In short, he's a man who cares..."

"He sure likes to kiss ass," said Kaufman to one of his PR associates standing next to him. "Can't seem to do it enough."

"He's also our coach. The head coach of this great team. Ladies and gentlemen, I present to you Coach George C.L. Simmons, Jr."

Kaufman could not believe it. Out from the wings came Simmons dressed in a baseball coach's uniform.

"Son of a bitch," whispered Kaufman to his PR colleague. "They finally convinced him to do it."

From time to time, Hawthorne and a couple of Simmons' other cronies had recommended what Kaufman considered "gimmicks." He had always been able to talk Simmons out of these recommendations, which he considered undignified and amateurish. But this time, they had won.

A short, portly, balding man, 63 years old, with a pot belly, Simmons looked like a caricature. He was welcomed by applause, cordial but not enthusiastic. There was also laughter, some of it derisive, although Kaufman was confident that Simmons would not notice.

"Thank you, Al. Thank you all. Yes, Al, I like being the coach of this team because of the caliber of players. Yeah, we are one helluva team, right?"

"Right," came the reply from the audience.

"I can't hear you. Right?"

"Right," the audience shouted a little louder.

About 250 employees attended, but the speech was beamed via satellite to another 20 divisions nationwide for a potential audience of about 10,000.

"Let me begin with a good news-bad news story."

Kaufman had not provided a joke for Simmons, hoping he would not remember and just deliver his speech.

"The joke involves a galley of slaves in chains rowing madly with the slavemaster stopping them with good news and bad news. 'The good news is an extra ration of bread for everyone.' Cheers went up. 'The bad news is the captain wants to go waterskiing.' "

There were a few snickers in the audience. The irony and implications of the joke escaped Simmons, who was visibly upset when his joke was met with more silence than laughter.

"Well, then, let me get right to the speech. Incidentally, I want to answer your questions, so please fill out the index cards on your seats and pass them up to Al Hawthorne.

"This was a good fiscal year. Sales increased from $100 million to $135 million." He stopped briefly indicating he wanted applause and the clackers went to work. "Earnings increased about 10 percent, from $3.6 million to more than $4 million." Again, applause.

"He has overdone it a bit," Kaufman told his associate.

"Hell, I planted five in the audience myself," his colleague replied.

"I think he's going to beat the record of the President of the United States. If this continues, we may be here for some time."

Simmons read the speech well. He had learned that discipline. The trouble was, Simmons, a slow-witted man, was not very good at speaking extemporaneously or answering questions. Kaufman always had to do some damage control after each public Q & A session.

Simmons delivered his formula speech in about 15 minutes and concluded to polite applause.

"Thank you to all of you. This company needs you; we need your contributions. Remember, ask not what your company can do for you but what you can do for Thompson Brakes."

Kaufman looked out into the audience which seemed angry and defiant. Simmons had just told them not to expect too much, if anything, from the company. Their obligation was to serve Thompson Brakes. With the only impromptu line Simmons delivered, Kaufman concluded, the chairman destroyed all the goodwill he wanted to create. Whatever the corporate culture of the 1990s, it was hardly politic to state it so coldly to the only audience that mattered.

On another occasion, Kaufman remembered he had heard Simmons tell his employees that if they were unhappy, they were free to leave – this, at a morale-building session.

As Kaufman digested and processed Simmons' latest employee relations disaster, the chairman stepped out from behind the podium to open the meeting to questions. He scratched his left arm with his right, straightened the bill of his baseball cap, rubbed his nose, thumped his breast, and for a fraction of a second, cupped his crotch.

The audience reacted with a mixture of laughter, boos and hisses.

Back behind the podium, he shouted, "I'm giving you the signal to steal first, steal second, steal third and then home. Be aggressive. Don't let anything stand in your way. And we're gonna win...yes, we're gonna win. Those who say that it's not whether you win or lose, but how you play the game, are losers. Only one thing matters: winning."

Simmons was warming up and he was talking with passion and emotion.

"Do what it takes to win. Don't let the weak make life difficult for you. They'll always find a reason why things can't be done. But if you've got the will, there's always a way. Remember that. And I'll bet you all agree. Do you?"

"Yes," the audience shouted collectively but halfheartedly.

"And now, Al, read me some of the questions my teammates have sent up to you."

"The first one asks, 'What kind of a raise can we expect this year given the improved earnings?'"

"Good question, Al. We're going over the budget now and it's a little premature to say. We should have a decision for you shortly. What else, Al?"

There were a number of other questions, most dealing with wages and benefits. Simmons was as vague as he had been to the question on wages. Finally, he said, "Thank you very much. That's all the time..."

"Mr. Simmons," a member of the audience shouted. "My question was not read. May I please ask it?"

Simmons peered out from the podium trying to find the speaker. "I'm sorry, I can't see you. What did you say?"

"I'd like to ask a question that was not read."

Kaufman had no trouble identifying the individual. It was Sue Merriman and he wondered how she got into the meeting.

"May I ask your name and what department you work in?" Simmons asked.

"I'm Sue Merriman from the *Detroit Blade*."

Simmons was thunderstruck and angry.

"Miss Merriman, this is a..."

"You never mentioned the issue of asbestos safety," said Merriman, one of the paper's top reporters. "As you know, we've written many stories on the subject and I've tried to reach you for comment, but couldn't. You never return any calls. So I would like to ask you here. Did your company change to semi-metallic materials because asbestos was not safe? Is that true?"

"Miss Merriman, this is an employee meeting. I don't think this is the appropriate setting to discuss this very complex issue."

"All I want to know is whether you changed to a semi-metallic material from asbestos because asbestos isn't safe," Merriman replied, ignoring Simmons' admonition.

Kaufman's prediction that sooner or later Simmons would have to make a public statement on the safety of asbestos had come true – but not under the best circumstances.

Tough broad, Kaufman whispered to himself. Come on, give her an answer.

"No, that's not why. We made the changes for many reasons. The new materials are better and the product is cheaper. Thank you, Miss Merriman."

"One more question and I'm sure your employees would like to hear the answer."

Her comment was greeted by light applause.

"Is Thompson Brakes looking into the correlation between asbestos exposure and so many of your employees contracting cancer?"

"Those are rumors. All rumors. Started by troublemakers. We don't comment on rumors."

"Mr. Simmons, with all due respect, these are more than rumors. The statistics are very frightening and all I want to know is what, if anything, you are going to do about it. Are you saying you aren't even going to study the issue? You'll do nothing?"

"Of course not," Simmons replied, slowly picking up on the public relations implications if he were not definitive.

"We are a responsible corporation. Yes, we're looking into it. If you need anything else, call our PR department. Again, thank you. Thank you everyone."

Simmons stormed off the stage. Hawthorne, among others, patted Simmons on the back and congratulated him for "telling it like it is." Other officers also commended the chairman for his insight, his delivery and how he had handled Sue Merriman.

Simmons thanked them all, telling them it was really their work and contributions that made the speech so successful. But he was shaken by his exchange with Merriman and was already preparing a mental list of who was going to pay for letting Sue Merriman into the meeting.

As he watched the entourage congratulate Simmons, Kaufman thought, I'm sure glad I don't work in security.

NINE

Kaufman headed to his office and by the time he reached it, only a five-minute walk from the auditorium, Simmons had already called. There was a message from Susan Gray on his voice mail to call the chairman immediately.

"What the fuck do you know about this?" he asked Kaufman.

"Nothing, George. I was as surprised as you. I guess security..."

"I'll handle them. What do you suggest about PR? Will she write a story? Can we sue them for trespass? What can we do?"

"She'll write a story. I don't think we should sue them and in terms of PR, I suggest we meet first thing in the morning. This will give me a chance to see what damage control, if any, we have to initiate."

"Be in my office at 8 a.m. I'll call all the others I want there."

He sure is pissed, Kaufman thought. Frankly, he has a right to be.

Kaufman worked for another few hours before deciding to call it a day. He headed for the Press Club. He could use a drink.

He sat at the bar by himself, sipping a scotch, when Sue Merriman tapped him on the shoulder.

"Want company?"

"Free country."

"Touchy, touchy tonight."

He ignored her teasing. Admittedly, he admired her work; she was a professional, thorough and responsible.

Kaufman had dealt with Merriman frequently over a two-year period and they had established mutual respect. She had warned him that she would do what was necessary to get an answer from the chairman on the asbestos issue.

He respected her persistence; indeed, he liked good investigative reporting, but he objected to a variety of unethical practices engaged in by reporters, including the use of hidden cameras and reporters misrepresenting themselves while in pursuit of stories. He had never expected her to use subterfuge to attend the meeting.

"Did I touch a nerve? Little angry at my intrusion, Mr. PR man?"

Again, he did not react.

"Come on, Tim. We're adults. Are you going to sulk all night? It was a fair question."

"I have no problem with your question. I have a problem, however, with trespass and the underhanded methods you must have used to get in."

She explained that she had simply walked into the meeting and no one challenged her.

"If you have a security problem, don't blame it on me."

He could see doubt in her eyes as she defended her position.

"Look, the asbestos issue is important. People have died and others are dying. I tried to reach him several times and he turns it over to you. I wanted an official comment, Tim. That is no insult to you." Becoming angry, she added, "And I don't need a lecture on ethics from PR guys who help corporations cover up asbestos deaths, faulty brakes on cars, contamination of our environment, breast implant screwups, the firing of people who reach 45 or 50, downsizing, safety problems on cars...you want me to go on?"

He stared at her defiantly and she immediately regretted her attack. Tim Kaufman was respected by reporters; he played it as honest as was possible in a highly political arena. She shared the respect others in journalism had for him.

"Screw you, Sue." She was startled by his angry retort because Kaufman, while no prude, was always gentlemanly. She started to walk away but abruptly stopped and turned around.

"Tim, I'm sorry. Really, I am."

"Apology accepted."

She knew he was hurt. "Tim, I..."

"You want to talk about ethics, let's talk about ethics. I feel cleaner now than when I was a reporter like you. At least people know what my job is. It's to make my client look good. There's no bullshit. You get exactly what you see. As long as I do my job honestly and ethically, I have no problem with that.

"But you – and this is no insult to you, to use your words – I mean the media, deliver what you consider the truth and you and I know that half of it is distorted in some way. It's superficial, it contains errors, it's slanted. And when those covered complain, you whine like little children. No sector of our society is more sensitive than the media, the very institution that holds everyone else accountable. Ethics has become almost a foreign concept in journalism. I don't care how you rationalize it; you trespassed and covered what was a private meeting.

"TV uses hidden cameras that others, in their naivete, might call wiretapping. You pay for news. You accept honorariums. Media frenzies, a term coined by the media, are almost weekly events. The list goes on and on. Journalism reviews discuss the sins of the media regularly and it's all so repetitious and nothing is done. Tell me, big city reporter, how do your readers find out about all the screwups that the journalism reviews write about? The public sure has a right to know, doesn't it?"

He was wound up. Merriman let him talk. She knew she had some of it coming and it sounded like he needed some breathing room.

"Tim, I said I was sorry. I went too far. You know I've the highest respect for you personally."

"It just pisses me off when I hear the sanctimonious condemnations of flacks like me by the media. Incidentally, *flacks* is such an endearing word. Sue, journalism can be an honorable profession and, all things being equal, I might consider covering politics again. But it's about time that the media not just take a look at themselves but do something about their own flaws.

"I'm tired of hearing about the First Amendment and the public's so-called right to know. The latter, I'm sure you know, is not a constitutional principle but a self-serving cliché promoted by the media. I don't need lectures from an institution that destroys organizations and people with superficial reporting and then whines when someone tries to hold it accountable.

"You use anonymous sources, for instance, never questioning their motivation, which is immensely important. You use them willy-nilly, the more indicting the quote, the more credibility it is given. Even Woodward and Bernstein sold out. Telling the public they check everything with two sources, they write a book detailing how Nixon acted while he was alone in the White House and what people *thought* about in meetings. How in the hell did they check that?

"Even your code of ethics is flimsy at best. It instructs reporters they should not do certain things, but if the story is at stake, they should check with their editors regarding the ethics policy in question. What kind of ethics are those? Talk about situation ethics.

"Again, whenever anyone protests your wrongdoing, you wrap yourself up in the First Amendment and issue that famous standby, 'We stand by our story,' which, I'm sure you understand, is the equivalent of the corporate 'no comment.'

"Incidentally, how in the hell do editors know when a story is accurate? They don't participate in the interviews, have no idea if reporters have their facts straight or what was omitted. All they can do is read stories for holes left in the piece, grammar, good leads and the like. I have never understood their automatic defense of reporters. The Janet Cooke case is an excellent example of editors not knowing what's accurate and what isn't. Her fictitious story of an eight-year-old heroin addict won the Pulitzer Prize and lost it when it was discovered her series was a hoax. The problem is we've learned nothing from that incident. So please, spare me the holier-than-thou attitude."

"The Cooke case is an anomaly. You can always find a fraud in any profession."

"Well, I'm not so sure it is an exception," Kaufman said. "The *New Republic* had a writer who invented all or part of some 20 different articles he wrote for the magazine and this scandal was followed by one at the *Boston Globe* where a columnist was forced to resign after it was discovered she had manufactured quotes and characters for her articles.

"But even the meaning of these incidents has been distorted or missed by the media. These cases received headlines because they were unique. But little is said or done about day-to-day news stories which are inaccurate, slanted, distorted or screwed up in some fashion. These are never dealt with. It's easy to be principled, moral and take action on stories that turn out to be pure fiction.

"The point of the Cooke, *New Republic* and *Boston Globe* cases is that editors do not know and have no way of knowing whether stories are accurate or not. Even fact-checkers can't help because while individual facts might be accurate, they may be used out of context and, most important, those checking stories have no way of knowing what has been omitted from stories. And, of course, the omissions might be crucial to the context of the story being verified."

Merriman was on the defensive and she knew it. She countered, "I didn't come to cover the asbestos issue. I came to cover a business meeting with your company's employees. With 250 people in attendance and with satellite transmission, it was hardly private."

"I differ, if you please. The size of the crowd doesn't matter. Suppose Simmons had spoken to 20 employees in his office. Then what? What's the difference between bribing your way in, or sneaking in, or putting a glass to the wall, or planting a bug? You violated ethical standards if, indeed, you did not violate the law."

"So, sue me."

"I wish I could tell you they won't consider that. I expect they will and guess who'll try to talk them out of it? Me. Not because you wouldn't have it coming. But strategically that wouldn't be the right thing to do. Can you just imagine the media hoopla over that? You, your colleagues and the journals would have a news orgy."

Although smarting and hurt, Merriman agreed with some of what Kaufman said. But she was not ready to give in on this story. She was not prepared to surrender yet.

"I got the message. As I said, I didn't come to cover asbestos. I came to cover the meeting overall. I still think what I did was fair. It wasn't any different than an annual meeting."

Kaufman shook his head. "An annual meeting is a public function. It's required to be public by law. It's not the same thing. This was a meeting for employees on company property. But I'm confident your editors are proud of you. You got the story.

"You see, Sue, each time a reporter does something like you did, you set very disconcerting precedents and these precedents lower the threshold on ethics a little bit more. And I don't like where we're headed. The best part, of course, is that you have no accountability to anyone. That's a wonderful job to have."

"What do you mean no accountability? I'm accountable to my editors and they to the readers."

"You're accountable to your editors in terms of bringing them good stories, as they define them. They have no way of guaranteeing whether what you have written is accurate or not. Obviously, they will always defend you publicly."

"They can fire me, you know."

"Tell me the last time a reporter, any journalist, was fired for writing an inaccurate story. And as far as readers are concerned, they make decisions on whether to buy your paper, but they hardly do it on a standard of accuracy. How the hell would they know?"

"You know as well as I that we run corrections and letters to the editor."

"After you screw someone on page one, you might run a paragraph on 12D that one sentence or fact may have been wrong. Big deal. You can have your letters to the editor. They are hardly corrections. I have the opportunity to tell the paper it was wrong. That's about it. On many occasions, they even prostitute that by adding a postscript."

"Sounds to me like you're just a little bit bitter. Maybe a little more than a little bit. Overall, I think whatever shortcomings we have, the First Amendment has worked pretty well."

"I wondered how long it would take before you wrapped yourself in the good old First Amendment. No one is questioning the constitutional right to screw up. I'm raising issues of ethics, of responsibility and your obligation to the public.

"Sue, the First Amendment gives you no right to break the law. You, the media, are not above the law. We don't let police officers or anyone in government get away with violations of civil liberties, even when we have to let murderers and rapists go free. You're not going to tell me that private, profit-making institutions should have these rights when public officialdom does not, are you?"

He waited a moment and then added, "But like your colleagues, I'm not sure you understand that. So let's just drink to the First Amendment."

He raised his glass and finished the drink in one gulp.

Angry and feeling insulted, she left without saying a word.

TEN

The alarm woke Kaufman at 5:30 a.m. the next day. Whenever he expected the morning paper to have a story on his client, Thompson Brakes, he would get up early, drive to the nearest newsstand and pick up a paper, not wanting to wait for the one delivered to his home. He always had a few jitters, even after all these years, when he knew his client was subject to news coverage.

This morning he was hung-over; he had closed the Press Club, drinking alone. In recent years, unlike his earlier days as a reporter, he seldom got drunk anymore. But Merriman had upset him.

Without shaving, he dressed in a sweatsuit and drove about a mile to pick up the paper. He did not read it in the car but waited until he reached home.

He scanned page one; nothing there. He immediately turned to the business section. The story was splashed across the page under the headline "Thompson Brakes to Look into Asbestos Exposure-Cancer Correlation" by Susan K. Merriman. The headline appeared above a huge picture of Simmons in his baseball uniform. Kaufman concluded that either Merriman or someone with her had used a hidden camera, or that a *Blade* photographer was somehow also able to get into the meeting – as she had – with no challenge from security personnel.

He read:

The chairman and chief executive officer of Thompson Brakes, Inc.

told the company's employees yesterday that Thompson Brakes would study whether there is a correlation between exposure to asbestos and contracting cancer. Addressing more than 200 employees at corporate headquarters, George C.L. Simmons, Jr., in answer to a question from a *Detroit Blade* reporter – the only newsperson covering the meeting – said Thompson Brakes would look into the issue. The meeting was also broadcast live via satellite to Thompson Brakes divisions throughout the country.

Commenting on another question, Simmons denied that the company switched to semi-metallic materials to manufacture brakes because it considered asbestos a health danger. Simmons said the company is using new materials because they are stronger and cheaper. He also attributed charges that exposure to asbestos has caused cancer among company employees to "rumors" that were being spread by "troublemakers."

In his speech, Simmons addressed a variety of issues ranging from the company's increase in sales, profitability, promotions from within and other company matters. He did not mention asbestos in his prepared text.

Reaction to Simmons' promise to look into the cancer issue was positive in the community, but some expressed reservations. Steven Marks, president of the local union that represents Thompson Brakes' employees, said, "It's about time, but I hope this is not a delaying tactic. I hope he really means it and isn't just creating a smoke screen, hoping that in a month or two we'll all forget about his promise." Marks has been pressuring the company to set up a fund for survivors of cancer victims. He claims the victims contracted the fatal disease because of exposure to asbestos.

City and state health officials commended the company. Overall, they praised Simmons for stepping up to the issue.

But one former employee, who wished to remain anonymous, said that the company has been covering up for some time. "Don't expect too much," he said. "They'll do just as much as is necessary so it won't cost them millions of dollars. Their don't-give-a-damn attitude already has cost many lives."

There was no immediate indication who will do the study, how long it will take or how much it will cost.

Except for the cheap shot of quoting an anonymous source, a former employee, Kaufman found the story fair. But, he knew, they'd be mad as hell in the executive offices at "city hall."

Then he read the short sidebar to the story detailing Simmons' baseball coach attire:

The Thompson Brakes, Inc. employee meeting yesterday was anything but what is usually expected in corporate America. George C.L. Simmons, Jr., the company's chairman, addressed the employees in a baseball coach's uniform, stating he was the "coach of our team." On one occasion during the speech, he gave signals like a third base baseball coach, even touching his crotch. He told the employees he was giving them signals to "steal bases" whenever they could because winning is all that matters.

Employees sitting near the *Detroit Blade* reporter covering the story were flabbergasted and reacted sarcastically. "What a farce," said one employee. "This guy must be nuts." Another called it "interesting," adding that it made this kind of meeting "more fun."

Thompson Brakes corporate executives contacted by the *Blade* for their reaction to Simmons' dress did not return phone calls. Executives at other companies said they preferred not to comment on the strategies of others.

Kaufman was amused by Merriman's sidebar, but he expected criticism on the story from Simmons and other Thompson Brakes executives.

He arrived at his office at 7:30 a.m., about a half hour earlier than usual. He wanted to be early, knowing Simmons and the others would call immediately when they reached their offices. His head was still pounding from his hangover.

At 8 a.m., the phone rang. "Get your ass down here." It was Simmons. Kaufman took a legal pad and headed for Simmons' office.

Susan Gray told him to go right into Simmons' office and when he entered, Hawthorne, Robertson and the vice president of environmental and health affairs, Glen Johnston, were already seated at the conference table.

"I got a few questions for you, Tim," Simmons said, glaring at Kaufman. "How the hell did that broad get into our meeting and how did they get that picture?"

"I really don't know, George. I'll check with security after this meeting."

"Don't bother. I already told my top security man, Lou Salter, to fire the jerks responsible in his department. They'll be gone by the time we finish."

As Kaufman expected, Simmons ignored the main piece Merriman had written and focused on the sidebar.

"So the broad didn't like my uniform?" he said, looking at Kaufman. "Doesn't understand the point, I guess. Probably one of those we-have-never-done-it-that-way people."

Kaufman concluded that since the incident was a fait accompli, he would go along with Simmons. "Lacks creativity and a sense of humor."

Simmons chuckled. "That's for sure. But let's move on. Where do we go from here? What do you make of her story?"

Kaufman knew this would not be easy. But his policy was always to give it straight to his clients.

"First, the anonymous source quote was bullshit."

"But you'll tell me, of course, there's nothing I can do, right?"

"Yes, George, that's right. It's not fair but, yes, there's not much we can do. The rest of the story was basically no more than a factual presentation of what happened."

"But the bitch broke into our meeting. And then she pokes fun at my baseball uniform. That's fair to you?"

Kaufman decided to ignore Simmons' criticism of the story on the uniform. "No, and I already gave her hell at the Press Club last night when I ran into her. Again, not much more we can do."

As he had predicted in his argument with Merriman, Simmons raised the issue of a lawsuit. "Let's sue the bastards."

"I'm not sure on what. I think a trespass case, George, will only make her a martyr among her peers and the rest of the media. And we'll get even more coverage. We need to let that go."

"We get roasted in the papers and you tell me there's nothing we can do."

"Not on that issue. On the substance of the story, your statement that we'll look into the matter, I think we should announce an independent study. That way we'll look responsible, but we must be prepared to reveal the results."

"You're telling me that we pay for a study and if it shows we caused some cancer, we need to announce it to the world."

Kaufman knew that he was the proverbial messenger of bad news. Hawthorne, Robertson and Johnston did not say a word. They pretended to be taking notes on their legal pads.

"Well, from all everyone has said, it shouldn't show that we caused cancer among employees," Kaufman said, picking up on Simmons' implication.

Simmons was upset by his admission of a possible correlation, telling Kaufman, "I have no doubt about the study. I just don't like being forced into this position."

"Right now," Kaufman said, "we need to follow up on your statement to Merriman. If we don't, they'll really kill us. As to the results of the study, let's worry about that when the time comes."

As he spoke, Kaufman wondered whether Simmons knew more than he revealed.

Simmons frowned, looked at the others and asked, "Well, what do you guys think?"

It was really an easy call since Kaufman had taken the brunt of Simmons' anger and frustration. There was no other choice.

"I agree with Tim," said Robertson. Johnston concurred as well.

"Al, how about you?"

"Well, this is more complex than first meets the eye," he began. Simmons cut him off.

"None of your legal bullshit, Al. I'm too busy. Do we do the study, yes or no?"

"I guess I'll go with a qualified yes," Hawthorne said. "I'm not happy about it, but let's do it."

Typical Hawthorne, Kaufman thought. Now he can always say he had "reservations."

Simmons turned to Robertson and Johnston, asking them which consulting company they would recommend.

"We've used the Ann Arbor Research Institute for many years," said Johnston. "They do a good job. And being located in Ann Arbor gives the impression they're associated with the University of Michigan."

"How much business have we given them?" Simmons asked.

"A couple of million in the last five years."

"Good, that'll put some pressure on them. That ought to be worth something."

Simmons ordered Hawthorne to contact the Institute and draft the contract and Kaufman to write the press release announcing the study.

"And get the release out as fast as you can. Today, if possible."

Kaufman left the office, but he did so very worried. He did not like Simmons anticipating the results of a health study and even less, the financial pressure he implied he might apply to the Institute to develop conclusions favorable to Thompson Brakes.

ELEVEN

The release, a no-brainer for Kaufman, took him no more than an hour to write. He would usually send a draft to all the executives involved, but given Simmons' orders to speed up the process, he sent it only to the chairman, asking him how to proceed with other approvals.

"He said he would get the approvals," Susan Gray told Kaufman in a phone call.

About three hours later, a messenger delivered a "confidential" envelope to Kaufman. It contained the draft of his release.

Basically, there were only a few minor changes. The only major edit involved a Simmons quote that Kaufman had drafted, stating, "Thompson Brakes will make the results public when the study is completed." That sentence was deleted; no substitute language was offered.

Kaufman did not like the deletion and, equally important, he thought it was bad PR. But he did not intend to argue the issue because he knew he would have to answer that question when reporters called about the release. And, of course, the statement would have to be that the results would be shared with employees and the public.

Kaufman had his secretary fax the release to Newservice, Inc., instructing the company to distribute the release through their computer network throughout the country, assuring wide dissemination.

The release read:

Thompson Brakes to Commission Independent Study on Asbestos

Detroit, Michigan – The chairman and chief executive officer of Thompson Brakes, Inc. today announced that the company will commission an independent study on whether exposure to asbestos has caused any health problems for the company's employees. The highly-respected Ann Arbor Research Institute in Ann Arbor, Michigan, has been asked to conduct the independent study.

"We are a responsible corporation that historically has been sensitive to health issues involving our employees," said George C.L. Simmons, Jr., the company's chairman. "While we are confident that exposure to asbestos has not caused any health problems for our employees, we want to verify that we are correct and put to rest any concerns Thompson Brakes' employees and the community may have. The researchers will operate completely independently with the full cooperation of our executives and management team."

Kaufman was proud that he drafted the release without using the word *cancer* and that the language approved by Simmons made some concessions regarding the independence of the research team.

Kaufman's secretary faxed the release with instructions to Newservice. About an hour after the release hit the wires, the telephone started to ring. One of the calls was from Sue Merriman.

"About last night..."

"Forget it. I got bombed. I don't even remember, so you're ahead of the game. Let's move on."

Somewhat defensively, she asked. "What did you think of the story?"

"I'm not sure how you got the photo, but I'm sure I don't want to know," he offered. "As to the story, except for the anonymous source, who may be some pissed-off employee who was fired for screwing his secretary, drinking on the job or stealing equipment, I had no problem. I did have a little problem with your attempt at some humor in the sidebar. But I was also amused, off the record."

"The photo is the result of our high-tech age," she replied. "That's all you need to know. The source, Tim, is a reliable one, believe me. You don't want to know who that is either."

"As I said, Sue, let's not get into that again. How in the hell do you know the source is reliable? No way for you to know. But, again, let's move on. I can't get drunk two days in a row anymore. What do you need?"

She laughed. "How long will the study take?"

"Two to three months."

"How much?"

"We don't discuss what we pay our suppliers."

"How can Thompson Brakes call this an independent study ? The people doing the study are being paid by you."

"We will not interfere. That's what the contract says and the Ann Arbor Research Institute, I can assure you, being a reputable organization, would have it no other way." He liked citing the professional integrity of the research firm; that was good.

She followed up on the point by referring to Victor Crawford, a former tobacco industry lobbyist, who had gone public on how he commissioned "independent" reports to prove that tobacco did not pose a health hazard. Crawford, a smoker, changed sides after contracting throat cancer and went on many television talk shows to explain how the industry literally bought support from so-called experts.

"Is this the kind of independent report we can expect?"

"I know absolutely nothing about what Mr. Crawford might have done. I'm speaking for Thompson Brakes."

"Will you share the results of the study with everyone?"

"Yup. We will. We want to create a level of confidence in the community."

"Can you expand on how and to whom you'll send the results?"

"Nope. I think my answer speaks for itself."

"Hardly very definitively."

He did not want to give an elaborate quote that could come back to haunt him. He'd have to explain his answer to Simmons in any event.

"Your boss says he doesn't believe exposure to asbestos causes cancer. How can he say that and then order a study?"

"That's what he believes and, his convictions notwithstanding, he wants to be sure."

"Nice job, Tim. Always said you're a real pro."

"Thanks." He didn't return the compliment. "Take care."

"Tim," she said hesitantly. "I really would like to talk to you some more. How about a drink later this week? Off the record."

Kaufman was surprised at Merriman's initiative. The "off the record" comment indicated to him that she might be asking him for a date.

"I'll call you," he said. She believed that he meant it.

Whether or not he was right in his assumption about Merriman's overture, his ego was stroked and he had an impish smile on his face.

While Kaufman was glowing in the aftermath of the end of his conversation with Merriman, Hawthorne was working on a contract with the Ann Arbor Research Institute. He was reviewing the draft proposal from the Institute, making minor corrections throughout. Then he read the section entitled "Reporting Results":

> "The study is being undertaken with the understanding that, whether or not the conclusions reveal a causal relationship between exposure to asbestos and the deaths of Thompson Brakes employees, Thompson Brakes will communicate the results to appropriate government agencies, Thompson Brakes retirees who worked at the company during the time period covered and its present employees.
>
> "Given the public interest involved, we are also conducting this study with the understanding that – whatever the results – Thompson Brakes will release the report to the public, primarily through the media, and the Ann Arbor Research Institute will be permitted to comment on questions about the study."

When he finished reading the section, he crossed it out and called his secretary into his office. "Please take down the following and fax it to Richard Collins, the president of the Ann Arbor Institute. 'The following language replaces your proposed language in the section on reporting results: Thompson Brakes, Inc. will release the results of the study to any authority as required by law.' Fax that to Collins and get him on the phone for me. That's all."

When his secretary left, Hawthorne continued to review the proposal.

"Mr. Hawthorne?" his secretary interrupted on the speaker phone. "Mr. Collins is on your line."

"Thanks," Hawthorne replied, hitting the button on the telephone.

"Dick?" Hawthorne said, "How are you?"

"Fine," Collins replied. "Have you read our proposal?"

"Yes, that's why I'm calling. It looks fine except for the section marked reporting results. I'm faxing you some alternate language."

"What's the trouble?"

"Nothing much. I've approved the cost of the study. Review the language. If you've got a problem, get back to me."

"Can you tell me what it is?"

"Just read it, Dick. Call me back within an hour if you have a problem. If I don't hear, I'll assume you accepted my suggestion."

Hawthorne did not expect Collins to call back and he was right.

TWELVE

At union headquarters, Steve Marks could not believe his luck. Sue Merriman had accomplished with a couple of questions what he had been unable to do for years. She had made exposure to asbestos a public health issue by confronting the chairman. Previously, all the questions on the issue regarding policy had been handled by Simmons' subordinates in the PR department. Now, Simmons was on record.

He could have kissed Merriman. But he also understood the nature of news; he needed to keep the pressure on. There would never be a more ideal time for a press conference, asking for medical and other benefits for Paul Ferguson and threatening or actually filing a lawsuit. Sure, it was exploitation. But he could envision the drama, how the media would eat it up, the pictures of Ferguson, the tears, the public sympathy.

He picked up the phone and called. "Angie? Steve Marks. How's Paul?"

He recognized the awkwardness of the question.

"I guess so-so, under the circumstances."

"And you?"

"Holding up and holding on."

"Angie, I'm sure you've seen the papers. Simmons finally has been forced to face the issue publicly. Remember, I asked you about Paul's participation in a press conference. Well, we'll never have a better opportunity.

"The issue is very public and the media are looking for what they call follow-up stories. If we're ever going to do it, it has to be now."

She had hoped for more time to decide on Marks' request. "Yes, I remember, Steve," she said. "I've not talked to Paul about it. I know I said I would, but I'm sure you understand."

"I understand, but Angie, this could mean financial benefits for you – for all the families who have suffered through the years. This could give all of you some security, if we win.

"And we will win," he added very quickly. "Think of it this way, Angie. It would be a wonderful legacy for Paul."

He knew the last point could be interpreted as crass or uncaring. He took the risk. If Angie Ferguson turned him down, it wouldn't be because he hadn't played all his cards.

He waited. Had he blown it?

"Steve, I think you make a good point." Her voice was firm. "I'll talk to him. When do you need to know?"

"Today is Tuesday. I'd like to hold the press conference tomorrow or Thursday. Not Friday because that would hit the Saturday papers, which isn't good. We try to avoid Saturdays because of the small paper, which doesn't permit much coverage. So if we don't do it this week, we'll have to wait until next week. It really should happen as soon as possible to keep the momentum going."

Angie promised him an answer within 24 hours.

"Thanks, Angie. Give Paul my best."

Angie was torn about what she should do. Her husband had been depressed since hearing the diagnosis. Never much of a talker, he was now even more introverted. Every time he coughed, she winced as if it represented a countdown to his death which, in a sense, it did. She felt chills whenever she heard it.

Marks had no right to make this request, to put so much pressure on her family. She did not even understand the dynamics of a press conference. What would it all mean? Would her husband have his picture in the paper? Would they get reporters calling their home like she saw on television and in the movies? Could they handle it?

She wrestled with the arguments, trying to separate her strong feelings for privacy from how public pressure might hold Thompson Brakes accountable. Even discounting the moral issue, maybe Marks was right. If it meant some money, it would help her and the other families. She had to consider the future. Other widows were suffering and she would be too.

She was struggling with her need for financial help, whether the union would or could win, her desire for revenge and the need to stand up publicly to share the family problems with the world. God knows she needed the money. The company certainly had it coming. But she was averse to having her husband plead his case before cameras and reporters. It smacked of vulgarity, but she had little time before she needed to make a decision.

Now she was committed to a quick decision – 24 hours. If she decided not to ask her husband, she would never tell him that Marks had made the request. No need to worry him with moot issues. If she finally agreed with Marks, Angie was confident she could convince her husband to participate in the press conference.

Then, a bittersweet smile came to her lips. The thought of making "them" pay, getting some revenge and exposing Thompson Brakes to bad publicity, felt pretty good to her.

Yes, she thought. I would like to stick it to them.

THIRTEEN

Tim Kaufman and Sue Merriman were sitting in a booth in the Splendid Cafe in a remote part of southwest Detroit. They met "off the beaten path" because they agreed that it would be better not to be seen together. They did not want to start any rumors about a possible romance or talk about involvement in some diabolical scheme relating to their mutual business interests.

"I'm glad you called, Tim."

He smiled. "Well, do we set some ground rules regarding on and off the record?"

She slapped his arm flirtatiously. "No need. I'm wearing a wire."

He laughed, realizing he was looking at her romantically for the first time. She was a very attractive woman. He had never even considered asking her out on a date. She was so professional, tough and unyielding when she called in her role as a reporter.

Just an informal date, first date, Kaufman thought. Don't flatter yourself that she would even be interested.

Neither knew much about the other so, as is the custom on these occasions, they recited a little biography.

Kaufman, 42, grew up in a low-income family. His father ran a drycleaning store. He was the first in his family with a college degree. He attended Oakland University in suburban Detroit. Periodically, throughout his four years, he wrote for the university's student newspaper. He loved being a reporter; indeed, he had worked on the school paper in high school as well. After graduation, he knew someone who knew someone and he landed on the *Detroit Blade*.

"I didn't know you're an alumnus," she said, expressing surprise at the revelation. "I'll have to look up your clips."

He covered politics and enjoyed it immensely. After about 15 years, he quit to join Thompson Brakes. No, he never married, and no, he does not date frequently.

"How about you?" he asked.

Merriman, 31, was a graduate of Ohio State University. One of four children, she was always a "rebel, wanting to change the world."

After two years covering courts, she became a "star" and the paper's top investigative reporter, although she also covers business. When a big story comes along, she usually gets the assignment.

No, she has never been married. Engaged once. Yes, she does date frequently. No, nothing serious.

"You're good, you know," he said.

"You don't have to say the right things just because we' re out together."

"I know I don't. I mean it."

"Well, thanks. I appreciate that. Tim, I'd like to ask you about what we talked about the other day. When we both got pissed. I really want to know how you deal with being in PR. Doesn't it bother you to manipulate the news?"

"You know I've heard the charges about PR and politicians manipulating the news and it amazes me that the media do not understand that they are indicting themselves," he said. "Why do they let themselves be manipulated? Consider that I distribute a press release or call a press conference that you and your colleagues consider manipulation. Why don't you just ignore me and my brethren? If you let yourself be manipulated, then I'll be glad to do it so long as I do it honestly and ethically. I have no ethical problem with so-called manipulation. What I suggest is that the media consider the implications of being used."

She had to admit he had a point.

"Food for thought. But explain how you deal with always working to make your clients look good regardless of what they've done."

Kaufman welcomed the opportunity to discuss some PR philosophy. "Yes, I feel apprehensive at times and I'll explain. I think all of us who are in PR, especially those of us who were reporters but even others who weren't in the news business, don't always feel completely at ease morally or ethically. I don't always know that what they tell me is the truth. When I write quarterly reports and annual reports, they may only tell me what they want me to know. I know the lawyers sanitize the copy, letting their clients go as far as they can without going to jail. The entire system of governing public companies is a sham, but that's another story.

"I don't know if exposure to asbestos has caused cancer. My colleagues at GM didn't know if side-saddle gas tanks on pickup trucks were dangerous. And so on. These are complex issues. And, maybe we don't want to know. I'm not a psychiatrist. But as long as I don't know, I will do what I can for my clients and do it ethically and honestly. I will not lie for them.

"Maybe we're a little like lawyers. I'm told some attorneys won't ask their clients if they're guilty. They don't want to know even though they say lawyers have an obligation to defend the guilty as well as the innocent. Well, I couldn't do that, particularly if it involved rape or murder or crimes of violence. Alan Dershowitz deals with these issues in his book *Advocate's Devil*. He discusses all kinds of moral issues and says he could not violate his professional responsibilities of confidentiality to his client even if he knew his client would commit murder.

"You see, that's bullshit. I couldn't keep a confidence if I knew my client would commit murder. Dershowitz has his main character, a lawyer, blow the whistle on his client when the client is about to murder the lawyer's daughter. So it comes down to whose bull is being gored.

"Same with reporters. They say they will not violate promises of confidentiality. Well, if it involves crimes – murder, rape and similar violent crimes – I think they have a responsibility to do so, particularly since they work for private, profit-making companies. My friends in the media say they can't do that because their sources would dry up. But you can bet your ass they'd talk if their families were involved. Well, what about other people's families?

"So I can live with myself as long as I know that what I am telling reporters like you and, in turn, the public is the truth as far as I know. Is it rationalization? Perhaps, but I can live with it."

Merriman was impressed. That's what she liked about Kaufman, his intellectualism.

"But suppose you know the truth, what then?"

"Good follow-up question," he teased. "I don't know and, you know, I hope I never have to find out, Sue. But I'll tell you this. I hope I do the right thing. No one can ever say what they'll do when the pressure is on. But I pray I do the right thing under the circumstances."

He sure is straightforward, she thought. No sanctimonious b.s. He did not promise to be moral, he only hoped that he would be.

"Last follow-up," she teased back. "Why did you leave the *Blade* and journalism?"

"Because I did the right thing, as I said, under the circumstances. I encountered my asbestos issue in journalism. I could no longer live with semi-truths. Sue, you know as well as I do that much of the crap that is reported is just that – crap. Terrible mistakes are made because of superficiality, the pressure to beat the competition, to be first, to be exclusive, to publish stories that sell papers, which means the more negative, the more sensational, the better. How many times have I called to correct stories for my client and heard, 'You're right, I'm sorry.' And that's it. I and my colleagues have received thousands of sorries, but they don't do me or them any good.

"We complain about politicians failing to address the issues and those who do aren't covered. We complain about negativism in campaigns, but it makes good copy. We ruin reputations with information obtained from so-called reliable sources and feel no contrition when it turns out the information was bad.

"Remember former Secretary of Labor Ray Donovan? He was the subject of major media coverage on corruption charges. Every leak about him made the news. Then, when he was found innocent, he asked, 'Where do I go to get my reputation back?' The media had no answers for him.

"When I listen to TV news, news mind you, I think I'm watching Geraldo or the tabloids on television. They use any means to get a story –

hidden mikes, recorders, whatever. Hell, even the venerable *New York Times* has quoted the national tabloids on the O.J. Simpson case. This shows you where precedents take you. We even have journalism textbooks that support and recommend use of this new undercover high-tech equipment and these books proclaim proudly that the ends justify the means.

"Regularly, I read editorials criticizing the media for their coverage of particular stories. Talk about irony and hypocrisy. They criticize the media, of which they are a part, and then defend their actions at the same time. I don't understand it. At journalism seminars, in periodicals like the *Columbia Journalism Review*, and in speeches by journalists, the media admit their failings, but nothing is ever done.

"Sue, it has nothing to do with the First Amendment. It is not a matter of freedom of the press. It is a matter of the responsibility and fairness of the press. We are setting new precedents every day. And the precedents are hardly in the public's interest.

"It's not only about the press and those they cover. The proverbial argument always pits the media against government, business, politics, sports, etcetera. But not a word, not a word has been written about the media's responsibility to the public. When they publish erroneous reports, they are cheating the public because the product is faulty. And the public is making its decision based on that information. They have no other source.

"Think about it in that context. Forget about those you cover. At worst, they are expendable, but the public's right-to-know, to give you the benefit of the doubt, is not expendable. All this happens with no accountability, as we discussed in the Press Club the other day – if discussed is the right word."

Merriman broke into Kaufman's monologue. "But we have accountability. Our readers and, in the case of television and radio, viewers and listeners. And ultimately, the courts. People can sue us for libel, you know."

Kaufman took over again. "Let's take your first point, that the public holds the media accountable. Buying a newspaper is a long way from a public mandate. Nor is watching a television station or listening to a particular radio station accountability. They are customers; they make commercial decisions. Just because people buy our brakes does not mean they endorse the company's overall policies. Just because readers buy your papers does not mean they endorse what you do. The way the media define accountability – people don't have to buy the product or they can turn off the TV – is pure bullshit.

"As for suing, yes, I can sue, spend thousands of dollars for lawyers, perhaps spend years in court and, ultimately, still lose on some constitutional concept that may, indeed, support that I was wronged but it was not libel, and the damn case is thrown out.

"For instance, Ariel Sharon, the Israeli military general and politician, accused *Time* magazine of libeling him by publishing an accusation that he was partially responsible for the massacre of hundreds of refugees in Lebanon. He sued the magazine and a jury found the story was wrong, that it defamed Sharon, but it did not find it libelous because it did not meet the Supreme Court test of malice. Big deal, Sue. It was wrong, it defamed a man, but *Time* crowed and boasted how it had won. They wouldn't even admit how they'd screwed up under those circumstances.

"Sue, all this on a wonderful and respected foundation created by Ernie Pyle, A.J. Liebling, Edward R. Murrow, Walter Lippmann, Ted White, "Izzy" Stone, Walter Cronkite, and others."

He stopped, collected his thoughts and continued. "You see, the media accuse corporations like Thompson Brakes of caring about nothing but the bottom line, of being prepared to do anything to assure a good bottom line. That may be true. But the media aren't any different. Your exclusives are analogous to good sales in brake shoes. They lead to more sales of papers. The sensationalist coverage on TV improves ratings, and high ratings permit the broadcast media to charge higher advertising rates. So the media's corporate objectives are not any different than those of the rest of corporate America.

"All these issues combined were my asbestos issue. I hope you don't encounter one. When you do, I hope you're ready. I could no longer live with it. So I quit. And, yes, just so you don't think that I'm the ultimate idealist and do-gooder, the money is better and I like the stock options."

He threw in the last sentence to lighten his monologue. He realized he was getting a bit heavy.

"Whew," she said. "Well, that's a mouthful."

"You asked."

"Yes, now I'm sorry…just kidding. No, I'm glad I did and I'd like to think about what you said."

"Whatever. May not be worth your time."

They both sat without talking for a few minutes before she broke the tension.

"Want to go?"

"Sure."

He paid the check and they left the restaurant. They got into his car. He moved close to her and kissed her. She returned his kiss passionately and sat next to him when he started to drive.

"Want to stop by my place for a nightcap?" Kaufman asked.

"Yes, I'd like that."

He drove while stroking her knee next to his.

When they reached his house, she did not wait for him to open the door. She got out as he did. He took her hand and walked up to the front door. He kissed her before unlocking the door.

Inside, they kissed passionately. They fumbled to unbutton each other's clothes, and tumbled into the bedroom where they made love.

With his arm around her shoulder and her head on his chest, Kaufman stared at the ceiling.

"A penny for your thoughts," said Merriman.

Kaufman only shrugged his shoulders.

"What do you see up there?" she asked, trying to interject some light-heartedness.

"I see some problems," he replied.

"Problems?"

"This is an interesting situation, and interesting seems inappropriate under the circumstance."

She knew what he meant but asked anyway, "What do you mean?"

"Well, you cover Thompson Brakes and I'm the PR man. I think we've got the potential here for a conflict of interest, no?"

"We're professionals, aren't we? I think I can continue to do my job and I believe you have the integrity to do yours. I'm not going to ask you for special treatment just because of a personal relationship."

"Well, right now, I am tempted to say yes, but I'm not sure. You must admit, it's awkward. But we'll see."

"I'm sure your bosses wouldn't approve."

"And yours? I assume they'll be tempted to believe you'll go easy on me. I hope they're right."

"Can't keep you from hoping. Maybe I'll be even a little tougher under the circumstances."

The banter continued but Kaufman was more disturbed than Merriman. Could he represent Thompson Brakes honestly while having an affair with the reporter covering his company? Would he help her out by giving her more information than other reporters? How could he withhold information from her?

While they did not realize it at the moment, their first test would come the next day when Merriman would cover a press conference at which Steve Marks charged Thompson Brakes with creating an environment that caused Paul Ferguson to contract mesothelioma. An hour or so after the press conference, she would call Tim Kaufman for Thompson Brakes' reaction to the charges.

FOURTEEN

Steve Marks' adrenaline was flowing. This was his chance at national publicity on an issue about which he felt very strongly. He also recognized the political benefits to his presidency of the union.

He was angry that "his guy" was dying while Thompson Brakes was playing hardball, as he knew all corporations do when they get involved in these kinds of high-profile issues.

Angie Ferguson had convinced her husband to be the focal point of the press conference, arguing that they could do some good for the survivors of the men who had died from cancer. But it had not been easy. He protested that he did not want to be pitied or to be put on display. What he did not tell her was that he also felt guilty about having contracted the disease; he felt "dishonored" in his own way.

"I don't want to be shown like some freak at the circus," he told his wife. "They'll all flash their cameras, ask me questions about my life. Angie, I don't like that."

"Paul, it's not like that," she said. "You're not on display. You're showing courage by standing up to the company, by fighting the system. And I think you'll be doing something for all the other wives and families. Maybe it will help me."

She did not like making the reference to herself because it suggested the inevitability of his death, possibly just six months away. But she convinced herself that she also had to deal with the reality of the circumstances.

They had a very long argument but he relented when – only when – she cited the fact that his participation in the press conference might force Thompson Brakes to make some financial concessions and provide her with some security.

He loved his wife and he wanted to help her. Whatever his doubts about the tactics recommended by Marks, he agreed to participate in the news conference only because of his love for Angie.

Marks had briefed him well. All Ferguson needed to do was give short answers about himself. Marks would handle all other questions. They would sit close together behind a desk and Marks would signal him under the desk by tapping Ferguson's knee when the union leader would speak. Basically, he would handle the political questions.

The union hall where the press conference was held was packed. Not only did the Detroit media attend, but other reporters represented the national media – the *Wall Street Journal*, the midwest bureau of the *New York Times* and the national TV networks.

Marks was experienced; he knew how to push the right buttons. It was the biggest day in his union career; he needed to score, as he had told his union officers.

"Ladies and gentlemen, thank you for coming. First, let me introduce the man at my left. He is Paul Ferguson, an employee of Thompson Brakes for 46 years. I am Steve Marks, president of Manufacturers Workers Local 100. You have a press kit containing a release, some bios, pictures and statistics.

"I will read a short statement and then Paul and I will be glad to answer your questions."

Ferguson coughed several times because of nervousness. He squinted into the TV lights. He did not like this at all.

"In the 1940s, 1950s and 1960s, Thompson Brakes did absolutely nothing to protect its workers against exposure to asbestos," Marks read. "As a result, in the last 10 years, 89 workers have died of mesothelioma or other cancers related to exposure to asbestos. Studies indicate very clearly that mesothelioma does not manifest itself until 20 to 40 years after exposure and Paul Ferguson is suffering from that disease.

"We have tried everything possible to have the company meet its financial obligations to Mr. Ferguson's family and the survivors of those that died. But we have failed. The company has rejected all our requests. They deny any responsibility when the facts and evidence are very clear.

"We called this press conference to announce a lawsuit against Thompson Brakes. In the lawsuit, we are asking for $90 million in compensatory and punitive damages. The damages in the suit will be used to provide benefits for families who have lost loved ones to this insidious disease, help pay medical costs for present victims of mesothelioma like Paul Ferguson and finance medical treatments for future victims.

"We can't bring back those who died nor can we make Paul Ferguson healthy again. But we can make life a little easier for all those who have been victims of the company's irresponsibility. Thank you. Now we'll take your questions."

Marks, savvy about the news business, particularly the interests of TV, kept his statement short. He included in it the key points, understanding that the electronic media would use no more than a sound bite that would run about 10 seconds. Thus, he had edited his statement to assure that one of his key points would make the airwaves.

"How do you know that asbestos caused the illness?" a reporter asked.

"You have the statistics in your press kits. They are irrefutable and well beyond mere coincidence," said Marks. "And we have discussed the issue with health experts."

"Why won't the company do anything?"

"You'll have to ask them and I hope you do. It's despicable and unconscionable."

"How can you prove that Thompson Brakes knew of the dangers of asbestos?"

"Obviously, I don't want to give our strategy away here today. But overall, I think you will agree that the scientific evidence was there. They knew; everyone knew. But they chose to do nothing because it would cost them money."

"You are accusing Thompson Brakes of being inhumane, killing people intentionally."

"I suppose that's the bottom line. There is no nice way of saying it."

"Mr. Ferguson, what is the status of your cancer?"

"Well," stumbled Ferguson. "I have cancer that is – I'm not sure..." He coughed.

"Ladies and gentlemen, Mr. Ferguson's case is inoperable," Marks volunteered, somewhat reluctantly, but in keeping with his strategic objective of playing to the media.

The press corps appeared stunned by Marks' statement.

"How long?" someone asked but the tone of voice indicated discomfort. "I mean, how long...have they told you how long you might live?"

Ferguson looked at Marks, then into the lights and hesitantly said, "They told me...six months to a year."

"How do you feel now?"

"Okay," he said and coughed. "Sometimes I think, I hope, the doctors are wrong."

"Mr. Ferguson, how do you feel about Thompson Brakes?"

"Well, I worked for them for a long time. Always put bread on the table. I don't know much about this sickness. But what Steve here says makes sense. They caused a lot of misery. They should do something to help. Angie, my Angie, and the others need some help. We helped them; they should help us."

Marks was pleased with Ferguson's somewhat naive and unsophisticated responses.

"Do you think you'll win this suit?"

Marks squeezed Ferguson's knee behind the desk and took the question. "Absolutely. We are very confident, given all the evidence."

Then Marks added, "I want to point out, this is important, that before considering this suit, we tried everything else. Unfortunately, we have to fight for every worker's compensation case and we have continually asked the company to voluntarily set up a fund to pay for medical costs and survivor benefits. But they rejected everything."

"Mr. Ferguson, how do you feel about your illness?" came a question from a television reporter.

"Feel?" Ferguson said uneasily. "I don't know what you mean."

"Well, how does it feel to know you have inoperable cancer...that you have six months...."

Ferguson was agitated and tense. "I really don't know what to say. I don't want to die. I love my family. I want to...."

"Is there pain?" the same reporter followed up.

"Yeah, some," Ferguson replied. "Not too bad yet, I guess...most of all, I have trouble breathing..." Ferguson hesitated for a moment, and then added, "I think they should do something. Isn't my life worth something?"

Marks was surprised by Ferguson's emotional appeal. He had not expected such a philosophical statement from Ferguson. Recognizing the public relations value of the comment, he was confident that the quote would be used extensively for sound bites by the electronic media and he was equally confident the statement would be exploited by the print media.

Wanting to end on Ferguson's dramatic statement because he feared that the quote might be lost if the conference continued, he quickly ended the meeting. "That's all. Thank you for coming. We'll be around to talk to you individually."

He immediately walked over to the television reporter who had asked the last two questions.

"You bastard," said Marks. "Don't you have any feelings at all? I assume you got the sound bite you wanted."

"Spare me the lecture," the reporter shot back. "You put him on stage. You called us here."

"Because of the issue involved. I didn't do it to improve my ratings."

"No, you did it to get more votes from your members when you're up for reelection."

Marks started to lose his temper and would have punched the newsman if he had not remembered that other reporters were still in the room.

"Fuck you," Marks replied. "You have no sense of decency. I'm sure you're going to leave here to ask some parents how they feel about losing a child. That's real investigative journalism."

Marks stormed away from the reporter and then realized he should not have left Ferguson, who was surrounded by reporters.

Ferguson was stammering as questions came from every direction. He had some help from a union PR official, but he felt bombarded nevertheless.

"Can you describe your working conditions?"

"Well, it was dirty," Ferguson replied. "Always had dust on my clothes, in my pockets and it got into my nose."

Marks, joining the group, beamed as Ferguson awkwardly described the plant conditions.

"Did they give you any masks?" a reporter asked.

"Masks? No, I never had a mask. I didn't think much of it. Guess I was wrong. But I remember one of the guys saying that is was not good. He pointed to the clouds of dust in the air. I just laughed."

"Will you continue working?"

"Well, I want to. Don't have much money and the doctor bills are piling up. But I can't breathe too good. After I do something, I have to sit for a few minutes. And I have pain. Really, I don't know what I'm going to do. I'll have to talk to Angie."

"Fellows, give him some room," Marks said as he worked himself through the circle of reporters. "Take it easy on him. It's been tough on him."

The press backed off a little.

"Let's call it a day unless anyone has something more, something major," Marks suggested.

"Thanks everyone," Marks said, concluding the interviews. "Call me if you need anything. Thanks again."

When the press was gone, Marks congratulated Ferguson.

"You did a great job, Paul. I would like to see the faces of those Thompson Brakes bastards when they see the evening news and tomorrow's papers. What I wouldn't give to be there."

"I don't know, Steve," Ferguson said. "I didn't like that at all. Those questions about my illness, how I feel...I'm really upset."

Marks felt guilty. "They can be rude and crass sometimes, I agree. But look at the big picture. Think about what we might accomplish. Think about Angie and all the other Angies."

"Angie is why I'm here. Steve, that's the only reason. I still don't like it. I sure hope this works. I sure hope I didn't do this for nothing. You think this will do it?"

"Remember, Paul, we're not done yet."

FIFTEEN

When Tim Kaufman reached his office at about 10:30 a.m. – he was late – the morning after his date with Sue Merriman, he already had calls from several reporters who wanted the company's reaction to the lawsuit and the charges made at the press conference. Kaufman called Simmons' office and suggested a short meeting to discuss strategy.

Simmons agreed and within 15 minutes, Simmons, Hawthorne, Johnston and Kaufman were debating their contemplated media strategy.

"I don't care how you tell them, Tim, we're not going to be blackmailed. This is extortion," said Simmons. "We're not caving in to their pressure of a lawsuit. If we were to settle with them now and give them what they demand, they'd come back and ask for more. It's a terrible precedent. Plus, I think it would be an admission of guilt and we aren't guilty, right Al?"

"Absolutely," Hawthorne replied. "Let them sue, but let's not give in. The courts would tend to look on the agreement as tantamount to a confession and we could be sued anyway even if we establish a fund voluntarily. I agree, George, we don't want that kind of precedent.

"This is defamation," he continued. "I think we can sue their asses for libel."

As Simmons beamed, Kaufman demurred. "Al, I'm no lawyer but even I know that what's charged in a lawsuit can't be used for a libel suit. Otherwise, no one could ever sue because charges in a lawsuit always impugn someone's integrity."

Not being able to restrain himself, Kaufman added, "This is even better than suing Sue Merriman for trespass. These are some strategies."

Hawthorne grimaced, recognizing that Kaufman was showing him up.

"When did you get your law degree?" Hawthorne asked rhetorically.

"I don't need one for..."

Simmons cut them both off. "Al, check it out and let's move on. Enough of this bickering crap."

Kaufman was pleased with the exchange, hoping Simmons would recognize Hawthorne's incompetence. "Is there any truth to their charges?" Kaufman asked, understanding the political risks he was taking in raising such a question.

"You have to ask?" inquired Hawthorne. "I'm a little surprised. Tim, we're a responsible company. We do what's right to protect our employees."

Kaufman noticed that Hawthorne avoided the question.

"The point is, Al, we need the best information to develop the best strategy. Good PR can't work in a vacuum."

Hawthorne did not appreciate Kaufman's admonition. He was obviously angry.

"I don't need a lecture on PR, Tim. We've been truthful, or are you suggesting otherwise?"

Kaufman ignored Hawthorne's challenge. "Regarding calls from the media, I suggest that I offer our best to Paul Ferguson and his family but reject the basis for their suit. I'll repeat, as we have, there's no proof of the charges. And I want to emphasize that we've a study underway to decide the issue. Any problems with that?"

"Yes, wish him well, Tim, good idea," said Simmons. "That'll show we care. And, yes, the study. That's good. Glad we did that. We'll worry about the results later. We can always, as Nixon said on the tapes, PR it."

The meeting adjourned quickly after that exchange and Kaufman walked back to his office. On his desk were about 20 phone messages. There was one from Merriman, whom he decided to call first.

"I called about the press conference," she said. "We could talk about other issues another time."

"Fine, go ahead. Shoot."

"What's your reaction to the suit? Should I assume it has no merit like every suit ever filed against your company and your colleagues in corporate America?"

"First, we want to extend our best wishes to Paul Ferguson..."

"I want to barf."

"...and to his family," he continued. "We believe there's no basis for the suit. No empirical evidence exists that Thompson Brakes has any legal or moral liability."

"How do you account for the number of people who've died?"

"Medical experts will differ on this subject. As you know, we've commissioned a study to put that issue to rest. The point is there's no proof. Thompson Brakes is a responsible company that has always worked to ensure the health and safety of its employees."

"But the union charges that you failed to protect employees, that you knew and did nothing."

"We'll answer at the proper time in the proper place and that's in court – not in the media."

He had doubts about what he was saying. But he hoped his misgivings did not reveal themselves in his voice. His mind kept drifting back to the implications of Simmons' and Hawthorne's comments at the last meeting.

"Thanks, got to go. I'm on deadline. Let's talk in the next day or so."

"I guess you're assured page one on this one."

"Yup, see you. Sure makes me feel good to make you guys feel bad – present company excepted. Enjoy the news."

Then, reflecting back on their previous night's discussion of professional ethics, she added, "See, it *can* work. I ask the questions, you give the answers between 8 a.m. and 5 p.m. After work, all that stuff is off the record. Unless, of course, you say something really juicy about your employer," she kidded him.

Kaufman listened. "I guess. But I'm still not so sure. Don't want to talk on the phone."

"You think you're being bugged? Wouldn't surprise me."

He hesitated, "No. But I think you'll agree, this is a bit ticklish."

"Not for me. Right now you're a PR man and I'm the news hound doing my job. Of course, if you want to do me a favor with some inside info, be my guest."

"Don't hold your breath," he laughed. "Talk to you later."

He sat behind his desk reflecting on his mixed emotions. He thought he had handled the questions well. Yet, no matter how hard he tried to rationalize his relationship with Sue Merriman, he knew that it was wrong, a conflict. But he was unable to bring himself to sever the relationship even though it was in an embryonic stage.

He would deal with the issue later. Given what he expected from the media on the press conference, he had to focus on the asbestos crisis.

SIXTEEN

It was a total PR disaster. The story was major news, not just in Detroit but in cities all over the country where Thompson Brakes had facilities.

The news stories, with photos of Paul Ferguson, described him as a man facing death which, of course, was true. Ferguson's soft, naive and almost inarticulate approach toward the company was devastating.

The news stories played up Ferguson's statement about the value of his life. His rhetorical question, "Isn't my life worth something?", was played up in newspaper and television stories.

As a sidebar, the *Blade* published a man-on-the-street interview, asking residents about their views on the issue. Given Ferguson's fatal disease and the sympathy his suffering evoked, along with the pro-union environment in the Detroit area, the man-on-the-street voted for the union and the survivors.

The juxtaposition of the company's matter-of-fact statement to the lawsuit against the emotional press conference with Paul Ferguson made the company appear as coldhearted as possible. A typical story read, "With Paul Ferguson, a Thompson Brakes, Inc. employee for 46 years who has no more than a year to live as evidence that Thompson Brakes did nothing to protect employees from cancer-causing asbestos, the local union that represents him and other Thompson Brakes workers, has filed a lawsuit accusing the company with having knowledge of the dangers of asbestos but turning a blind eye to the evidence for financial reasons.

"The suit, asking for $90 million in damages, charges the company was aware that employees might contract cancer by being exposed to asbestos but did absolutely nothing to warn anyone in its plants."

The headlines were even worse. Most dropped any attribution on the accusations that exposure to asbestos had caused cancer, making the charges fact:

Thompson Brakes Refuses Financial Aid for Employees
Who Contracted Cancer at Company;
Union Sues for $90 Million for Medical Costs, Survivor Benefits

At the end of the piece in the *Blade*, the paper reported that it was planning a series of stories on the Thompson Brakes issue. In a special box, the *Blade* said:

> "About 90 employees, who worked for Thompson Brakes, Inc. since the 1960s, have died in recent years of cancers purportedly related to exposure to asbestos. We will take a look at their lives and their families. We want to tell the public about them because we believe they should be remembered as more than a statistic. You'll read about how they lived, how they worked, how they died, and how their families are doing.
>
> "Most important, we will try to answer the question whether exposure to asbestos – a known carcinogen – contributed to their deaths. And we will investigate what kind of scientific evidence existed on this subject and what Thompson Brakes knew and did not know about asbestos-causing cancer. The stories will be written by Susan K. Merriman, award-winning reporter for the *Blade*."

As Hawthorne, Johnston, Robertson and Kaufman met with Simmons to assess the impact, the chairman was furious. He was pacing the floor and was more profane than usual.

"What the fuck is going on?" he screamed. "Those bleeding heart liberals are going to kill us. The stock is taking a goddamn beating."

Simmons was right. The impact on the stock was devastating, with

Kaufman receiving hundreds of calls from upset shareholders who wanted to know what plans the company had for damage control.

"They are literally ruining us," the chairman continued. "I'm going to sue the fuckers. I'm going to destroy them. This has gone too far. Now they're going to write a series of tear-jerking stories that will really make us look like bastards. Tim, where the hell do we go from here?"

"Hate to say this, but there's really little we can do. Here are our options: (1) Negotiate for an out-of-court settlement, make a counteroffer, or (2) continue in court and fight the suit. But we should release our study as soon as possible, and I assume it will verify our position. Even if it does, the union will charge the study isn't accurate because we paid for it. I think, as a first step, we need to get the study into our hands as soon as possible."

Hawthorne confronted Kaufman's suggestions.

"We can't pay or give them what you call a counteroffer, Tim," the attorney said. "I already told you, from a legal point of view, it sets precedents."

Simmons took over. "For the time being we hold the course. Tim, keep saying what you have. Get that in about extending our sympathies to...what's his name?"

Hawthorne volunteered that perhaps the corporation should give a donation to a medical facility. "Let's give them about a $50,000 donation. That will show we care. Earmark it for research."

Kaufman objected. "It'll look like we're trying to buy support and only make things worse. The union and the papers would crucify us."

"Well, maybe we should make it a hundred grand."

"Al," said Kaufman. "You're not getting the point. We can't buy our way out of this. We need to deal with the issue."

Hawthorne gave up, although he refused to acknowledge the weakness in the strategy.

"A hundred grand buys a lot of goodwill. Let's think about it."

"Al, as I said..."

"Let's get back on track," Simmons sneered angrily. "Anything on a possible libel suit, Al?"

Hawthorne had hoped that Simmons would forget about the suggestion he now regretted he had made.

"Still checking," Hawthorne said. "From the research we've done, I don't think it will work. Really somewhat complex legally. If that changes, I'll let you know."

Kaufman had a sly smile on his face while Simmons frowned. "This meeting is over," he said abruptly.

He looked at Johnston and told him to stay.

"Al, you stay, too," Simmons said.

After Kaufman took the cue and left, Simmons' entire demeanor changed. He became very serious.

"Listen, we need to get this thing under control. Al, with this suit, can they subpoena our records? All of them?"

"Yes, with discovery motions. I assume they'll do that. They can go back as far as they want."

Simmons cringed. "I want you guys to start thinking how to end this, understand? I don't care how you do it, just do it. Got it?"

Simmons then addressed Johnston, his vice president of environment and health.

"Glen, you know we have a lot of sensitive records. Some are no longer relevant, some are outdated, some won't be understood in the context of the times. I'm sure you agree with me that these records could be inaccurately interpreted. They were written at a different time under different circumstances and people today wouldn't understand that. You do agree, don't you?"

"Of course," Johnston said, but not very enthusiastically.

"Some of the records are nothing but old information and, frankly, I always thought they were totally inaccurate. What I'm going to say, no one else knows. You and Al are the only ones I'm trusting with what I'm going to say."

Simmons then discussed records that contained citations from governmental agencies charging the company with poor ventilation systems and many other asbestos-related health hazards. The records also included, he said, many memos written by executives over the years warning the company of the asbestos dangers and recommending, sometimes in very strong language, that Thompson Brakes institute remedial action.

"But the thing we need to remember is that all this happened many years ago," Simmons tried to reassure Hawthorne and Johnston. "The situation was much different."

Hawthorne listened passively but Johnston, anticipating Simmons' upcoming request, was worried about where the conversation was headed. He did not interpret the chairman's expression of trust as a compliment.

"Go through the records. Take a good careful look. And destroy what's useless, redundant, outdated. Do you understand?"

Johnston, looking very disturbed, said he did.

"Good. Like I told the others, just do it. I know you're a team player, a good soldier, and in times like these we need team players. You'll have a great future here. Thanks for your help."

After Johnston left, Simmons asked Hawthorne, "I assume this was all protected under client-lawyer privilege?"

"Absolutely," Hawthorne said confidently. "We did everything according to the law to protect the company. This conversation is protected by the law."

But Hawthorne was wrong and the bad advice would eventually haunt Simmons.

SEVENTEEN

Simmons had more on his mind than the asbestos issue. For the last several years, the earnings of Thompson Brakes had been anything but stellar. He was facing severe pressure because, with the tacit agreement of his board, he had been using intricate accounting procedures to hide a major financial loss. The pressure was building to make the loss public. Ronald W. Mathison, the chairman of Mathison, Hatchett, Emerson and Lewiston, the company's independent auditing firm, was very concerned about his company signing off on Thompson Brakes' financial statements.

Mathison was sitting outside of Simmons' office waiting to meet with the chairman, and Simmons assumed he was going to push – and push hard – for the company to report the loss publicly.

Mathison and Simmons had been friends for many years. They socialized in the same circles and Simmons frequently was Mathison's guest at a private, exclusive country club.

Thompson Brakes represented $500,000 to Mathison's firm and Simmons was convinced that Mathison would not want to lose the account, not because it was very large, but he realized that Mathison enjoyed the relationship for political reasons. Still, $500,000 was a significant figure, "nothing to sneeze at," Simmons would say, and he understood the use of financial pressure and the role it played in convincing independent auditors, at times, to look the other way.

"George," Mathison began when he joined Simmons in his office, "we have been friends for a long time. I think I've been very supportive."

"Yes, you have, Ron, and I appreciate your friendship and support. And I think we've been a good client."

"Yes, of course, George. I don't mean to imply anything else. But some of my people and I as well, frankly, are deeply concerned about certain issues regarding our audit."

"What do you mean?" Simmons asked, knowing exactly the point Mathison was making.

"I think you need to take the write-off in the next quarter – the fourth quarter. Even now, I'm very worried that you might face some lawsuits for delaying taking the hit. We've gone along with the interpretation given by your financial people, but I can't subject my company to the risks involved if we wait any longer."

Mathison was disturbed because his staff on the Thompson Brakes account maintained that the company was not "totally realistic" in the figures it was providing. But he was very careful in the language he used with Simmons. He had been convinced by his staff that Thompson Brakes was overestimating the value of its inventory, understating accounts payable while overstating accounts receivable.

In addition, the company was projecting sales artificially to achieve budget forecasts and reporting decreased administrative expenses on the books while they were actually increasing.

This was not an unusual procedure used by public companies to delay announcing losses. Although other public companies engaged in this kind of deception, at least they did so based on realistic evaluations that they would attain their goals. Mathison's staff had told him that Thompson Brakes "could not make up the red ink." His staff had briefed him thoroughly, stating that a careful analysis indicated a fiscal mess.

"If this isn't cleaned up, we'll all go to jail," one of Mathison's accountants told him.

The staff believed and told Mathison that the company had used sophisticated computer programming to finesse the actual financial status of the company, a strategy that required the involvement of at least four or five top officers. They also believed the chairman had to be involved, given the gravity of the financial situation. They did not believe the figures could be adjusted so dramatically without Simmons' approval and that of the board. Senior management, including the board, at least gave its implicit go ahead, if not outright approval.

"Maybe I should've come forward sooner," Mathison continued. "But my people gave your people the benefit of the doubt. They also understand the value of this account to us. But George, the risk is getting too great. I can't take such a risk. If we can't resolve this, I'll have to take it up with my board. This is too much responsibility for me to shoulder alone."

Simmons tried to downplay the gravity of the financial crisis.

"I don't think it's that bad," Simmons said, but not very convincingly. "Ron, sales are looking up; I think we can turn the corner. We need another quarter or two."

Mathison looked dismayed, but did not relent.

"George, I'm sorry. I'm sorry we didn't act sooner. I'm sorry we have to have this conversation. I want to help, but this is serious stuff."

Simmons became angry and started shouting.

"You don't have to tell me this is serious, Ron. I've been sweating blood. I could end up in the can."

He immediately regretted his statement because it implied complicity. Trying to recover, he added, "I'm no financial whiz, you know that. I rely on people who are supposed to know what they're doing."

Mathison, breaking the tension, agreed with Simmons, stating "it was probably the fault of the financial staff."

"George, I understand how staff can succumb to pressure and mislead you with the numbers," he said, indicating to Simmons he did not believe the chairman was involved in a financial conspiracy. "They want their promotions and their bonuses and they don't always want to be the bearers of bad news. But my advice is to take the hit now. Talk to your board. You'll take some flak in the short term, sure. But it beats the alternative."

Mathison was trying to be as diplomatic as possible. He had wooed the account over several years, defeating formidable opposition. Having Thompson Brakes as a client not only provided a half-million-dollar account, but it gave the accounting firm prestige. He enjoyed the camaraderie with the chairman and he liked being recognized as Simmons' friend at the country club. But he decided to risk losing the account because he, like Simmons, feared a possible investigation and, ultimately, criminal charges.

Mathison was also very alarmed because, a year earlier, the chairman sold 1,000,000 shares of his stock while the company was going public with a stock offering.

He had stated his case clearly at the time. The perception, he had told Simmons, of the chairman selling while urging the public to buy "sent some very troubling messages, not to mention the negative PR implications."

Simmons, however, would not change his mind and the reaction of the financial community, particularly Thompson Brakes shareholders, was one of outrage. Mathison was cautious about bringing up the matter but he felt he had little choice.

"George, there's the matter of the sale of stock last year..."

Simmons cut him off sharply. "I don't need your reminders. I said at the time I did that for tax and inheritance planning and that was the truth."

"That may be, but the Securities and Exchange Commission..."

"Ron, I heard you. I don't want to discuss it anymore. I know the implications and I'll defend that decision if it comes to that. For now, I don't want to hear fucking complaints about something a year old."

Mathison was shocked and intimidated by Simmons' reaction. He knew the subject was sensitive, but had not expected such anger. He wanted to make certain that Simmons understood the seriousness of the implications, if not to Thompson Brakes, then at least to his auditing company.

"I'm worried about a class action suit besides a possible SEC investigation," Mathison told Simmons. "It happened to Arthur Andersen in the John DeLorean case. They got hit with a $100 million judgment. The ruling was that if they hadn't known of the precarious financial situation, they *should* have known."

Simmons was not impressed. "I would start hiring some good lawyers."

Mathison was angry at Simmons' snide remark, but did not show it.

"Lots of records would implicate us," he said.

"Well, as I tell my people, take care of the problem. Just do it. Cover your ass. Do what you have to do. Those records can be taken care of."

Mathison decided his efforts to elicit some understanding from Simmons were futile.

Without saying another word, Mathison stood up to leave. He shook Simmons' hand and left the office, still feeling unsure and worried about what Simmons would do.

If Simmons ignored his advice, could Mathison's firm accept the risk? If not, could it afford to lose the account? A public controversy, Mathison knew, would give credence to the argument that independent auditors are hardly independent when they are paid by the very people they audit. While the two should work at what is called in the industry "arm's length," the cynics argued that many firms like his work with the client in an embrace.

While Mathison wrestled with those issues, Simmons was deciding to go public with the loss. Some of the directors had told him the time had come to "face the music." Even Hawthorne told Simmons that outside counsel advised to report the loss in the next quarterly report.

All feared an investigation by the Securities and Exchange Commission if Simmons continued to stall the release of the bad news. Hawthorne explained that even if the loss were reported, the SEC might investigate on the suspicion that Thompson Brakes had misled investors with promises of increased earnings while camouflaging the real financial picture.

The company's shareholder communications in recent years contained many promises of "improved earnings" and "increases in return of investments." Unfortunately, the reports did not reflect reality. Even before Mathison's direct appeal to the chairman, Simmons had been warned by directors and his financial advisors that the company might be violating SEC requirements on disclosure and, in addition to an investigation, it might face class action lawsuits from disgruntled shareholders.

Frankly, he considered the financial loss more devastating to Thompson Brakes than the asbestos issue because most investors feared, as he did, a major write-off would reduce the potential return on their investment. It would also reflect negatively on Simmons' ability to effectively manage Thompson Brakes and depress the value of the company's stock. The asbestos issue, however, could be dragged out for years in the courts and the company might even win.

If he agreed to report the financial loss, it would be released in the fourth quarter along with year-end results, which meant he would have to face questions from shareholders at the next annual meeting only two months away. The timing was not good, to be sure, but time had also run out. He needed to act.

Simmons called Kaufman to his office to brief him on the fourth-quarter report and to ask him to prepare a press release as well as begin working on the CEO's speech for the annual meeting.

"What I'm going to tell you is strictly confidential, Tim," said Simmons. "We are going to have a major loss – about $35 million – in the fourth quarter.

"It results from complex inventory issues and wrong projections on accounts payable and accounts receivable. The lawyers will fill in the reasons for the loss," Simmons said, while trying to assess Kaufman's reaction.

Kaufman showed no sign of being surprised by the news, but he was shocked, fully understanding the very serious implications.

"Tim, take down the following on your legal pad and listen carefully. I want you to draft the release emphasizing that this is a one-time write-off, that it was totally unexpected, that we intend to recoup quickly, that we've solved the problem to make sure it never happens again and so on. I want the release to put shareholders and the financial community at ease about Thompson Brakes. You understand?"

"Yes, but this is going to be a tough one out there."

"I don't need you to tell me that."

Kaufman regretted stating his assessment. He changed the subject.

"Given everything else I have on my desk, I need your approval to have Ruth Sanderson involved. I'll need her help on this."

"Can you trust her?"

"Absolutely," Kaufman said, vouching for his assistant in the public relations department.

"But warn her of the sensitivity of this issue. I also want you to start on a draft of my speech for the annual meeting, covering the same theme. I want shareholders to leave the meeting with confidence. I know it's early, but this is going to need lots of work and many drafts. So get right on it. Also, start the Q & A process."

Kaufman was stunned by the news as he left Simmons' office. He expected a major PR disaster, particularly in the Wall Street community. He would be the first to agree with Simmons that investors would consider the loss more critically than the asbestos issue. But Kaufman would judge their priorities to be immoral whereas Simmons sympathized with them.

Kaufman headed to his office deeply concerned about what he had just heard. He did not understand how a company suddenly, without warning, loses $35 million nor would Wall Street, the institutional or individual investors. He knew he would face tough questions about why the company had failed to warn investors of such a major loss.

It's going to be fun around here when this breaks, he thought.

After processing the disastrous news he had just received, Kaufman wrote a memo to all senior executives asking them to submit to him questions that might be expected at the annual meeting.

"I will develop a master list from the questions received, prepare responses and then send them to all of you for comments and approval," he wrote. "I need these in no later than one week. I appreciate your assistance and cooperation."

Kaufman, however, found the process as practiced totally useless. It rested on assumptions that the questions would be posed exactly as drafted by those in the organization and that those responding would memorize all the answers.

That, of course, was not the case. Thus, Kaufman frequently told his staff, while corporate America spent endless hours and huge sums of money to sanitize Q & A drafts, they were useless because interviews never followed the prepared script. Kaufman argued that if the executives were thoroughly briefed on the issue involved, no Q & A papers were necessary.

But Kaufman, after some futile attempts to change the exercise, surrendered. After receiving the questions, he would prepare recommended answers that would be edited by all departments involved directly or indirectly, and generally the answers were so vague as to be totally unresponsive. As he told his trusted assistants in one-on-one conversations, communications for shareholders, like other information on controversial matters in corporate America, were based on the principle of obfuscation – not candor.

Reflecting on the upcoming press release, Kaufman expected the stock to drop at least three or four points, if not more, when the news and magnitude of the loss became public and was digested by the financial community.

He walked into Ruth Sanderson's office to brief her about her assignment on the project. Sanderson was a bright, talented writer who had joined Thompson Brakes five years earlier. At 33, she'd had some previous PR experience at a much smaller company and had not been involved in the brutal politics of a large organization. She shared many of his philosophical misgivings but still retained some idealism. She thought he was too cynical, although she understood the reasons for his distrust in the system.

Kaufman briefed her on the loss and asked for her help in preparing the Q & A.

"They're going to raise hell when this gets out," she said. "I guess you're right again about the system."

"Ruth, the governance of public companies is a complete farce," he said. "We've talked about this.

"Inside directors aren't going to take on the chairman. He holds their future in his hands. Outside directors are generally friends of the chairman, carefully screened by the chairman. They socialize together, play golf and they get a good stipend. The last thing they think of is the shareholder. They really protect the chairman, and the directors at GM, Kmart, Bendix and Morrison Knudsen, where they had disasters, finally acted but only after the ballgame was almost over. And then only because of major pressure and publicity.

"When outside directors start to challenge the chairman, he gets rid of them. Ruth, how many releases have you written in your short time in PR about resignations to pursue other business interests? Or because they no longer have the time to serve?"

"But the shareholders vote for these directors."

"Ruth, that's a joke. What do you know about candidates mentioned on proxy cards? Nothing, nor do you have the resources to do the necessary research on them or on financial issues management asks you to approve or reject on proxy cards.

"What's more, even if you were to launch a fight, the rules are stacked against you. They have the bylaws in their favor, and given their stock ownership, they control substantial percentages of the vote that you can't overcome. Those people who fight management on nuclear power and the environment generally fail."

"What about the independent auditors?"

"I assume you're kidding. Who pays them? The companies they audit. The entire investor relations field is one of cover-up versus revelation. Hawthorne – or I should say, our outside counsel – works hard to sanitize everything you and I write. They let us say just enough to keep them out of jail."

Sanderson did not like what she was hearing.

"Well, I still think you're overstating the case. I'd like to maintain some faith in the system otherwise I might as well try something else."

Kaufman smiled understandingly and continued by citing the duplicity of research reports by so-called independent brokerage houses.

"Ruth, the latest report that recommends a buy on Thompson Brakes comes from a firm Simmons pressured to write the report in exchange for giving them the public offering of new stock. What else are they going to write? They can't recommend that investors sell when they're trying to get the financial community to buy the new stock issue. Their commission rests on a successful stock sale.

"And the other reports? Half just report what you and I tell them. Very few have the ability or resources to do any independent analysis. Hell, many send their drafts to me to read and edit. True, I can't touch their opinion on whether to buy or sell, but I sure can affect their decision by what's in the report. The investor relations discipline is one of incestuous relationships and conflicts of interest, not to mention some incompetence.

"But, Ruth, I am still fighting with myself. You may be right and only by retaining a degree of doubt can I do my job. So let's develop some good strategy on the latest news."

Kaufman was developing PR strategies on the $35 million loss as Johnston pondered Simmons' instructions to destroy corporate documents dealing with the health issues relating to asbestos. He called his assistant, John Barrister, to his office. Using the instructions Simmons had given him, he told Barrister to purge the records of material that was "useless, redundant, outdated."

"I know you can do this job," Johnston said. "We need to clean up our files and get rid of outdated material that no longer has any relevance to our present environment. You know what I'm saying?"

"Absolutely. Don't worry. I'll take care of it."

Johnston knew Barrister would not protest. His assistant was ambitious and basically a "follow orders" kind of guy.

Johnston was violating Simmons' orders of confidentiality, but he could not bring himself to personally carry out the chairman's mandate. Moreover, he was worried that if he were called as a witness in a lawsuit, he might be asked if he had ever destroyed company documents.

With his instructions to Barrister, he felt satisfied he could answer honestly he had not. For the moment, he did not consider his complicity or that he might be asked whether he had knowledge of the destruction of documents. He simply did not want to engage in the destruction himself.

Barrister started on his assignment immediately. He searched through company records and collected documents relating to issues of health, particularly those dealing with exposure to asbestos and cancer. He created two piles, one that he would review very carefully after a cursory examination and the other contained material he would discard.

Some documents he read quickly; others more thoroughly. It was a laborious task, but he did not mind. He was dealing with extremely politically and legally sensitive issues for Thompson Brakes. And he wanted Johnston – and Simmons – to think he was a team player.

Of course, he did not know that Simmons was unaware that the task had been assigned to him or that Johnston had been instructed to do the housecleaning himself. What Johnston did not know was that Barrister would not destroy all the incriminating documents.

For instance, he made a point of saving one written by a senior executive to the chairman, which read:

To: George C. Simmons, Jr.

From: Bob Alterman

Subject: Asbestos, CONFIDENTIAL

Date: February 21, 1993

"As I have indicated in previous discussions with you and other executives, I think we are sitting on a time bomb regarding the asbestos issue and whether we were responsible for causing cancer. We need to deal with this issue. The pressure that we have some responsibility in this matter is mounting and becoming more public.

"In my view, it is absolutely essential that we create a task force to study the issue and recommend a course of action. I think we should do this immediately. I would be most pleased to discuss this matter in more detail with you at your earliest convenience. Please let me know."

Below Alterman's signature was a note to him. "Bob – Agreed. We'll talk next time you're in my office." The note was followed by Simmons' initials.

After several hours of research, he even found a memo written by Simmons to his predecessor.

"The asbestos issue may cause us some problems soon," he wrote. "We should talk about it and develop a strategy for a possible public posture. I know we can't give in because it could cost a fortune. I agree that we must avoid the impact on our profitability at all costs. But to achieve our goals, we need to develop a comprehensive plan."

He found another memo, written by one of Alterman's staff members that read, "Any headway with the chairman on the asbestos issue? We need to move. It's dangerous."

He also discovered documents from OSHA charging Thompson Brakes with health violations such as poor ventilation, not posting warning signs and similar infractions. These Barrister considered most incriminating since they were government citations.

As he examined the files, Barrister carefully collected documents that he knew indicted Thompson Brakes. He put them in the pile he intended to take home.

After the third day of his review, Barrister ordered a cart from the maintenance department. He placed several cartons of records containing materials he considered very important and potentially damaging on the cart and wheeled them to the elevator.

When he reached the lobby, he looked at the security guard and donned a casual demeanor. "I got some big projects for the weekend at home, Sam."

He walked over to the guard. "Bastards always give me a deadline project when the weekend comes up."

"I know how you feel," the guard replied. "Guess you won't be watching the big game."

"Big game? You got to be kidding. I'll be lucky if I have time to get lucky."

The guard roared as Barrister returned to his cart and wheeled it out without being asked about the contents or having to sign for the documents.

Barrister was taking home what he hoped someday might help him become vice president of environment and health of Thompson Brakes, Inc., the job now held by Johnston.

EIGHTEEN

Tim Kaufman was unaware of the behind-the-scenes activities as he sat in the Splendid Cafe with Sue Merriman. It was their first meeting since they'd made love.

"So, how's it going?" Merriman asked.

"I've had better days," he said. "You're making my life tough – I mean professionally."

"If you want to stop..."

He shook his head. "No, I suppose if James Carville and Mary Matalin could handle representing opposing candidates running for president of the United States, I think I can handle this."

She had read about Carville, who was President Clinton's strategist in the 1991 presidential campaign, and Matalin, his fiancée at the time, who worked for George Bush, the incumbent President who lost the election. After Clinton's victory, the two strategists for the Democratic and Republican presidential candidates married, wrote a book and made lots of money promoting their unique relationship.

"Well, think of the marketing potential."

He did not laugh. He was preoccupied with the asbestos issue and his relationship with Merriman. Regardless of how the Thompson Brakes case developed, he wanted to maintain his integrity. That was important to him. He did not want to create even a perception of a conflict of interest or any impropriety.

"No one will know," she volunteered, anticipating his concern.

"I will," he said. "And I don't like hiding out with you."

Then he asked, "What if you get some info on me? A good story, a real good one. Would you go with it?"

"Absolutely," she quipped. "No problem whatsoever. The juicier the better." Then, more seriously, she added. "You know something I don't?"

"Just wondering. How would you report a scandal on the man you're sleeping with?"

"Tim, let's get serious. I don't even want to think about it. It's not going to happen and you know it."

"I don't know it, Sue. You can joke all you want, but your clashing with me is a possibility – a very good possibility – and, frankly, I expect it to happen. This asbestos thing is a hot issue. And that's only part of the overall conflict."

She had to admit – at least to herself – there was merit in what he said. As they sat sipping their drinks, neither noticed the photographer, seated several booths away, taking their pictures.

"So, what's the answer?"

He scratched his head. "I wish I knew. I know I want to see you. I know I enjoy your company. You're bright, attractive..."

"Don't stop now," she joked.

"We're compatible. The sex is good."

"Thank you," she offered with a seductive smile.

"I just don't know the answer. But then, maybe I do and I don't want to admit it."

"What do you mean?"

"The answer, of course, is to stop seeing you – even if it may be too late already. But I don't want to do that."

"For now, why don't we just put it on hold and get out of here?"

As Kaufman and Merriman left the cafe, Steve Marks called the Ferguson house. He had not talked to Ferguson or his wife since the press conference.

"Angie, things are going just great," he said, immediately regretting his choice of words. "I mean, the pressure is building on them.

"We've filed a class action suit in Paul's name asking for the $90 million and we couldn't have been luckier. It's been assigned to Wayne County Circuit Judge John Faulkner. Angie, he's a liberal concerned about the environment, a civil libertarian. We could not have done better."

"That's great."

Feeling bad that he had not asked about her husband, he quickly inquired about Ferguson's health.

"Sometimes he seems the same, sometimes worse. Maybe I'm just more sensitive to it now. I guess he's the same. That's good news about the judge. Congratulations."

"Thanks, but not much I did. It's a blind draw, but we sure were lucky. I can't tell you how much Paul helped at the press conference. If we have a jury trial in this county, everyone is going to remember him. They can't tell me that has no influence in court or on the judge. Given his history, it's going to be helpful."

"Steve, I can't think about that now. I have to put my energies into making Paul as comfortable as I can."

Marks, picking up on Angie Ferguson's emotional turmoil, said, "I understand, but just remember, we're going to win this one."

"I hope you're right," she replied, knowing only too well that whatever the outcome in court, she would lose a husband.

NINETEEN

At Thompson Brakes headquarters, Hawthorne was briefing Simmons on the suit and Judge Faulkner. The chairman also had asked another new member of management to attend the meeting. Lou Salter, vice president of security, had joined the company six months earlier after retiring as a detective from the Detroit Police Department.

"Shit, what more can happen to us? Who knows anything about this judge?" Simmons asked.

When no one answered, he called Kaufman, put him on the speaker and asked him if he knew Judge Faulkner.

"Don't know much," Kaufman said. "When I was a reporter, I covered a few cases in his courtroom. He's known as being very honest, lots of integrity. Once or twice, several years ago, he called me with a couple of questions about things we reported. Just a few phone calls. Really don't know him personally."

"Is he a bleeding heart liberal?" Simmons asked.

Answering carefully, Kaufman said that he was considered "a liberal and an environmentalist. But he doesn't let his politics influence his decisions, I've read."

"How the hell can he do that?"

Kaufman had to admit that was a good question.

"I really don't know, George."

Simmons hung up and asked his advisors, "What can we do to get another judge?"

"I'm afraid not much," said Hawthorne. "It's a blind draw system and we don't have much of a choice. We can do things to stall but not much about the judge."

Salter volunteered, "Well, let's not be too hasty. You never know. George, can my department look into it?"

"Hell, yes. As I said, just do it."

"We will, George, and on the other issue we discussed, I may have some interesting information and photos for you."

"Good, get the stuff to me when you're ready."

Hawthorne did not know what the two were talking about nor did he ask, although he was curious. He excused himself, stating he had to meet Richard Collins to discuss the status of the asbestos-cancer research.

Richard Collins was waiting outside Hawthorne's office with a draft of his report. He was there on Hawthorne's order. Hawthorne had called a few days earlier, asking when the study would be ready. When told it would not be finished for several weeks, Hawthorne demanded a quicker result.

Collins protested, indicating he did not want to hurry his staff and, subsequently, have a flawed report. But Hawthorne insisted, demanding an immediate meeting.

He also instructed Collins to come without any staff support. Again, when Collins tried to explain that he had no hands-on knowledge and might not be able to answer complex questions, Hawthorne ignored Collins' concern.

"I said no staff, got it?" Hawthorne demanded with impatience.

Collins did not like any of Hawthorne's instructions and worried about their implications. But he pressured his staff to complete the report to meet Hawthorne's deadline and was outside of the lawyer's office alone.

"Good to see you, Dick," Hawthorne greeted Collins. "Let's go in and have a frank discussion, just you and me."

Despite the deadline constraints, the report was thorough and professional. Admittedly, he was worried about Hawthorne's – and the company's – reaction. The results were not good for Thompson Brakes.

"Let's see it," Hawthorne said.

Collins handed the 92-page document to the lawyer. Marked "Confidential," the study was entitled, "A Mortality Study of Thompson Brakes Workers and Exposure to Asbestos."

Hawthorne turned to the executive summary. He read: "The mortality experience since 1940 of former employees at Thompson Brakes' various facilities has been reviewed. The statistics indicate that there exists a direct relationship between employment at Thompson Brakes plants, the exposure to asbestos dust and such diseases as mesothelioma and other cancers which are caused by such exposure."

Collins could see Hawthorne wince.

"There have been many deaths related to these cancers and these occurred mostly when employees had long exposure to asbestos dust. The occurrence of cancer was much less in employees with very little exposure and there were no cases reported among Thompson Brakes office employees.

"There is also a relationship between those who contracted mesothelioma and smoking. The research indicates that smokers were also more likely to contract this cancer. While smoking, therefore, may not be related to contracting mesothelioma, it does enhance the chances of contracting this cancer."

Hawthorne raised an eyebrow and stopped to make a note on his pad. He continued to read the summary which contained an explanation of research methods and statistics. He read the conclusion: "We feel compelled to observe that other cancers, such as cancer of the nervous system, also showed a statistically significant excess over that which would be expected in a comparable U.S. population. We recommend further study of this issue and we would be pleased to assist the company in informing retirees, employees and government officials of the findings and health implications of this study.

"In summary, there is a pattern that suggests a relationship between contracting cancer and employees' exposure to asbestos. The statistics and occurrence of cancer are too high to ignore a cause-and-effect relationship. We do not believe the relationship can be attributed to coincidence. We recommend further study and more comprehensive analysis of this complex subject."

It was signed, Richard A. Collins, president, Ann Arbor Research Institute, Ann Arbor, Michigan.

Hawthorne looked up. "Not very good, Dick," he said. "I expected better. Let me ask a couple of questions, Dick, and I want you to understand how important this is to us."

"Of course."

"I'm going to get right to the point. There's room for doubt, isn't there?"

"Yes, but the statistical..."

"Just answer my questions, please. If there's doubt, then we could stress this doubt, couldn't we?"

"Yes, but..."

"I made a note that you state smoking is a contributor in these cases, right?"

"It's a little more complex than that..."

Hawthorne continued, "Then why can't we make a stronger case citing smoking as a – the – cause, the primary cause?"

"But, as I said, this is really much more complex. It's not that simple. The statistics..."

Hawthorne again did not let Collins finish.

"Dick, we've been a good client, haven't we? We want to continue to do business with your Institute. I would like a rewrite and I want you to make the report more concise. We don't need all those numbers. Do you understand?"

Collins was very perplexed and began to sweat. He and his company enjoyed a good reputation. He had never experienced anything like this. Now he understood why Hawthorne had insisted that he not bring any staff to the meeting.

"There's much at stake here, Dick. We need your cooperation."

"Al, I don't know what I can do. Our research was pretty thorough and comprehensive. The numbers say it pretty clearly. I just don't know."

Hawthorne did not let up. "I guess I can't tell you what to do. All I know is that this is serious stuff. I think you understand what a report like this will do to the company, right?"

"Yes, Al, I know. I thought about it when I reviewed it before coming here. It's pretty damning."

"Yes, it is, especially since it seems unnecessary, because you agree there's room for interpretation. That's right, isn't it?"

"Of course, nothing is ever beyond question. But..."

"Dick," Hawthorne said as he walked over to Collins. "All I want you to do is to explore the doubt we're talking about. That's all. I don't want you to compromise your integrity. That's not what this is about."

He handed Collins the report and patted him on the back as he led him out of the office.

"You have a family?"

"Yes, and three kids."

"How old?"

"Three, six and eight."

"Very young, very young. I'm sure that your family has significant financial obligations. But with a client like us over many years, that could sure help. But then, if business is good, you may not need Thompson Brakes."

Hawthorne continued. "Please understand, Dick, we just want you to review this draft, and it is a draft, and just see what you can do. That's all. I know the chairman will be grateful. This could be the beginning of a very long and productive relationship between the Institute and us."

Collins took the report and, almost sheepishly, replied, "I'll see what I can do."

"Good, we appreciate that. And we need it in a couple of days. If the report says what I think we agree it should say, we'll make it public, hopefully, in the same week. I believe it was your recommendation to make this public as soon as possible, wasn't it?"

Collins felt immense pressure as he left Hawthorne's office, torn between his professional obligations and the not-so-subtle threat from Hawthorne.

Thompson Brakes represented substantial revenues for his research firm. He could not afford to lose the account. Hawthorne must have done some checking on him. Collins did not like the choices facing him. What if he succumbed to Hawthorne's demands and word leaked out? He'd be destroyed in the research industry. If he did not change the report, he would lose his most lucrative client, not to mention the possibility of Thompson Brakes pressuring others not to use his firm.

While he debated the dilemma, he also knew that he did not have the fortitude to fight Thompson Brakes. As he accepted the fact that he would give in to Hawthorne's demands, Collins decided that no one else would be involved; he would take the appropriate measures to guarantee absolute confidentiality.

He drove off, suddenly stopped the car, opened the door and vomited.

TWENTY

A week later, Richard Collins was sitting in Alfred Hawthorne's office as Thompson Brakes' chief lawyer read the executive summary of a new report.

"After an exhaustive study and careful examination of the records of hundreds of present and former Thompson Brakes employees who were exposed to asbestos dust, the evidence is inconclusive whether exposure to asbestos causes cancer. While some Thompson Brakes employees contracted cancer, there is no scientific proof that exposure to asbestos dust in Thompson Brakes plants caused the disease.

"However, the statistics reveal a strong relationship between smoking, exposure to asbestos and cancers such as mesothelioma. The statistics indicate that if those employees who contracted mesothelioma had not smoked, they may not have – indeed they probably would not have – contracted mesothelioma.

"Much more work needs to be done on this very complex issue and we recommend further study."

Hawthorne looked up and smiled. "Excellent, Dick, just excellent. Be assured I'll recommend a further study and I'll recommend that your Institute conduct it. Just excellent. Leave this copy with me and get me about 50 more. I'll take it from here. I only read a little bit but I assume the numbers support the conclusions in the summary."

Collins looked at the floor to avoid eye contact with Hawthorne.

Then, as Collins was leaving the office, Hawthorne added, "Please make sure that earlier draft is destroyed. We don't want that kind of misleading information around. You never know who may pick it up and misinterpret it. Right?"

Trying to reassure Collins, Hawthorne added, "There's nothing to worry about. Dick, don't worry about this leaking out. This is covered by lawyer-client confidentiality."

With Collins gone, Hawthorne called Susan Gray, Simmons' secretary, asking her to have the chairman call a meeting immediately.

"Tell him I have good news."

A few minutes later, Hawthorne briefed Simmons on the report, telling him, while stressing the lawyer-client confidentiality relationship, of the rewrite.

"Good work, Al," Simmons said. "Work with Kaufman and get a release out as quickly as possible. You handle it. I don't need to be involved."

Hawthorne called Kaufman to his office, handed him the report and asked him to draft a release as quickly as possible.

"Want to get it out tomorrow. Just send it to me. No one else needs to be in the review loop."

It will be fun working alone with this idiot, Kaufman thought.

"Give me a few hours. I'll have a draft before the end of the day."

"Good, Tim. This is good news as you'll see."

After studying the report, Kaufman was still worried. It was good news, but the report contained holes and the press would see right through some of the language. But, he thought, at this point, it may take some pressure off.

Independent Study Shows No Causal Correlation Between Asbestos Exposure and Cancer

That was the headline Kaufman wrote on his release. The lead said: "An independent study conducted by a prestigious Ann Arbor, Michigan, research firm has reported there is no conclusive evidence to link exposure to asbestos to cancer. However, the Ann Arbor Research Institute also said that employees who smoked and were exposed to asbestos were at greater risk of contracting such cancers as mesothelioma than those who were nonsmokers."

He used all the "tricks" of his trade – using such words as "independent" and "prestigious" when referring to the Institute – and drafted a seven-paragraph release.

He also quoted Simmons in the release: "Obviously, we are very pleased with the results. We have always maintained that exposure to asbestos did not cause health problems and this has been confirmed by this study. But we're going to conduct more studies because we want to assure our employees and the community that our plants are safe and always have been safe."

When the draft was completed, Hawthorne and he wrestled over language – as they always did – but this time Kaufman did not seem to care. The entire issue had taken some strength and determination out of him. Given his doubt about the company's credibility, he played a passive role.

The approved press release was distributed the following morning. He received a few follow-up phone calls. Simmons and the others might have expected a major story, but Kaufman knew the news value of the study would not be as great as the union's charges; thus he expected mediocre coverage. It would hardly be a banner story.

Sue Merriman called. "A little good news, huh?"

"I guess," he said unenthusiastically.

"On the record, please. The study is not definitive, is it? It doesn't rule out the possibility of asbestos causing cancer, does it?"

"It makes a very strong statement that the study didn't find a causal relationship between the two. We're very pleased with it."

"You didn't answer my question."

"I gave you my answer," he said, somewhat irked.

"Once more, the study didn't rule out a causal relationship, did it?"

"As I said, it didn't find a causal relationship. Come on, Sue, get off my back. Let's move on."

She did not react to his anger. "This independent Ann Arbor company, how much did it get paid for the study?"

"Obviously, what we pay our suppliers – any of our suppliers – is confidential, as I told you when we commissioned the study. We never make those kinds of figures public."

"Was it in the hundreds of thousands?"

"As I said, we're not making that public."

"Gee," said Merriman, sarcastically, "this is fun. We're still on the record. How can they be objective when they're paid by the organization they're investigating?"

"I think everyone in the community has the highest regard for the integrity of the Ann Arbor Institute. It has a proven record over many years. That's why we hired them. They received very clear instructions to be as thorough and objective as possible and we're confident that's exactly what they were."

Then he added, "Enough already. Aren't you on deadline?"

"But I'm enjoying this too much. Just kidding. Off the record, see you later this week?"

"I'll call." Then he added facetiously, but making a point, "I assume, of course, that this will receive as much coverage as the Ferguson press conference."

"Of course. I reserved page one."

TWENTY-ONE

The next morning, Joe Sutherland at the Ann Arbor Research Institute was reading the paper in his office when he noticed a short story on the front page of the business section relating to the study he had worked on for Thompson Brakes.

"Thompson Brakes Study Denies Asbestos-Cancer Correlation," the headline said.

"Damn," he said to himself. "This isn't right. Son of a bitch."

After finishing the story, Sutherland called Collins' office seeking a meeting with the president of the firm. After putting him on hold for several minutes, the secretary told him to come down and meet with Collins immediately.

Throwing the paper on Collins' desk, he demanded, "What the hell is that all about? That's exactly the opposite of what we found."

"It's not exactly the opposite..."

"Bullshit, Dick. It is. May I at least have an explanation?"

He was putting his job on the line with his tone of voice. Collins, after all, was the boss. But he also appreciated Collins' integrity, at least until now.

"Joe, I wish I could explain. This isn't easy. I really can't explain nor do I want to."

"Dick, this is..."

"Joe, that's all, I'm sorry."

Sutherland stormed out of the office. He slammed the door and thought long and hard about what he should do. He was angry, sad, depressed all at the same time.

He was a loyal employee, hardworking and dedicated. He liked Collins; he liked his work. But he could not let this go. It would be sacrilege to the memory of his father, a Thompson Brakes employee who died of mesothelioma about two years earlier. He had been troubled for a long time that the company had not been held accountable.

Maybe this was his chance. He decided to act. What he was about to do, he knew, would cost him his job and, if he was discovered, might make him unemployable anywhere.

He opened his file cabinet and removed the draft he and two of his colleagues had prepared. He made a copy and put it in an envelope with a covering note that said, "I will call you soon to discuss this."

He addressed the envelope to Susan K. Merriman at the *Detroit Blade*. He held on to the package for a few days during which he did some checking on Merriman. When his information indicated she was a reporter with integrity, he mailed the report.

Two days later, Merriman received the special delivery envelope. She noticed it had no return address and was marked "Confidential and Personal." The postmark was from Ann Arbor.

She opened the package, read the note and then the study. She looked up from the report, certain she was on top of a big story, but not quite confident she understood all the implications. The report, obviously, was the opposite of the one made public. What does this mean? Who sent it? Is it a forgery or authentic? What do I do now? These and other questions ran through her mind. She decided not to say anything to her editors. It was premature. Nothing to do but wait.

The next day, she came to work an hour early. Perhaps the contact would call early. She did not want the individual on voice mail. It was a long day. She answered every phone call with excitement and anticipation. He did not call until late in the day.

"Did you receive the envelope?" he asked. "Do you know what it means?"

"Well, I think I do but, of course, I have lots of questions."

"Will you give me anonymity if we meet?"

"Yes, absolutely."

"How can I be sure?"

"Check me out around town. Ultimately, you'll have to trust me. I've never violated a confidence."

"I already did some checking before I called. You have a good reputation. What about you and Tim Kaufman? There are rumors, you know."

She was stunned. No, she was not aware of the rumors. Her silence was too long already, she knew.

"I don't know what you mean," she lied.

"As I checked you out, I picked up that there's something between the two of you and he is Thompson Brakes' PR guy."

"I deal with him for my stories all the time." Then, sounding offended, she added, "I don't know about any rumors. There are always rumors about someone. I don't know what you're talking about and, frankly, I resent it."

"I'll go with my instincts and risk it. I've enough on the line already. Meet me at Splendid Cafe in two hours. Alone. No photographer or other reporters."

"Fine, but not that cafe. Pick another spot."

"Why?"

"It's no big deal. Just another spot."

They agreed to meet in a small neighborhood bar in northwest Detroit. She arrived first and ordered a light beer while waiting on a bar stool. A half hour later, a man in his early 30s walked up to her, asking, "Sue Merriman?"

"Yes, nice to meet you. Let's go to a booth." Merriman took inventory. Well-dressed, clean, very professional-looking. He made the same analysis of her. Attractive, rather tall. If Kaufman is not involved with her, he should be, he thought.

"I'm going to trust you, basically you might say, with my life, my career," he started. "My name is Joe Sutherland and I work for the Ann Arbor Research Institute. I've been there for about five years. I'm one of three staff people who wrote the Thompson Brakes study. What you reported in your story isn't what we discovered. I sent you the report that we submitted to Thompson Brakes – or the report that was supposed to be submitted to Thompson. That's the story."

Merriman worked hard to assess Sutherland's credibility.

"Then how…"

"I don't have the answers. I don't know who rewrote it, how the results were changed or what happened. I confronted my boss, but got no answers."

"Richard Collins?"

"Yes, he signed it. He didn't give me an explanation. I like Dick and I don't like doing this to him, but it galls my ass. Don't use the following, because he'll know it came from me. I was the only one there. He just refused to answer any questions. Again, please don't use that."

She would call Collins anyway, if she decided to write a story, so she agreed.

"Before we go on," Sutherland said, "I need one commitment from you. My assumption is that you would call the three staff people named in this report. Publicly, in your stories, I want to be reflected as issuing a 'no comment.' That's important so the Institute and Collins don't think I'm the leak. They may still suspect me, but it gives me some cover. Agreed?"

Merriman processed the demand, concluding she had nothing to lose; she really didn't need him except for his leak and if she refused, he wouldn't talk.

"Deal," she replied.

"How do I know all this is true," she asked, "that you don't have another agenda, that this is really the authentic report?"

"To quote you, you'll have to trust me. I want this out and if you decide you can't trust me, which I can understand, let me know."

I'll go elsewhere, she finished his thought in her mind. She could not even think about losing a story, especially a big story like this one.

"Why? Why are you doing this?"

"Professional integrity."

"Spare me the bullshit. You're not putting your career on the line for a report unless you're telling me I'm sitting with someone who's campaigning for sainthood."

He smiled slyly, appreciating her candor.

"It's a bit of a long story," he said. "It's also a little schmaltzy, but true, nevertheless. I'll be brief."

Her interest was piqued. "I'm all ears."

"My father worked his ass off for that company," he said. "More than 40 years. Two years after retirement, he's gone. Mesothelioma. They gave my mother nothing. No special medical benefits, no life insurance, nothing. We tried everything. They stalled us. Killed our family with the corporate bureaucracy while those bastards voted themselves millions of dollars in raises, stock options, you name it."

He was angry and Merriman thought she noticed tears in his eyes.

"So you want to get even."

"You're damn right. But it won't help my family."

"Since you're not an objective third-party observer, and I think you'll agree with that assessment, how do I know this is accurate? How do I know you didn't slant the study?"

"You don't. You'll have to take a risk as well. I'm sure you're going to call Collins. Then you can call Johnson and Canham, the two staff people I worked with, whose names appear in the report. Their reaction to your questions may help you make a decision. My guess is they'll give you 'no comment.' That should tell you something.

"This may not make sense to you, but when I got the assignment, my first instinct was, because of my father, to use legal jargon, to disqualify myself. Then my next instinct, and this is the absolute truth, was to hope the study wouldn't indicate a correlation. I had so much anger, I wanted to put this behind me and my family. I could live with it maybe if I knew he got cancer from smoking or other causes. But to think those bastards knew what they were doing, knew the dangers and now refuse any responsibility was too much for me to bear.

"It's like the coal mining companies or the government using civilians as guinea pigs for atom bomb experiments and covering up when the facts start to come out, and so much else we've all read about. So now, here's a chance. My chance. And I want to use it."

She listened very carefully to all he said. It made sense. He appeared credible. After some checking, she would know more and be in a better position to make a decision.

"Why me?"

"Two reasons. You're the reporter on the story and while I hate to flatter you, you have a good reputation. At least, that's what my sources say. But," he added, looking her in the eye, "I have to admit I was worried when I heard things about you and Kaufman. You never did answer my question about whether you're involved with him. I guess it's a little too late for me now anyway. So I'll have to live with the consequences."

"You can trust me," she told him. But she avoided his question about her relationship with Kaufman. "Give me a few days. I need some time to make phone calls."

"No problem, but I want a decision – one way or another – in no more than a week."

"Fair enough. I'll call you. Don't worry, I won't call you at work."

They shook hands. He went to his car, she to hers.

What a story, she thought. Then she felt a little sorry for Kaufman whom she would call after checking the veracity of this report with Dick Collins.

TWENTY-TWO

"Hello, Mr. Collins. This is Sue Merriman of the *Detroit Blade*. Thank you for taking my call."

"No problem," he replied. "I'd be glad to answer any of your questions."

"I want to ask you about your report on exposure to asbestos and cancer."

"Be glad to be of help."

"Mr. Collins, as you know, we published a report that your Institute found no causal correlation between exposure and various cancers."

"That's right."

"Well, I've obtained a copy of a draft of a report written by your Institute that reaches just the opposite conclusion."

He felt a sharp, piercing pain in his head. He was unable to speak. But recognizing the implications of his hesitancy, he recovered quickly. "I don't know what you're talking about."

"As I said, I have this report...let me read you some of the conclusions."

"I'm not interested," he said angrily. "Miss Merriman, we issued our report. You wrote about it. There's nothing more to say."

"Then what is the report I have? Aren't you interested in what I have?"

"I have no idea and I don't care. I don't give a damn. Write whatever you want. You guys do anyway. I have no further comment."

He slammed down the telephone. He was devastated. He sat reviewing his options, realizing he had few, if any. However, he called Joe Sutherland to his office.

"Joe, the *Blade* reporter, Sue Merriman I think is her name, called me to discuss our Thompson Brakes report."

"I suppose that's to be expected."

"But not the report we sent to Thompson. She apparently has a copy of the other draft. How in the hell did she get that?"

Collins watched Sutherland carefully for an indication of complicity. There was none.

"I'm shocked," Sutherland replied, feigning surprise. "I haven't the foggiest."

Collins anticipated as much. He did not expect a confession.

"Keep your eyes open in your office," he said. "We obviously have a fucking leak and I'm mad as hell about it."

Sutherland started to leave – he wanted to end the meeting quickly – when Collins added, "One more thing, I don't want you talking to reporters. If you get a call, send them to my office. Understood?"

"Yes, I understand," he replied. "I never liked talking to reporters anyway. Glad to give you the privilege."

Collins had similar meetings individually with Bob Canham and Sam Johnson, the two who worked with Sutherland on the report.

Canham and Johnson expressed shock and told Collins they had no information regarding the leak. He also ordered them – as he had Sutherland – not to talk with the media. "Under no circumstances," he emphasized, "are you to discuss your work on the Thompson Brakes report with the press."

Canham and Johnson, while surprised by the news reports on the leaked report, had no strong feelings about the deception. What's more, they did not want to get involved. Collins went to work developing his damage control strategy.

When she arrived at her office, Sue Merriman called Tim Kaufman.

"Sorry, but I got a toughie for you," she said as he answered the phone at Thompson Brakes.

"So, what else is new?"

Merriman explained what she had uncovered.

"Tim, this is strong stuff. It implies some hanky-panky by someone in your company. I don't think I have to tell you what this means."

"I think I understand the implications. How do you know your source is good?"

"I'm satisfied," she replied. "Institute won't talk. They hung up on me. Something is up."

"But you really don't know."

"Tim, I said I was satisfied. It's my call. You don't have to worry."

"But I do. If you have a bogus report, we're the ones who'll pay, not you. Remember, as we discussed, we'll stand by our story."

"Tim, you have a comment or not?"

"Call you back in half an hour."

Kaufman called Hawthorne and outlined the situation.

"So tell her we know nothing about it. That should take care of it."

"She's going to write a story; I can promise that."

"Did you tell her she might have a phony report? Probably has one and probably from the union."

"I told her that she may have bad information. No, I didn't point at the union and I'm not sure we want to do that without any supporting documentation. Should we call Simmons?"

"No, just tell her she's way off base. Someone is using her. Make her have doubts."

As Kaufman prepared to return the call to Merriman, he was troubled by Hawthorne's calm demeanor. Hawthorne should have been very angry and disturbed, but he wasn't. He used phrases like "she might have a bogus report" and qualified his statements with "probably."

Damn, he should have been pissed and insistent that Sue not write such a story, Kaufman told himself.

Kaufman put his doubts on hold as he called Merriman. "On the record, Sue, we know nothing about the report you have. Nothing at all. We stand by the one we made public. Off the record, Sue, someone may be using you. The union. An unhappy Institute employee. Someone else. You understand that?"

"I may not be a 25-year veteran, but I know the ropes. My editors agree and, very frankly, I think we, as they say, gotcha."

"Sue, I wish I could be as sure as you are on this report. I really hope a story doesn't come out that you'll regret."

"Appreciate your concern. Right now, given all I know, I think I'm sitting pretty. See you."

As he reflected on his answers to Merriman's questions, Kaufman felt very compromised. He did not believe Hawthorne; his confidence in what he was saying as Thompson Brakes' spokesman was continually eroding.

He expected the worst for the next day. The *Blade* would play the story for all it was worth and his prediction proved entirely correct.

The story was the lead item on the front page. Marked "exclusive," the story reported how the *Blade* had obtained a draft of a report prepared by the Ann Arbor Research Institute that concluded a strong correlation existed between exposure to asbestos and cancer.

Merriman reported that the company had released a study that concluded the opposite. Then, she wrote, Institute and company officials could not explain the discrepancies between the two reports.

Quoting "reliable sources, who wished to remain anonymous," the story said, "the sources speculated the report was rewritten for legal and financial reasons. Sources told the *Blade* that if the actual report, the one finding a correlation between exposure to asbestos and cancer, had been made public, it could be used in court as evidence and could cost the company millions. 'So they just rewrote the results of the report,' sources told the *Blade*."

It was not good, to be sure, Kaufman thought. He received numerous calls and gave the standard reply: "Thompson Brakes stands by the report it made public."

Simmons called to ask what Kaufman knew about Merriman's story. "Doesn't the broad know she has a forged document?"

"I guess not," Kaufman replied, deciding not to confront the issue with Simmons. "I don't know much. How about Hawthorne?"

"I talked with him. He pleads innocence. Tim, I'll say it again. This has got to stop. I'm very tired of all this crap. I don't give a shit what you tell me, I'm calling Bob Harrison at the *Blade*. If he wants my advertising, he's gonna have to give me something in return."

TWENTY-THREE

Bob Harrison, the *Blade*'s publisher, sat in Simmons' office, expecting the worst. He had expected to be asked to meet with the Thompson Brakes chairman much sooner.

"Tough time, eh, George?" Harrison said, trying to be lighthearted.

"Tough? Bob, you guys are killing me, all of us here. Do you get your rocks off on this kind of stuff?"

Harrison's strategy was to let Simmons get it all off his chest and perhaps he would feel better.

"We've been in this community for many years. We pay taxes, create jobs, contribute to the community and what do we get in return?"

He paused, waiting for Harrison to answer, but he didn't.

"Our stock is taking one fucking beating. Shareholders are calling every hour. They want to hang me by my balls and, frankly, I don't blame them. Every time I pick up your rag, there I am on page one. Bob, I demand that you put an end to it."

Harrison still did not offer a reply, making Simmons angrier.

"Fuck, Bob, are you just going to sit there and not say a thing?"

"I'm not sure what I can say," Harrison said finally. "You're, unfortunately, involved in a major public controversy and we're doing our job covering it. The good news is, like everything else in this world, George, it'll blow over. The public's attention span, and ours in the media, is relatively short."

Simmons, his face reddening, was furious.

"What are you telling me?" Simmons shouted. "It'll blow over? When? When our stock amounts to nothing? When our net worth is shit? When the board cans my ass?"

Simmons was breathing heavily as he paced the floor behind his desk.

"George, I know..."

He did not have a chance to finish before Simmons roared, "...how I feel? I'll tell you how I feel. I feel like I'm being fucked every day by your pinko rag. I feel betrayed by you, a friend, a colleague. I feel..."

Now Harrison interjected.

"I am your friend, George, but you have to understand there's not much I can do. This is an important community story."

"Don't give me that shit..."

"Please, George, let me finish," Harrison pleaded.

Simmons sat down in his chair behind his desk, glaring at Harrison.

"So go ahead."

"I don't like what's happening to you and your company. I'm a businessman, too. But this story is now bigger than the *Blade*. The snowball is rolling downhill and I couldn't stop it if I wanted to."

"Are you telling me that the owner of the *Blade* can't tell his employees what to write?"

"It's more complex than that. George, I wish I could help."

Simmons put his hands together on the desk and leaned forward.

"How much do we spend on advertising with you each year? How much, Bob? In round numbers."

"About $12 million."

"There you have 12 million reasons to put a stop to this at the *Blade*."

"George, I can't succumb to this kind of threat. The story is too big now."

"You're telling me you never compromised before in doing favors for advertisers?"

"Of course not. I'm a realist. We've cut corners many times. But we'd look silly dropping this story with everyone else on it."

"You're going to look silly? Geez, I'm so sorry. Does that mean your paper won't win the next journalism award? Bob, I don't give a shit how you look. You want my advertising, you stop it. Understood?"

"George, I can't."

"So, the facts are, as you see them, I have to pay for my own funeral? You sit there, look me in the eye, tell me I'm your friend who has to keep making your company profitable while your rag continues to tear me and the company apart? Now, that makes a lot of sense."

"If word got out that you threatened us by cancelling your ads, I hate to say this, George, the entire media will be at your doorstep. Nothing turns them on more than being threatened. There'll be stories galore about the First Amendment and that they won't be intimidated. I don't think that would serve your interests."

"I know. That's what the asshole Kaufman, my PR guy, told me many times. But answer my question. You maintain I have no choice but to finance the demise of my own company. Is that right?"

Harrison avoided the point.

"George, I really do know how you feel and I really am sorry. Let me see what I can do. Let me talk to my editors and I promise we'll be as helpful as we can. You're a valued customer, of course. But even more important, you've been a good friend. We've gone through many wars in this town."

Simmons calmed down. He rubbed his chin several times.

"I don't think I have to tell you, we don't have much time. Get on it and get on it right away. I can't take much more of this shit."

"I will, George. I promise."

TWENTY-FOUR

But the pressure did not stop, at least not immediately.

John Barrister, working at his home, sifted through the documents he had taken from headquarters, compiling the ones that were most damaging to Thompson Brakes. He made copies of all of them at a local office supply store, packaged one set and, like Joe Sutherland at the Ann Arbor Research Institute, mailed it to Sue Merriman.

He wanted the job of his boss, Glen Johnston, and was not averse to using whatever tactics were necessary to achieve his objective. He had never encountered a better opportunity to inflict what he believed would be a fatal wound. This kind of opportunity might not come again for a long time.

Once more, as Merriman opened her mail, she could not believe her luck. The material could not be more damaging to Thompson Brakes. There were numerous memos from several executives dating to the 1950s and 1960s which warned management of the dangers to the health of employees.

One read, "We are guilty of complicity." Another, addressed directly to the chairman at the time, stated emphatically, "We have a moral, legal, medical and ethical responsibility to take some action to protect these employees. To do nothing is unconscionable."

She was particularly delighted with the memo from Simmons recommending development of a strategy to avoid the potential costs to Thompson Brakes.

Some of the material contained statistics, indicating the high percentage of cancer cases expected in upcoming years, a percentage, which the material stated, could not be attributed to coincidence. She considered copies of OSHA citations extremely important because they gave the other memos credibility.

Merriman and her editors agreed that this material offered enough for at least two or three separate stories.

When she called Kaufman for an overall statement, he referred to the one he'd offered on the leaked study.

"You can use the following for any leaked material. We stand by all the documents we have made public. We know nothing of the material obtained by the *Blade*. We suspect they may be bogus or forged documents, documents being sent to the media by those who have special political interests."

But Merriman would not let him off the hook.

"I also have a memo from Simmons when he was an executive vice president in which he warns about the costs if the company were to meet its obligations."

"As I said, all the papers you have could be forgeries."

"Tim, are you saying these government documents are not authentic? You know I can check these and I'm going to do just that when we hang up. Come on, Tim, you know I will get confirmation from OSHA."

He felt trapped and lashed out.

"Get whatever you need, Sue. You have my statement, now back off. What the hell do you want me to say?"

"Tim, I'm sorry to put you in this position, but I have to pursue..."

"Not with me you don't, Sue. I don't like this at all. I'll talk to you later."

He was angry, frustrated and in turmoil. Kaufman had never felt so compromised in his years in PR. He had no doubts that the documents – the OSHA documents, Simmons' memo and the others – were authentic. He felt pressured by his professional responsibilities to Thompson Brakes and by being caught in this quandary by his lover.

Merriman also did not like pushing Kaufman so hard. Like Kaufman, she felt similarly compromised, and almost guilty, in her dual role as girlfriend and journalist. As she followed up on her exclusive, all those contacted by her, those who allegedly authored the papers, gave her a "no comment." Politically, the "no comments" were incriminating and Merriman understood they gave her story increased credibility.

The next day, after Merriman's newest revelations appeared on page one, Simmons called Johnston to his office.

"I thought I asked you to do a job," Simmons said.

"I did," Johnston replied. "Maybe there were other copies."

"Not a good job, Glen. You know you've left me no choice. You'll get a severance package, assuming you keep your mouth shut and don't sue the company. If you violate this agreement," he said waving some papers, "Glen, not only won't you get all the money but I'll make life miserable for you."

Johnston, after years in corporate life, understood the circumstances all too well.

"No need to go back to your office to clean up. We've already done that. One of Salter's people is outside my office to walk you out. You disappointed me, Glen. If you agree with what I've said, sign the papers in this folder."

Simmons slid a manila folder toward Johnston. Johnston opened it slowly, skimmed the documents and took a pen from his shirt pocket. He was familiar with these forms; indeed, at times, he had had subordinates sign them as well.

After signing six different forms in areas marked with an "x," Johnston stood up and walked out without saying a word. Outside Simmons' office, an employee from the security department was waiting. He escorted Johnston to the front door of the building. Johnston walked out and headed to his car in the parking lot.

Simmons picked up his telephone and called Barrister. He explained to him that Johnston had just resigned to "pursue other business interests."

"Sorry to lose him," Simmons told Barrister, who listened with self-satisfaction. "Very unexpected.

"John, you're acting head of the department. Congratulations. Two points of advice: don't screw up and don't screw with me. Again, congratulations."

"I appreciate that, George," said Barrister, who felt proud having achieved his objective.

TWENTY-FIVE

"Are you asking me to back off?" asked Joseph Brennan, the *Blade*'s managing editor.

"I just want to talk for a few minutes," Harrison said. "There are two sides to every story and maybe we're overplaying it."

"We're not," said Brennan, his voice rising. "Thompson Brakes killed people and it's paying the price."

"Environmental issues are complex ones, Joe," Harrison said. "What if we're wrong?"

"Again, we're not," Brennan replied and then suddenly asked, "Did Simmons get to you?"

"That has nothing to do with this discussion."

"So you met with him," Brennan concluded. "Let me guess. He threatened to cancel his advertising."

"Joe, back off. I'm still in charge. He did, but I promised him nothing. I want to talk this through with you and I don't need any Journalism 101 lectures about freedom of the press."

Brennan retreated quickly. "I'm sorry. You're right."

Brennan respected Harrison, who had served as publisher for almost 20 years. Brennan recognized that Harrison occasionally accommodated advertisers by either having stories buried or killed and he understood the realities of the business. Brennan was no idealist and he knew that other media institutions succumbed to pressure from time to time as well.

But overall, Harrison did not interfere in the newsroom. Brennan received much more pressure from the paper's advertising executives, who asked him frequently to either run stories in favor of advertisers or kill bad news. Knowing he had the support of Harrison, Brennan was able to ignore the pressure.

"Joe, you know that I've defended the editorial department throughout my career," Harrison said. "At times, I give in. We all have to. I think you'll agree I'm hardly setting any precedents, the media's public posture notwithstanding.

"The larger the paper, the more we can stand up for principle, not because of any ideals but because of our power. But you know as well as I do that the smaller the media institution, the more it has to surrender its independence. Small papers could not survive unless they gave in to the wishes of advertisers."

"I didn't mean to come on so strong, but it does piss me off."

"It should and I'm glad it does; otherwise you wouldn't be my managing editor."

Brennan smiled. He liked the compliment.

"So what do we do?" Brennan asked.

"First, this is all between us. I don't want a rebellion in the newsroom. Those reporters don't have to meet payrolls or meet the expectations of my shareholders. Simmons isn't the only guy who has to be accountable to investors and the young turks in the city room can afford to be idealistic. I wish, at times, I were one of them.

"We both know full well if we end our coverage, everyone in the city room will know what happened. To get even, they might leak information to competitors to keep the story going and show me up. I understand that. It's happened before in this business. There would probably be a revolution and neither you nor I could explain it to them – at least not give them an explanation they'd accept."

Brennan repeated his question. "So, like I said, what do we do?"

"Assign someone other than Merriman to do a profile on Simmons.

This isn't public yet, but I think he's going to receive the Civic League's humanitarian award."

Then Harrison added with a smile, "No smart remarks. The award will give us a chance to do a good profile on him. Frankly, such a piece doesn't have to mention the asbestos issue. Make it a community-oriented piece."

"I don't like it, but I can live with that," Brennan replied.

"And see if you can bury a couple of the asbestos pieces. Keep them off page one."

"Off page one?"

"Joe, I'm asking you to use your judgment. Don't go out of your way but if it's a coin toss, make it come up heads. Make it come up heads even if you have to work the coin. Help me a little bit."

"But I still don't like it."

"I don't like it either but neither one of us has to. Like those idealists in the city room, you don't have to answer to shareholders either. Moreover, $12 million is nothing to sneeze at."

"He wouldn't do it."

"But he has a point. I mean, does he have to give us money to continue to put the screws to him? Can we defend the idea that he has to pay us for his own demise? While we cry bloody murder when an advertiser like Simmons threatens us, I think he has an argument."

Brennan offered, "There's such a thing as the First Amendment."

"Joe, he isn't arguing that we don't have the right to print the stories. Frankly, I don't think he has the foggiest idea what the First Amendment is all about. But he is asking why he has to give us $12 million or any money if it's used to cut him to pieces."

Harrison waited but Brennan still did not offer a counter argument.

"You do know we're a pompous bunch. We rip people to shreds, have no accountability, seldom run meaningful corrections when we screw up, roar louder than a wounded lion when criticized and then still expect advertisers to pay us when we attack them. Joe, that's chutzpah."

"I don't think he'd do it," Brennan speculated. "He has no place else to go."

"True. With only two papers in town, he has little choice. Another great idealistic defense. But that aside, are you asking me to risk it?"

"I'd like to."

"Are you ready to risk your salary or a layoff? Don't just give me a yes because you know we're talking in the abstract."

"I get the point. I'll see what I can do."

TWENTY-SIX

For the next month, the story quieted down, but not because of any intervention by Joe Brennan. The story simply died temporarily, mostly because of no new major developments.

The next assault on Thompson Brakes would come when the court hearings began before Judge John Faulkner. Given the relief from the asbestos issue, Kaufman was spending most of his time trying to placate shareholders who were livid.

The stock had taken a beating, dropping from $33 a share to $28. The market was anticipating that Thompson Brakes would be forced into multimillion dollar class action settlements, seriously weakening the firm's cash flow and balance sheet. In the company's letters to shareholders drafted by Kaufman with the company's lawyers, Thompson Brakes tried to convince the investment community that it expected to win the lawsuits without making any serious additional financial commitments. The lawsuits were "without merit," the communications assured shareholders.

George Simmons went on the road along with his chief financial officer, Robert Jameson, making presentations to Wall Street analysts and major institutions who owned the stock throughout the country.

They discussed the "excitement" in the company about new brakes and other products that were being developed, but at almost every meeting, the questions were about the asbestos issue. Simmons and Jameson tried to defuse concern as much as possible but their explanations were not helping improve the stock price.

Kaufman appreciated the change of pace from the daily grind of fending off reporters' questions. He had always liked the interplay with the press; he enjoyed the give-and-take, the intellectual challenge of matching wits. But he did not enjoy the present adversarial atmosphere involving the asbestos crisis and being constantly on the defensive.

Worse, he did not like the implications that Thompson Brakes was guilty, if not legally guilty, certainly morally and ethically guilty. Slowly, he was losing faith in the company and beginning to wonder what he should do to maintain his integrity.

He wrestled with his conscience, continually asking himself what he would do when and if he knew the truth – without doubts. That was a question he could only resolve when – and if – the time came. He hoped it wouldn't. He also worried that he was already compromising since he had some very powerful evidence. For the time being, he convinced himself to continue to do his job as professionally as he could.

He and Merriman had several dates and she informed him she had been told there were rumors about the two of them. He said he had heard that also. Thus, they became even more careful and circumspect when planning meetings.

He enjoyed her company. She was smart, talented, dedicated – a pretty good reporter, he had to admit. She had not yet become troubled with the ethical weaknesses of journalism. That was good and bad. Good because he loved watching her enthusiasm, her total dedication to "doing good, to getting the bad guys." It was bad because the principles of journalism, he believed, needed refinement. She never really considered that the draft report she received might be a "setup." In this case, he admitted to himself, she was probably right. But overall, he found too much superficiality and hypocrisy in journalism.

He continued to be troubled by his relationship with her, by the conflict of interest issue, but did not want to end the relationship. He realized that he was rationalizing but he decided not to break up with Merriman.

With the asbestos issue out of the public limelight temporarily, he worked on the CEO's speech for the annual meeting only three weeks away and compiling a very thorough Q & A. He had received more than 100 questions from management and he compressed them into a master list of about 50.

The speech was basically a rewrite of the one delivered to employees a few months earlier. The subjects covered were the same: sales, earnings, technological improvements, promotions of executives and two paragraphs on the one-time loss.

"We want to state as strongly as we can, this unexpected write-off is a one-time loss. This is all behind us. As we look to the future, we are optimistic about continued growth in sales and earnings and we expect to meet shareholders' expectations."

He cringed at this corporate language, but experience had taught him that attempts at creativity, candor, forthrightness were futile.

Then he went at the Q & A:

Why have sales only increased about five percent?

A. We believe that the economy is generally stagnant in the country. Also, bad weather impacted do-it-yourselfers from repairing brakes this winter. They are waiting longer than usual to replace brake pads. We are optimistic that this will change in the new fiscal year.

When will earnings improve?

A. We are confident they may improve soon. We have instituted cost control measures and cut travel and expenses. All this we expect to show up in the bottom line.

How can a company lose $35 million in one quarter with no warning to shareholders?

A. That's a good question. The issues involved are very complex and I wish we had time to discuss them fully. But, again, it's behind us. And we're looking ahead.

Was the company remiss in not protecting employees years ago from asbestos dust, causing them to contract cancer?

A. As we have said many times, no proof exists that this is true. But, being responsible, we'll continue to study the issue.

Are the media reports true that the asbestos study was altered and that, at various times, management knew of the dangers of asbestos exposure and alerted senior management to take action?

A. We know nothing about the rumors printed in the media. We stand by what we have said publicly and we don't believe it serves any useful purpose to speculate about reports which may be based on forged or bogus documents.

What is your response to the class action asbestos lawsuit?

A. It has no merit. Since it is in court, we cannot comment beyond that.

Given all the troubles at the company and its continued poor financial performance, how do you justify your raise and bonuses?

Kaufman did not develop a reply but instead wrote:

> George: I recommend you don't answer any questions regarding your compensation. Have the chairman of your board compensation committee do it. I believe that's good strategy for several reasons: (A) obviously, it would be awkward and appear self-serving for you to outline your contributions to the company; (B) you really don't vote on your raises and bonuses, the committee does; (C) the committee can make all these points and indicate that you're not involved in these decisions.

As he worked on the paper, Kaufman drafted statements that reflected the lowest noncommittal common denominator. And even these answers were generally watered down even more during the review process.

He also worked with executives to control stockholder gadflies who persisted in their questions. The methods included the chairman stating that others should be permitted to answer questions and directors taking the CEO off the hook by interrupting critical shareholders.

Kaufman had won his battle over the years not to have critics physically removed as the chairman suggested in strategy meetings. Kaufman did not want a photograph of a Thompson Brakes security employee walking a shareholder out of the meeting on the front pages of the newspapers' business sections. Indeed, such a picture might be picked up by the wire services and published nationwide.

He finished the draft of the Q & A along with a draft of the fourth-quarter press release which stated:

"SUBJECT: Thompson Brakes Reports Fourth Quarter

"Detroit, Michigan – Thompson Brakes, Inc. today reported its fourth-quarter and year-end sales and earning results."

The release summarized sales and earnings and in the fourth paragraph stated, "due to a one-time write-off in inventory, accounts receivable and payable and sales projections, the company is incurring a $35 million loss in the fourth quarter."

"This is a one-time loss," said George C.L. Simmons, Jr., the company's chairman and chief executive officer. "It is all behind us and we have taken the necessary steps by installing state-of-the-art technology to better track financial indicators in the future. We now have some early warning systems and we are confident about the first quarter of next year and the years ahead."

He delivered the materials personally to the offices of Simmons, Jameson and Hawthorne, marking the envelopes "Confidential."

Kaufman headed home. At the same time, Wayne County Circuit Court Judge John Faulkner, severely depressed because of a personal crisis, was seeking advice from a long-time friend.

TWENTY-SEVEN

"That's prior restraint," said Frank B. Hartman, a well-known attorney who had practiced in the Detroit community for more than 30 years. "John, you know that won't work."

Judge Faulkner countered, "But I think it's worth a try."

"You know we're wasting our time. The courts did not approve it in the Pentagon Papers and they won't now. You're reaching. And, as a liberal, you know it runs counter to everything you believe in."

"Yes, it does. But I need help."

"Even if we filed the suit to keep the information suppressed, our efforts probably would attract even more attention. The media would really focus on it if you sought a restraining order and the practical result would be an admission of guilt.

"You know what would happen. I file the suit to suppress the information against you, the media report on your request, but worse, they report the information you want suppressed. You know they would get it quickly, without much trouble."

Faulkner knew his friend was right.

"It isn't fair, Frank," the judge replied. "I've seen reputations ruined by information leaked to the press. Never liked it and now I could be the victim of the process. It isn't fair."

"No, it isn't fair," Hartman said. "But this isn't about fairness. It's about damage control."

Faulkner sat down, his face in his hands. He was breathing heavily, the muscles in his face twitching.

"You really don't need legal advice," said Hartman. "You need PR advice and I can't help you there."

"Frank, the story is untrue and, if it's published, it'll destroy my career and all that I tried to work for in my lifetime. You know how these things go."

"I'm not disagreeing about the potential results. I just don't know how we can keep the story out of the papers – true or not."

"But it's simply not true," the judge repeated plaintively.

"John, you know as well as I that truth has nothing to do with it. In the public arena we, unfortunately, deal with perception most of the time. The media don't deal with the truth; they deal with what people tell them and cover themselves with attribution."

Faulkner was hardly listening to his friend; he was in no mood to discuss media ethics. Right now, he had a major personal crisis to deal with. Hartman, noticing his friend's preoccupation, returned to the issue before them.

"Perception is much more important than reality," he told the judge. "You need to deal with the perception created by a motion asking the court to approve your attempt at prior restraint. I don't think, as I said, the court would approve that but, as I also indicated, it may produce a larger problem for you."

Faulkner, trembling, asked, "So what do I do?"

"As I said, you need PR help. Do you know anyone in the business?"

"No, not really."

"No one?"

"There's a PR guy at Thompson Brakes. I see his name in the paper from time to time, Tim Kaufman. He used to cover occasional cases in my courtroom. That's as close as I can come to any connection to PR."

Hartman was not encouraged.

"Would he remember you and, if so, would he help?"

"I don't know, Frank. I don't know. I don't know anything right now."

"Call him. What've you got to lose? All he can do is say no. You haven't lost anything and he may have some ideas. PR is his business."

Faulkner picked up a cup of coffee and the cup rattled against the saucer.

"I suppose you're right. The phone book is in the closet, Frank. Would you mind looking up his number? Tim Kaufman."

Hartman found the number and Faulkner dialed. Kaufman was sipping a beer when the telephone rang.

"May I speak to Tim Kaufman?"

"Speaking."

"Mr. Kaufman, this is John Faulkner. I don't know if you recognize the name."

"Judge Faulkner?"

"Yes."

"Yes, I remember, of course. What can I do for you?"

"I want to apologize for this inconvenience, particularly at this hour but I didn't know where to turn."

"What is it, Judge?"

"Forgive me for asking, but would you come to my house? This is a matter of utmost urgency."

"Tonight?"

Kaufman was not interested in meeting with the judge. He tried to beg off. "Judge, I understand you've been assigned the suit filed against our company. I'm not sure it would be proper to meet you under the circumstances."

Judge Faulkner, understanding Kaufman's point, stated firmly, "You raise a very valid point but I want to indicate as strongly as I can this has nothing to do with that case or Thompson Brakes. This is completely unrelated."

"Still, Judge, I really don't know what this is..."

Faulkner, his voice quivering, literally begged, "I implore you to please consider my request."

"Could you give me some idea..."

"Not on the phone, Mr. Kaufman. It's really very sensitive. My life is at stake."

Kaufman was moved by Faulkner's dramatic characterization and relented. "I have to admit, under the circumstances with my company's case before you, I'm not confident this is right, but I'll come if it's important." Kaufman recognized desperation in the judge's voice.

"I'll need an hour or so. Could you give me your address and some directions?"

As Kaufman had told Simmons, he knew little about the judge except that he enjoyed an impeccable reputation. He was a staunch defender of First Amendment rights and liberal on most issues.

Kaufman remembered the judge as a man of ethics, a man who felt very strongly about his integrity, who had the utmost respect for the office he held. Indeed, many in political circles considered him somewhat aloof with a holier-than-thou attitude.

But Kaufman did not believe that was fair. Faulkner was a loner, that was true, but he did not preach. Faulkner accepted no political contributions for his elections and that disturbed others who thought he was suggesting, by implication, that other judicial candidates should do likewise. He also refused to socialize with attorneys who practiced in his courtroom. Moreover, he did not attend fund-raising events for other candidates for judicial, legislative or executive offices.

In his personal life, Faulkner was devoted to his family. Frequently, he would have his grandchildren visit the courtroom as had his children when they were younger. He was extremely proud of them and felt honored to be on the bench.

Kaufman dressed and drove for about 30 minutes to Faulkner's home. When Kaufman rang the bell, the door opened immediately, as if Judge Faulkner had been waiting at the door which, in fact, he had.

"Thank you so much for coming."

"Judge, nice to see you. I must admit that I'm a bit puzzled and still very concerned because you're presiding over the Thompson Brakes case."

Hartman had left earlier. He and the judge agreed that Faulkner should meet with Kaufman alone. The presence of Hartman, an attorney, might give the wrong signals.

Faulkner was also pleased that his wife had left to visit relatives; he did not want her to know of his crisis and never would have invited Hartman or Kaufman to his home if she were in the house. He loved her too much to share his burden with her. He was hoping for a solution so she would never have to know of the crisis he faced.

"Mr. Kaufman, let me put you at ease about that case. This has nothing to do with Thompson Brakes. So you don't have to worry about that. Can I get you something? Coffee? A beer?"

"No thanks, I'm all right. Why did you want to see me?"

"Again, I apologize. I readily admit my phone call to you must seem strange. But frankly, I just didn't know what to do. I called you because you know something about the press, how the dynamics work."

He paused and looked at Kaufman to evaluate his reaction. Kaufman looked interested but still puzzled.

The judge continued. "I remember you covered a few cases in my courtroom. I need advice and some help now; I need it very badly and I don't have much time."

"Judge, I don't know what I can do for you, but why don't you outline the problem."

Judge Faulkner, 62 years old, was pale and his voice cracked as he told his story. He had received a call from a *Detroit Blade* reporter, Sue Merriman, who said she had learned about charges that he had molested a seven-year-old boy in his chambers. The boy's stepfather, Roland Stern, was convicted by a jury of nearly killing his wife, the boy's mother, in a beating. Stern was scheduled to be sentenced by Faulkner in two weeks.

"The reporter called me two days ago and said the father had accused me of molesting the boy when, during the trial, I asked the boy, who had seen his mother beaten, some questions in my chambers."

Judge Faulkner was in a cold sweat. He appeared on the verge of collapsing.

"Mr. Kaufman, this is just not true."

"She can't use this information based on his charges, Judge."

"Mr. Stern took a lie detector test and passed. The reporter claims that the boy also said that I molested him. And, finally, I took the test because I wanted to put this to rest as quickly as possible, but I am told my test was inconclusive."

"That's quite a scenario, you must admit that," said Kaufman, immediately regretting his comment.

"I agree. Again, Mr. Kaufman, I don't know what I can say to make you believe me but there's absolutely no truth to the charges. Let me anticipate your question. Why would Stern make the charges? I have no idea. Maybe he's worried about the possible sentence. Maybe he thinks I didn't rule fairly. Maybe he thinks, with me out of the way, he'll get a more lenient judge. I don't know."

Kaufman noticed tears in Faulkner's eyes.

"My whole life is on the line. Everything I've worked for all these years. Can you help me?"

"What do you want me to do?"

"Talk to the reporter. You know the business. You're in PR. I really don't know. Use whatever argument works. Please. I know this is a terrible imposition, but will you try?"

Kaufman did not reply right away. Call Sue? She'll ask why, and rightly so.

"I don't know, Judge."

"Mr. Kaufman, this is a matter of life and death. I'll pay you, if that's an issue. Frankly, you can name your price. It's my whole life we're talking about."

Kaufman's tone of voice indicated that he was offended by the financial overture. He told Faulkner, "Money is not the issue here, Judge. Frankly..."

Faulkner recognized he had insulted Kaufman.

"I'm sorry. Really, I am. I just don't know what I'm doing. Please forgive me."

"No problem, Judge," Kaufman said, accepting the apology.

"Did she say when they'll run the story?"

"She called me today to ask another couple of questions and she said it's being published tomorrow."

"That means, Judge, I need to call now."

Judge Faulkner looked ill. He was breathing very hard and having some difficulty doing it.

"That's why I asked you to come this late."

Kaufman asked the judge if he had met privately with the boy. The judge told him he had. He explained that at the beginning of the interview, he had a stenographer in his chambers as well. But as he asked the boy questions, the judge said, the boy kept looking at the stenographer and was reluctant to open up.

"The boy was scared when I asked him about his father and the beatings his mother endured. I told the stenographer to leave us for a few minutes. I don't like putting children through this kind of trauma and it appeared the boy was hesitant with someone else present. I didn't want to talk to the boy alone but under the circumstances I asked the court reporter to leave."

"I think it was a mistake."

"On hindsight, you're right. But, Mr. Kaufman, I never, never thought this could happen."

Kaufman listened sympathetically, finally telling the judge, "I can't promise anything, but I'll call. I must also tell you I don't think this is going to work."

"Thank you, Mr. Kaufman. All I can ask you to do is try."

Kaufman looked at his watch. It was 12:30 a.m. He purposely asked for a phone book, pretending to look up Sue Merriman's phone number. He dialed and heard a sleepy "Hello."

"Hello, this is Tim Kaufman, Sue," Kaufman started sheepishly.

"Oh, hi, and why so formal?" she asked. "Calling with a news tip this time of night?"

"Sue, I'm sorry to call this late but I have a serious issue I want to bounce off you. I'm at the home of Judge Faulkner."

"John Faulkner…the judge? What the hell are you doing there?"

"To tell you the truth, I really don't know." Then he recounted his entire conversation with Judge Faulkner.

"So what do you want me to do?"

"Sue, the story is razor thin. You have to admit that. Stern and the boy could be lying."

She was angry. "Tim, you're not calling me at this hour to ask me to hold off, are you? Tell me you're not."

"I guess I am. The guy is beside himself."

"Maybe you went into the wrong profession. You'd make a good priest."

"Sue, let's just talk about it for a minute. They could be lying."

She was getting angrier. "They passed the lie detector test. Your client didn't. Is this a little moonlighting? Are you charging by the hour with time and a half after midnight?"

He ignored the insult.

"Tim, I didn't mean that but what the fuck – excuse my French – do you want me to do at this hour?"

"He's not my client. I'm doing a favor. The man's life is passing before his eyes," Kaufman said, trying to whisper into the phone. "He may have a heart attack."

"I'm sorry about how he may feel. That's not my responsibility and, frankly, I resent your using our relationship to make this call."

"Sue, calm down. I am not using our…," he stopped abruptly, momentarily embarrassed and fearful that the judge might deduce his involvement with Merriman if he used the word *relationship*.

"Would you call another reporter with whom you're not having an affair to make such a request? And at this time of night?"

He hesitated. He was the one who worried about potential conflicts of interest and now she was using the argument against him.

"There's a strong case for not using the story – not yet. Check some more. Why is Stern doing it even if it's true? He has nothing to gain. Frankly, he may get a worse sentence from the next judge for accusing this one. It doesn't make sense."

"It may not make sense to you, but I do know I have charges by someone who is willing to put his name to them. This time, no anonymous sources. I have his son who says it's true and I have the accused failing a lie detector test. And authorities are investigating."

"The test was inconclusive and what if he's innocent? These could be phony charges. He hasn't failed the test. Sue, you know that lie detectors don't mean anything. They aren't admissible in court. They're subject to error."

"I'm going to print Faulkner's statement that he's not guilty, and if the investigation proves him innocent, I'll write that."

"Sue, you and I know that the story is going to be splashed across page one. The entire dynamics of publishing such stories is tilted toward guilt. You'll write five lead paragraphs of charges, Faulkner's two-paragraph statement and then more charges. The *Blade* may even run sidebars of reaction in which colleagues express surprise at the charges. These are even more irresponsible because they build on a premise of guilt.

"I understand this is journalistic objectivity. I've been there. I've been part of it. I'm still part of it. Sue, this man's reputation is going to go down the drain. I know you'll also write a story on the investigation if it proves there was no merit to the charges. That will come weeks later after his reputation is ruined and it will appear in the inside pages, much too late to help him."

Kaufman stopped briefly and then added, "Sue, you have to think of the consequences. A man's life is involved." Kaufman was surprised at his own compassion, how he warmed up to defending a man he hardly knew.

"You've been away from journalism too long," she replied. "Consequences are not my obligation. If I have a story that asbestos exposure causes cancer, I'll write it and I don't give a damn if your stock takes a dive. The issue of consequences is appropriate for debate in journalism schools. But professionally, I think you know that once we start considering the consequences suffered by those we write about, we'll probably publish very little because consequences hurt politicians in elections, public companies like yours and everyone we write about."

Kaufman countered that the consequences of publishing news stories should be considerations in certain situations. "Sue, some of what you say is true, but consequences, at times, need to be considered. You know you wouldn't – I hope – print the movement of U.S. troops to alert an enemy even though you may have the facts. I assume you'd consider the consequences to their lives if their secret movements were published.

"I understand that a journalist's obligations regarding the consequences of publishing are complex issues. But in this case, since many questions are still unanswered, I think it's fair to weigh them before you publish."

He heard Merriman sigh with impatience. He knew he was losing the battle.

"I'm not in the mood to take on the system at this time of night. I don't have the energy right now to debate the nuances of journalism with you. We have some precedents. As a matter of fact, come to think of it, this story is similar to the case of Clarence Thomas and his Supreme Court nomination. The press printed charges of sexual harassment against him despite the fact that the consequences might have cost him the nomination."

"You're absolutely right. That's my point. Put your politics on sexual harassment aside for a minute. That story should never have been published. The charges that he harassed Anita Hill were leaked with no warrant ever signed or issued. I'll bet all the money in the world they were leaked by someone who did not want him on the Supreme Court bench. All the editorial writers in the nation condemned the leak, yet published the story. Well, if it's wrong to leak, then it's wrong to publish leaks. There was no warrant. Hell, you wouldn't use a story about your neighbor being arrested for drunk driving unless there was a warrant. There were no warrants or official charges by the prosecutor in the Clarence Thomas case and there aren't any now. At least wait until there are official charges. Then, even the judge will agree that it's fair game. It would be public record.

"Remember the alar scare, that the alar spray on apples caused health problems? The charges almost destroyed an industry. The story disappeared as quickly as it surfaced. All of the media institutions worried about losing a good story. This time it's about a man, a man's life."

"If I wait for formal charges, I will lose exclusivity. Tim, if I don't run with it, someone else will."

"Now we've come to the root of the problem. It's really about being first, losing a story. The reporter who broke the Hill-Thomas story would never have done so except for fear of losing it, knowing that whoever leaked the story would go somewhere else with it. Assuming no other news outlets existed, the story would never have been used. But it's easy to be principled when nothing is at stake.

"So it's all about competition. The bottom line. While the media accuse corporations of caring about nothing but the bottom line, exclusivity is your bottom line. It helps the paper's bottom line. Same thing. But sometimes, Sue, we have to look beyond that. A man's life is more valuable than an exclusive."

"Tim, I'm tired and it's out of my hands now anyway. You know that. You don't think I'm going to call my editors at this time of night and tell them to kill the piece, do you? On what basis? On the basis of Thompson Brakes' PR man? What do I tell them? You called me while you were on a good Samaritan mission and I agree with you? Come on, Tim. I'm sorry. Tell the judge I'm sorry. I need some sleep."

She stopped, then added, "Frankly, if it weren't for our relationship, I might have a story of your meeting in the wee hours of the morning with the judge who is hearing the Thompson Brakes case. That could be a real good piece."

He ignored her sarcasm but agreed with her that she could not call her editors to kill the story, even if she were convinced by him that the story was premature. It was too late. He gave up.

Judge Faulkner could tell that Kaufman was losing the argument. He took the phone from Kaufman. "Miss Merriman, please I beg...." But all he heard was a dial tone.

"She didn't listen, did she?"

Kaufman shook his head. "I'm sorry."

Faulkner was shaking. He asked for an assessment of how the story would play, but Kaufman was purposely vague.

"You really can't tell," he lied. "Maybe it's a busy news day and the story will be buried."

"Mr. Kaufman, I appreciate your kindness, but I know a little about the media. Very little, I admit. But on this one, I think even I understand it will be a major story in the *Blade* and – what do you call it? – it will be picked up by the wires.

"Here I am a circuit court judge who is accused of molesting a boy in judge's chambers. Even I know that's a good story. Mr. Kaufman, I don't know how I will live with that."

"Judge, sometimes we're stronger than we think," said Kaufman, surprised at his own philosophy.

"I don't know. I really don't know. I'm grateful for your effort. I'm sorry to have bothered you. I'll see you out."

Kaufman backed his car out of the driveway and then stopped at the curb in front of the judge's house. He was surprised at how disturbed he was over the issue since he did not know Faulkner well and had no relationship with him.

Kaufman sat in the car for about 15 minutes, wondering whether he should go back and talk with the judge. At one point, he actually left his car and took a few steps to the front door, but he decided there was nothing more that could be said.

As he got back into his car, he noticed the lights being turned off in the house. He finally started the motor again and turned on the radio which drowned out the sound of the gunshot from the house he had just left.

TWENTY-EIGHT

Kaufman got up early the next morning because, anticipating the story on Faulkner, he wanted to read the paper before he went to work.

He was very upset after his meeting with Faulkner and did not sleep well. A man's life was on the line and he regretted not being able to help. He did not blame Merriman; she really had very little choice, especially since fierce media competition was driving the story. He realized she could not delay publication and risk losing the exclusive. Worse, there had been no time to debate the issue with *Blade* executives given the eleventh-hour call from Faulkner.

He drove to a newsstand, put his change in the box and grabbed a paper. The story was the banner in the *Blade*.

Circuit Court Judge Accused of Molesting Boy;
Respected Jurist Charged by Youngster's Father;
Judge Issues Denial, Maintains Innocence

Wayne County Circuit Court Judge John A. Faulkner, a 20-year veteran of the bench, has been accused of sexually molesting a seven-year-old boy in court chambers. The charge was made by Roland Stern, the boy's stepfather, who has been convicted of aggravated assault in a jury trial in Judge Faulkner's courtroom. The boy's name has been withheld by authorities because he is a minor.

Authorities told the *Blade* that Stern passed a lie detector test, that the boy also confirmed the charges and that a lie detector test taken by Judge Faulkner proved inconclusive.

"We have not completed our investigation," said Assistant Prosecutor Yvonne Simpson. "These are serious charges that we'll investigate very closely."

Police said that Stern told them the molestation occurred when Judge Faulkner talked to the boy alone in the judge's chambers.

"When my son came out of the judge's office, he looked scared," police quoted Stern as saying. "When we got home, after talking to him for some time, he told me the judge touched him. I asked him where and he pointed to his penis."

Judge Faulkner strongly denied the charges. He said he could not explain why Stern would make the charges or why his lie detector test was inconclusive.

"I have done absolutely nothing wrong," said Faulkner.

The story continued for another 10 inches. It included more details about the boy's alleged statement and background on Stern and his trial. As Kaufman expected, another story included reaction from other judges on the circuit court bench and a third story detailed Faulkner's career in the law.

The sidebars reported that Faulkner's colleagues on the bench were "shocked" and that others "could not believe that Judge Faulkner would do such a thing," with one judge stating, "I can't believe he would molest a young boy in his chambers."

All the quotes in these stories, Kaufman reflected, did nothing but imply guilt, a concept that seemed to escape or was generally ignored by editors.

As Kaufman read the stories, he simply shook his head.

His reputation is gone even if ultimately the charges are proven to be false, Kaufman thought. Poor guy, he's had it.

He decided to call the judge. He assumed that Faulkner probably bought a paper early as well. Kaufman wanted to express his regrets again at being unsuccessful with Merriman and prepare him for the media frenzy he could expect.

They're going to be all over him, he thought. Radio, TV, more print media.

As he dialed the phone, he turned on the TV to watch the morning news.

The phone rang several times. There was no answer nor was he connected with an answering machine.

Probably still out getting a paper or in the shower, Kaufman concluded.

He hung up just as a local TV reporter came on, live from Judge Faulkner's neighborhood.

"Bob," the reporter said, addressing the anchor, "I'm here where Judge Faulkner lives, talking to some of his neighbors. Many are shocked by the charges but I must add, some are not."

The reporter paused, looked down waiting for his cameraman to play a tape.

"What's your reaction to the charges made against your neighbor, Judge Faulkner?" the reporter asked a woman behind a screen door.

"I don't know much. He was always nice, but a bit of a loner."

"What do you mean?"

"Well, he didn't talk much and he used to run his fingers through the hair of children playing outside."

"That made you suspicious?"

"I don't know about that. But I didn't like it."

Kaufman watched, feeling himself get increasingly angry. He had witnessed this kind of reporting all too often.

"Do you believe the charges against Judge Faulkner?" the reporter asked a man behind the steering wheel of his car.

"Can't say. But you know where there's smoke there's fire. I seen him give candy many times to kids."

"What did you make of that?"

"Well, you can draw your own conclusions. Feel sorry for him."

Then the reporter was shown interviewing a woman in shadow.

"I'm not really surprised," said the woman, who the reporter said wished to remain anonymous. "He always acted suspicious around here. I once approached him about how he dealt with the children outside. He just smiled and walked away."

The tape ended with the reporter wrapping up his story: "So you see, Bob, while the judge has a very good reputation on the bench, and while many here think he is innocent, some aren't so sure. Back to you, Bob."

"Thanks, Jim. I guess we don't always know people as well as we thought. Good job, Bob. Next, a fire destroyed..."

Kaufman turned off his television in disgust. He showered, shaved and drove to his office, arriving a few minutes before Merriman called.

"So, what do you think?" asked Merriman.

"Your colleagues in the Fourth Estate will be very proud of you and, of course, envious. Me? I feel sorry for the son of a bitch."

"Tim..."

"Sue, you don't have to explain. I know the game. I just don't like the way it's played. It stinks. And it's getting worse. You can't tell me after reading page one that anyone in the world will believe him innocent. Wait till you see what I just saw on the electronic media. And this is just the beginning."

She asked him to hold on for a minute. Then he heard her exclaim, "Oh, my God."

"What's wrong, Sue."

"Oh, my God. Oh, my God."

"Sue, what is it?"

He heard the click of the telephone. He called her back but the switchboard operator said, "Sue Merriman isn't available now. May I take a message?"

He left his name and phone number. What the hell had happened? What had shocked her? He hoped he would hear from her soon, but he didn't.

The all-news radio station, which was always turned on in his office – even all night – quickly gave him his answer. Kaufman listened to the radio somewhat subconsciously, but his antennae were always tuned to business news important to Thompson Brakes. Suddenly and intuitively, when an important story was aired, he would listen attentively to the radio.

This time, the name Faulkner caught his consciousness but by the time he turned his full attention to the report, much of the story had been aired.

A note was found beside the body, the announcer reported, and it was addressed to the Faulkner family. The note, released by police, stated: I simply cannot face the day tomorrow. It will be filled with shame for me but, more importantly, for you whom I love so very dearly. Please believe me when I swear to you that I have done nothing wrong. I have always tried to live a principled life. My strength came from your love and support. With tomorrow's news, I am afraid I might lose that. Thus, I have chosen to end it this way. I'm sorry...very sorry. With love and affection, John.

The county's medical examiner said an autopsy will be conducted but police and the coroner said such an autopsy was routine. In this case, they said, there is little doubt that the death was a suicide.

We'll update you on the story later in the day with reaction from other judges and the community.

Coming up next, the weather.

Kaufman was shocked and dazed. Judge Faulkner had committed suicide. All kinds of disjointed thoughts raced through his mind. His conversation with Faulkner the night before to Merriman's "Oh, my God."

That's what she found out while I talked to her, he said to himself. She must be going through hell. Judge Faulkner's family must be going through hell.

Kaufman sat for a half hour not knowing what to do. He thought about calling Merriman again, but decided against it. Should he go to the paper? No, that would blow their cover. He decided to wait until late in the day. Maybe she would call.

Then he realized that maybe he should call the police. He probably was the last person to see Faulkner alive. He convinced himself that was the right thing to do.

But first he wanted to get more details on the story since he'd heard only part of it. He called the radio station and talked to one of the reporters with whom he occasionally shared a drink at the Press Club.

"I caught only the last part of a story on Judge Faulkner," said Kaufman. "What's it about?"

He was hoping that maybe he had misinterpreted what he had heard on the radio.

"Old man Faulkner put a .38 in his mouth and pulled the trigger," the reporter replied. "Guess the bastard did not want to face the charges. I assume you saw the *Blade* today?"

"Yeah, thanks. Thanks, appreciate your trouble."

Kaufman broke out in chills. He went to the bathroom to wash his face. Then he sat another half hour in his office trying to make sense of it all.

Despite the fact that it would not look good if it were revealed that Thompson Brakes' PR man had been at Judge Faulkner's house, Kaufman knew he had to call the authorities. So finally, he picked up the phone and called the police. After being transferred to several departments, he told an officer that he had visited Judge Faulkner's home about midnight and he thought the police might want to know.

"We'll have someone out to talk to you before the day's out," the officer said. "You'll be in your office?"

Kaufman said he would. While waiting for the police, he went through the motions of working but was unable to concentrate.

When the two detectives arrived, they asked him to describe his meeting with Judge Faulkner.

Kaufman summarized Faulkner's telephone call, his discussion with the judge and his call to Sue Merriman.

"Why did you go to the house? You said you didn't know him well."

"I didn't. I really don't know why I went. I thought I heard a plea, desperation in his voice."

"You mean you thought he was going to shoot himself?"

"No, no, not at all. He was in pain, yes, but I never thought he would commit suicide."

"What time did you leave and did you hear anything?"

"I think I left at about 2:00 a.m. No, I heard nothing."

"The time of death is put between 2:00 and 5:00 a.m. You heard nothing?"

"No."

"What did you say to the reporter?"

Kaufman again summarized the conversation, emphasizing that he thought the charges were false and leaked to "get the judge."

The two detectives laughed. "You can bet your ass on that."

Kaufman was curious about their reaction, asking them to explain.

"He was hated by the cops. We work our asses off to clean up the streets and this liberal bleeding heart sends them back out on technicalities. All of us hated to get him as a judge for our cases. We know this Stern guy is a pathological liar. So he makes these charges to some cops…can't tell you why…but you can bet the cops tell Merriman."

"You know Stern?"

"Record as long as your arm. Assault, burglary, con man, you name it."

"But why did he want to get Faulkner?"

"Beats the hell out of us. Tell you the truth, not many tears shed at police headquarters over Faulkner. Anyway, good you touched base with us and we may be back. If you remember anything we didn't cover, call."

They started to leave when one of them turned and asked, "We have to talk to Merriman. Know anything about her?"

"Not much. She covers our company and also does some investigative reporting. Good reporter."

TWENTY-NINE

At the end of the day, Sue Merriman called. Her voice was weak. She sounded terribly distraught.

"Can we meet?" she asked almost meekly. "Somewhere quiet. Can you come to my apartment?" She anticipated his concern about being seen. "I don't give a damn who sees you. Please come as early as you can."

Before Merriman was able to leave the office, she received a phone call.

"I hope you sold a lot of papers," the female voice said.

"Who is this?"

"This is Mrs. Faulkner. My husband was a good man, decent, caring. Incidentally, as a civil libertarian, he cared about the First Amendment but he also cared about fairness and responsibility. I hope you can live with yourself."

Merriman was almost speechless. "I'm very sorry, Mrs. Faulkner. I feel I did everything proper. There was an investigation..."

"I don't know your business. I know that gossip destroys lives and that's what happened here. You destroyed my husband and you destroyed my family. The irony is that if my husband were alive, he might even defend what you did. But I can't. As far as I'm concerned, you and the *Blade* killed him.

"And, I assume, by the time we finish the funeral, you'll get a promotion and a raise for your exclusive. Maybe you'll even win the Pulitzer."

"Mrs. Faulkner, I really am sorry…I know this is a difficult…"

She stopped because she heard Mrs. Faulkner offer a cold "good-bye."

Merriman was shaken, feeling totally humiliated and guilty. She could not wait to talk to Kaufman.

He arrived about an hour after her call. When she opened the door, she immediately collapsed into his arms in the hallway and broke down crying. They both walked into her apartment and sat on the couch. He held her hand, trying to console her.

"Sue," he finally said, "it's not your fault. His death is not your fault. We can differ on the merits of the story, whether it should or should not have been published, but his death isn't your fault or responsibility."

Merriman dabbed her eyes with a handkerchief.

"I'm not sure, Tim. You told me I was wrong in reporting it. Others said the same. His wife called me and blamed me and I assume other members of the family and community will surely blame the *Blade* and me as well. And right now, I can't absolve myself of responsibility. I thought I had it all in place."

She was torn between her journalistic responsibilities and feelings of guilt. Where did one begin and the other end? Are the rules flawed, as Kaufman insisted?

"This isn't the time to talk about the principles of journalism," he said, trying to avoid the discussion that would only make her feel more guilty. "Moreover, remember this wasn't an independent decision. It wasn't your call. You have bosses and they had the final say. As I said, this is not the best time to rehash our conversation.

"You and I are struggling over similar problems. Faulkner is your Paul Ferguson and Paul Ferguson is my Judge Faulkner. There are some very frightening parallels. We are both having problems with some of the dynamics of our respective professions. It's almost a reverse mirror image. We are both struggling with ethics, truth – whatever that is – and our professional obligations, which are tempered by political and practical considerations.

"You're torturing yourself wondering whether Faulkner was innocent and I'm having trouble wondering whether Thompson Brakes is guilty. Until we resolve those questions beyond doubt, we'll do our jobs, even if what we're doing turns out to be flawed.

"I don't know any way out of it. But I do know this; both of us are ahead of the game because we recognize the shortcomings. The key question is, and we've talked about this before, what we'll do when we know the truth."

She listened, hoping that what she heard would lessen the pain. It didn't.

"But what if he was innocent? Did I cause an innocent man to die for the sake of a story?"

"That's hypothetical, so I can't answer that, but just suppose he was...then we'll have to consider this a tragedy and maybe, just maybe, someone somewhere in this news business will reflect on the terrible injustice and implement some changes. That would be a good legacy for the judge.

"But now, let's help Sue Merriman. It'll take some time, to be sure. You need to keep working. Hell, your series on the victims at Thompson Brakes ought to keep your mind off this story. When does that begin?"

"In a couple of weeks," she said. "I don't know, Tim, I just don't know. Even if he was guilty, it doesn't seem right, although I think, I don't know, I might feel better if he was. Will we ever know?"

Kaufman put his arm around her. "Probably not since it's over. Probably not."

He kissed her and then kissed her several times. Their mutual need for support from each other overpowered them and, without thinking of anything else, they made love on the couch.

Neither spoke for about 10 minutes before Kaufman tried to ease the tension with what he recognized was dark humor.

"Feel better?" he asked.

"A little. No insult to you intended." At least, he thought, she had retained her sense of humor.

Kaufman then told her of his interview with the police and said that they would probably interview her within the next few days.

"They can save their time," she told him. "I'm certainly not going to tell the cops anything, especially about my sources."

Kaufman told her the police believed that one of their own had leaked the charges to her because the police did not like Faulkner's politics.

"Tim, you've made your point on motivation," she said with some annoyance. "I'll handle them when they come."

She dressed and decided to go to the office. When she arrived, the police were waiting for her. The two detectives were blunt and to the point. They wanted to know her sources.

"Don't hold your breath," she said. "I don't reveal my sources, not even to my editors and I'm sure not going to give them to you. First, it would break a promise and second, no one would ever talk to me again off the record."

They tried every trick, but Merriman held her ground. "No way. You can state your case any way you want; I'm not giving you that information. Everything and anything I would tell you is in my story. Read the paper."

Exasperated, they left Merriman, indicating strongly that they would probably interview her again.

But one of the detectives had a final word. "You do know, don't you, that some cop used you. They were out to get Faulkner and they did. Stern has about as much credibility as the Wizard of Oz. He may have passed the lie detector test but it don't mean shit, remember that. So you're protecting some son of a bitch who, in effect, killed the judge."

"You don't scare me," she said. "You want the snitch so he doesn't make you and your department look bad by telling me and others like me of all your fucking screwups. Get the hell out of here."

But his charge did get to her, although she tried not to show it. She continued to worry that she had been used. As Kaufman said, she'd have to work it through, process it.

Merriman also worried about a second interview with the police. What if they came back with a search warrant or subpoena? She assumed the paper's lawyers would handle it and fight any legal documents demanding the release of confidential information.

She had read about the continuous conflict between the media and public authorities in the trade journals. As she remembered, most of the time the media won. However, sometimes, journalists would refuse to honor subpoenas or demands to testify and would go to jail on contempt-of-court citations.

While she admired the courage and convictions of these reporters and editors, at this time she had no interest in becoming a cause célèbre among her brethren. Martyrdom had little attraction at a time when she was dealing with her distress and anxieties.

She decided she did not want to risk the paper's lawyers losing a court battle over whether she had to surrender her notes. That, on top of all her other problems, would be disastrous.

The Faulkner story, she convinced herself, was a one-day story anyway. With his death, she would no longer need much of the information. She collected from her desk all her important notes on the case, walked about 30 yards to the end of the office and destroyed them in a shredder.

But she would soon learn that the Faulkner affair was not a one-day story.

THIRTY

Tim Kaufman had attended several meetings on the $35 million fourth-quarter loss and was ready to make it public. As he reviewed the press releases, he noticed that aside from the usual nitpicking, the original quote attributed to Simmons explaining the loss was now given to Robert Jameson, the company's chief financial officer. Nice touch, thought Kaufman, protecting the chairman from some press coverage and Jameson, a decent, quiet man, was a team player who would not object to being the point man.

The quote stated: "The one-time loss occurred due to forecastations not being maximized to the extent that met projections formulated earlier in the year. Optimization was also not realized on inventory as expected due to a variety of difficulties related to receivables."

He concluded that the lawyers had developed the quote and was about to call Simmons to discuss making the language more understandable when he noticed a note in the margin.

"Tim, this is not negotiable. Very complex legal issues. Language must stay." The note, signed "Al," was from Hawthorne.

Total gibberish, Kaufman said to himself, but he decided to forego a battle that he knew under the circumstances he would probably lose.

About an hour after the release hit the wires, Kaufman received a barrage of calls from reporters and shareholders – institutions and individuals. The financial community was furious.

Kaufman, as well as two other staffers in the PR department he had briefed, handled the calls as well as they could. The stock dropped three points immediately and trading was the heaviest in the company's history.

Merriman called. "Just what you needed, right?"

"Yup. On or off the record?"

"On. Anything you want to add? How the hell do you lose $35 million in one quarter? And explain forecastation and maximization, please."

Kaufman laughed. "You reporters just don't understand language. I think it speaks for itself. Not very clearly, but it speaks."

Merriman chuckled, but proceeded to question him on the substance of the earnings release.

"Come on, Tim. A little more candor, please."

"Sorry, that's it. Gotta go. Have oodles of calls."

"I bet," she replied.

Simmons, wanting an update on the crisis, called Hawthorne, Kaufman, Lou Salter from security and Judy Robertson from human resources to his office.

"I want to know where we stand." He looked at Kaufman, signaling him to begin.

Kaufman started: "Things were bad enough with asbestos, but now this loss. The shareholders are really angry. We're going to need a very good first quarter to settle them down. The annual meeting is going to be a donnybrook.

"As for asbestos, for the time being, barring unexpected developments, the story is not dead, but it should quiet down. The next publicity will come when the court hearings begin. Also, you remember, the *Blade* is planning a series of stories on the deaths of former employees."

"Can we stop that somehow?"

"I don't see how."

Salter interjected. "Can my department give it a try, George?"

Kaufman, protecting his turf, plunged in. "What do you know about PR?"

"Let's not be defensive, Tim. You may not have much respect for us former cops, but you should be open to ideas. One never knows. Right?"

"He's right. This is a team. We need all the brains we can get," Simmons said.

Kaufman realized he had overreacted, but he was puzzled by what Salter could do to keep the *Blade* from publishing the series.

Simmons asked for a legal update.

Hawthorne reported that the company would file an answer to the union lawsuit. It would still be a matter of weeks before a hearing took place, particularly in light of Faulkner's death.

"I guess we got a little lucky there," said Salter. "Old Faulkner, according to this guy Stern, was fiddling with his kid. Stern and little Bobby spill the beans and he couldn't take the heat. Bingo, we'll get a better judge for our case, right Al?"

Hawthorne said it was fortunate that, although the suicide was a tragedy, most of the other judges are more conservative.

Simmons did not like having Kaufman present in the meeting and suddenly asked him to leave.

"Tim, thanks for your help," he said. "We're only going to cover some legal, security and human resource issues. You can go, and thanks again."

After Kaufman left, Robertson spoke up for the first time. She was a weak manager, lacking backbone, especially when confronting Simmons. She recommended a meeting with Angie Ferguson.

"We should at least try," said Robertson. "Maybe we can convince her to drop the case. If she pulls out, it might weaken the rest of the suit and maybe the union will have to rethink its legal strategy."

Hawthorne knew that he was violating legal ethics by participating in a discussion that offered an out-of-court settlement to a pending lawsuit. But he liked the idea that Robertson was proposing and, despite the ethical violations, he did not want to leave.

"I'm not sure that as your legal counsel, George, I should stay in light of this discussion," Hawthorne said somewhat meekly. "There are some problems here if I stay, but I can handle them."

Simmons did not understand Hawthorne's warning. "What's the problem?"

"I really shouldn't get into it. I guess I'll stay since I've heard what Judy is proposing and I like her idea. Remember, everyone, I was never at this meeting." Hawthorne felt better because he had alerted Simmons, his client, even though the chairman was perplexed by the issue Hawthorne had raised so vaguely.

Simmons was glad he had asked Kaufman to leave. Then, turning to Robertson, Simmons commended her. "Good, you go. You're a woman. Promise her anything, a good settlement that'll make her more comfortable than she has ever been. But, of course, in confidence. Whatever she agrees to must not become public. Talk to her woman to woman. Tell her she can be set for life when her husband dies."

"I'll see what I can do," Robertson said.

"Remember, money isn't an issue if she agrees to keep her mouth shut. Let's keep the ideas moving. Like I said at the other meeting, I don't care how it's done, just do it."

Simmons then turned the discussion to the annual meeting. "I want tight security. I don't want hecklers, Lou. You and your people be ready. I want to get out of there quickly. I am going to end my speech indicating that we are having a special board meeting immediately afterward and I can only take a few questions."

The meeting adjourned. Robertson headed back to her office and immediately set up an appointment with Angie Ferguson for later that day.

Robertson braced herself for what she knew would be a sensitive meeting as she drove to the Ferguson home. She was sorry she had volunteered the idea but she wanted to impress Simmons and have him think well of her.

At the house, she met with Angie Ferguson alone. Paul Ferguson, she was told, was sleeping in the back bedroom.

Robertson described her position at Thompson Brakes and offered "a proposal that will help you and your family."

She explained that Thompson Brakes would pay all the medical expenses plus a significant life insurance benefit and a weekly salary for the rest of her life.

"That's generous," Angie Ferguson replied. "What do I have to do?"

"You must keep the agreement confidential and withdraw from the lawsuit."

Angie Ferguson did not hesitate in refusing the offer. "I can't do that and I won't do that."

"Mrs. Ferguson, if we make the agreement public, it would set a precedent for the others. We can't do that because we don't know if the exposure caused the illness. Indeed, we believe it did not. The lawsuit could go on for years, cost us a lot of money and, remember, you might lose. We believe we have a good case. Please accept our offer."

"It's not an offer. It's blackmail and it's pressure. There are many other families involved. They're suffering terribly. I'm not going to abandon them. I may lose, we may lose, but I have to live with myself."

Robertson tried again, adding, "You may not only lose, but remember, this is going to be in the courts for years. Even if you win, which is unlikely, you won't see any money for maybe ten years or longer."

"I'm not arguing with your facts," said Angie Ferguson. "You may be absolutely right. I hope not, but you may be right. That's no longer the issue."

"What is the issue?" Robertson asked, immediately regretting that she posed the question.

"I'm sorry that you don't understand and that I have to explain it to you," said Angie Ferguson. "The issue is that my husband is dying because of Thompson Brakes. The company killed others. And the issue is that you're trying to buy me off with what amounts to a bribe."

Her anger was rising as she spoke. "To accept your *offer*," she said, pronouncing "offer" with all the sarcasm she could muster, "would be equivalent to forgiving you and your company. It would imply that I don't care about my husband, his impending death or all the others that died. That's the issue, Mrs. Robertson."

"I think you're overstating...," Robertson started to say but she was stopped abruptly by Angie Ferguson.

"Please, no more. I'm upset as it is. This isn't doing either of us any good. The answer is no and that's it."

Robertson stood up, preparing to leave. She told Angie Ferguson to "give it some thought; don't be too hasty in your decision. This could give you security for some time."

"Nothing to think about."

When she reached the door, Robertson turned back. "You're a courageous woman, Mrs. Ferguson. On a personal level, let me say I'm sorry. I'm just doing my job."

"I understand. You might consider getting another one."

Robertson winced slightly at the admonition. As she opened the door to leave, she heard coughing. She turned around and saw Paul Ferguson, hunched over, standing in the living room, clutching his chest.

When Robertson was gone, Angie Ferguson described the conversation to her husband.

"Bastards," he said. "But Angie, maybe you should take the money. You'll need it."

"I'll be okay, Paul. I think we're going to win."

But there was no joy in the observation, knowing that her husband would be gone in a few months.

"Let's call Steve Marks," she said. "You want to tell him?"

"You bet I do. The sooner the better."

Ferguson called the union president at his office.

"You were right. They came. They made the offer. Just like you said."

"Did you do what I told you?"

"Right after they called for the appointment, I wired Angie as you instructed. I felt a little like the FBI. You can pick up the tape whenever you want."

THIRTY-ONE

The Detroit Civic League, a nonprofit organization dedicated to improving relations between races, religions and cultures in the city, annually selects an individual for its coveted Humanitarian Award. The award, the league maintained, symbolizes "all that is good in man," and is bestowed on the person who "has made outstanding contributions for the betterment of mankind" in the Detroit metropolitan area.

The league was meeting to nominate its honoree in the midst of the controversy at Thompson Brakes, and George C.L. Simmons, Jr. had been the favorite to receive the award.

With the controversy about asbestos, some league directors had second thoughts about nominating Simmons, at least, this year. They argued that he was a "good man" but with "this asbestos thing" maybe they should wait and give him the award "when all the hullabaloo has died down."

The debate became very heated at times. Those favoring Simmons argued that Thompson Brakes had created jobs, was a major taxpayer in the city, had made many contributions to civic institutions and Simmons had been "a fine example of philanthropy."

Those opposed retorted that, indeed, Thompson Brakes was a very "prominent and outstanding corporate citizen and George Simmons was a very fine man." But they did not believe it was "good timing" to give the award to Simmons when he and the company were facing serious charges.

"We have to think of our image," several of the opponents argued.

"I'd like to say something," offered Herman Porter, the league's president, a businessman who was also president of the area's largest retailing firm. "It's the media, in all due respect to publisher Bob Harrison here. We all know how they sensationalize these things. We have all suffered at the hands of the media. This is a media thing. We can't blame Thompson Brakes because the *Blade* – again, sorry Bob – wants to sell more papers."

Harrison, a member of the board, smiled following Porter's assessment of the Thompson Brakes crisis.

"It's no problem, Herman. You can't imagine how many times I've heard that as publisher. I don't mind being the scapegoat. Everyone from the president on down blames the media. I guess if we dish it out, we ought to be able to take it. But, let me add my opinion on George Simmons. Bottom line, he deserves this award. And if this board votes for him, we'll give it a huge spread in the paper. We do report good news from time to time. That would be good for George, the company and for this league."

The debate did not end, although blaming the media as the culprit seemed to galvanize the board. Supporters of giving Simmons the award identified with Porter's assessment of the media. None of them had much respect or love for the media because, at various times, all of them had had to face some tough questions regarding their respective businesses.

They agreed the media was to blame. There was no proof that Paul Ferguson suffered from cancer because of asbestos dust. Anyway, he was a smoker and, they were confident, "the cigarettes did it."

"And let's be practical," Porter said. "Who else can sell more tickets? We need vendor lists and no one has more vendors than Thompson Brakes. If we choose Simmons, you know he'll pressure the hell out of his suppliers to buy tickets and tables. He'll have the company place a major ad in our program book. That's another few bucks.

"He's got a big ego. He likes awards. He likes speeches praising him. And he likes to give speeches. That's a perfect formula for a successful dinner. And that's what this Humanitarian Award is all about. Having a good, fun event and raising some bucks.

"Let's even admit that Thompson Brakes may have made some mistakes. Who hasn't? No reason to penalize them and penalize us by choosing a nominee who can't raise money. What if we get someone who really made a major contribution to important causes but can't draw a crowd? Then what've we got?

"The issue isn't what Simmons has done for mankind. The issue is whether he can fill the hall and he can because he will apply pressure to his constituencies. That's what this is all about. What's more, there are a lot of businesspeople around this table and any one of us could find himself in such a stew. That's when we need support. I would hope I could count on my friends when, I mean if, I got into that kind of trouble. That's how I feel."

There was more debate but Porter had been persuasive. They had discussed similar circumstances before because, basically, the award was rotated in the community from one executive to another. And, at times, others were the target of controversy.

As the Detroit Civic League directors voted to bestow its prestigious Humanitarian Award on George C.L. Simmons, Jr., Sue Merriman finished writing the first in her series of articles on cancer victims who had worked at Thompson Brakes.

The series would be titled, "Working with Death in the Air," and promoted under that slogan.

The lead on her first story read: "When Robert Pillar went to work for Thompson Brakes, Inc. in the mid-1950s, he was a man with high hopes. He dreamed of having a family, living a long time and retiring to a life of fishing.

"At retirement, Pillar's lungs had been destroyed by an incurable cancer – mesothelioma – a disease that many experts maintain was caused by Pillar's exposure to asbestos dust in Thompson Brakes' plants.

"About 90 Thompson Brakes employees have died of the disease or other cancers attributed to exposure to asbestos in the last 10 years, statistically an usually high number.

"Pillar was 24 when he joined the company, a young man filled with optimism and dreams about the future. Some 40 years later, his dreams and family were shattered by X rays that revealed lung cancer. Doctors could not offer him any hope for a cure. Robert Pillar died seven months after the diagnosis, leaving his family destitute.

"Worse, Thompson Brakes, maintaining that no proof exists that Pillar's exposure to asbestos caused the illness, has continually refused to assist the Pillar family fearing, sources have told the *Blade*, setting precedents that might require the company to make some kind of restitution to Pillar's family and other survivors of cancer victims who had worked at the company.

"Pillar, who never graduated from high school, joined Thompson Brakes as a laborer."

Merriman was pleased with the story, which ran about 25 inches and would be accompanied by pictures of the Pillar family. One photograph showed Mrs. Pillar at her husband's grave.

She clicked off her computer, cleaned her desk and prepared to go home. It was 9 p.m. and she was tired. She grabbed her purse, walked down the stairs instead of waiting for the elevator and headed for her car in the company's adjacent covered garage.

Her footsteps echoed in the building which was almost empty. She reached her car and just as she was about to insert her key into the lock, a huge, gloved hand covered her mouth. The other arm of her assailant grabbed her around the waist and picked her up.

She could hardly breathe or think. She struggled but was unable to free herself. It was useless; he was too strong. As she tried vainly to escape, he held her in the air, warning her not to scream.

"Listen closely, don't scream and don't fight. If you listen, you won't get hurt."

She attempted to calm her trembling body and to obey the assailant. She was thrown to the ground on her back, seriously bruising her hips. She felt pain throughout her body. As he bent down, straddling her, she began fighting again.

She tried to scratch his face. Her left hand flailed away and her right hand caught in his shirt pocket. She pulled, tearing the shirt.

"Listen, you bitch. I told you to relax. I won't say it again."

He took her wrists and pinned them against the ground. She could not move.

"Listen very carefully. I'm only going to say this once. Lay off asbestos. You understand? That's it. Lay off. Next time you might not be so lucky. Just nod if you heard what I said."

She obeyed her attacker, nodding with fear in her eyes. She looked at her assailant, who was wearing sunglasses and a knitted hat pulled down just above his eyebrows.

"I'm going to let you go. Don't scream. Don't get up till I'm gone."

The man stood up, freeing her, and trotted to a car she had not noticed. He started the motor and drove off.

When he was gone, Merriman broke down, crying convulsively. She pushed herself up against a wall and sat for several minutes trying to regain her composure.

Finally, her breathing turned normal again. Her heartbeat slowed. Then she noticed her fists were still clenched. Indeed, she had clenched them so tightly, her hands hurt.

She opened her fists slowly and she felt a little pain. In her right hand she noticed a piece of her assailant's shirt. Along with the piece of cloth was what looked like a crumbled business card. She smoothed the card. On one side, in handwriting, was her name.

On the other side, she read: Louis Salter, Vice President – Security, Thompson Brakes, Inc.

THIRTY-TWO

"Tim, I need to talk to you and I need to talk now."

"Where are you? You sound weird."

"Never mind that. Stay home. I'll be there in a few minutes."

Kaufman had planned to leave, but the urgency in Merriman's voice convinced him that her request – demand – was important.

She arrived within a half hour and Kaufman was shocked at how she looked. Her clothes were rumpled and dirty, her face pale and her eyes red from crying.

She embraced him, breaking down again. She sobbed uncontrollably while he held her in his arms, trying to comfort her. He walked her to the couch. He did not ask any questions until she regained some of her composure.

Then she told her story, showing Kaufman the business card. "What do you think this means?" she asked him.

"I just can't believe they would be so stupid. I can't believe that Salter would try intimidation. But now I understand what Salter meant when he said in a meeting that he wanted his department to look into what could be done to stop the bad publicity. He got very sarcastic with me when I asked him what the hell he knew about PR. I guess we have our answer. And he hired a real Einstein. Did you call the police?"

She decided not to because she did not want to be the center of news coverage. Admittedly, she said it was an ironic philosophical posture for a reporter who convinces others to "go public." She added that she was worried that she would lose exclusivity if, indeed, Salter and Thompson Brakes were behind the attack. She would have to tell the police about the business card.

"Always the reporter, even under these circumstances, right?"

She smiled weakly, finally asking, "What do we do now? I can't write this and accuse Thompson Brakes without proof, even if we both know it's true."

"Let's sit on it for a while," he replied. "Let's just think it through."

He mixed her a drink, fixed some food and for the next hour they talked about Thompson Brakes, the attack and Judge Faulkner.

"Still feel very guilty about that, too," she said. "But the tragedy must be good news at your company. You'll get another judge and none of the others on that bench is as liberal as Faulkner was."

Her statement triggered a thought in Kaufman. Reassignment. That's what Simmons wanted. Was there any connection?

She noticed a sudden change in him. "What are you thinking?"

"I don't know yet. I'm wondering if there's any connection between Faulkner, you and who knows what else. Right now, I'm just probing."

"A little paranoid, aren't we?"

"Maybe. But let's follow it up. Stern makes an accusation. It's leaked to you. No, I don't think they could anticipate suicide, but even if Faulkner had not committed suicide, he probably would not have been able to conduct any business from his bench. He'd take a leave or be suspended while an investigation goes on. Mission accomplished. All someone had to do was get to Stern and Stern to Bobby, his son."

"How did you know the kid's name?"

"I don't know. I remember Salter using it at one of our meetings."

"How did he know it? I don't even know it and I wrote the story. The cops wouldn't tell me because he's a minor."

Kaufman jumped to his feet. "That's it," he said, planting a big kiss on her cheek.

"What?"

"When we talked about the case in Simmons' office, Salter sarcastically rehashed what happened, saying something along the lines that Faulkner committed suicide after being caught fiddling, I think he said, with Stern's son, Bobby. If you and the others didn't print the boy's name, how the hell did he know it?"

She planted a big kiss on Kaufman's cheek. This was too good to be true. They laughed at their discovery, hugging each other with joy.

But her elation faded quickly, giving way to depression. Merriman felt dizzy as she realized the story she had written, based on false information, had cost a man his life.

He did not have to ask why her mood changed. He came to the same conclusion.

Trembling, she asked Kaufman, "How do I live with this?"

He had no answers for her. He sat quietly, holding her hand.

"Tim, how will I come to grips with this?"

He felt he needed to say something, but was stumped for words.

"I don't know, Sue," he said. "It's all too fresh. They used you and they have the responsibility."

He knew that was a weak argument, but he did not know what else to say.

"But I share in that responsibility," she said as he held her close, stroking her hair.

This is a tough one, he thought. She won't get over this easily.

"We can't do anything for Judge Faulkner, Sue. But perhaps we can make them pay and pay dearly.

"As I told you, the real test for us comes not just when we suspect the truth, but when we know it. Sue, give me some time. I'll handle it."

Then he added, "Don't worry." It seemed a very silly and patronizing thing to say at the moment.

She was terribly distraught and all she could do was cry.

THIRTY-THREE

Simmons was interrupted in a meeting with Hawthorne and Salter at his home by a phone call from Herman Potter, president of the Detroit Civic League.

"I'm sorry to bother you at night, George, but I thought you'd like some good news, given that you've been under the gun lately. I'm pleased to tell you that you're the Humanitarian Award winner this year. We just voted and you'll get official confirmation in a few days. The vote was unanimous."

"Herman, thanks so much. Thank the board. I'm flattered."

"No problem. We feel for you. The fucking media, liberal bleeding hearts. They're more concerned about the spotted owl than jobs. How many jobs has the spotted owl created? Or what have these fucking owls done to maximize shareholder value? The media don't care whose reputation they damage. They care about nothing but sensationalism. Even if it's true, what did we know about asbestos 40 years ago? Right, George? We try to do the right thing and they fuck us. Anyway, congratulations George. You deserve this honor."

"This means a lot to me, Herman, thanks. And I also appreciate your thoughts about the media. It's been a little tough, but you know what Nixon used to say, when the going gets tough, the tough get going. And we're gonna get going. Thanks for the call."

"Just one thing," said Potter, "I think it would be helpful if you could indicate to me for the board – when I thank them on your behalf – what we might expect your contribution to be."

Simmons paused, contemplating his donation, and then offered, "How's $20 grand?"

"Come on, George. For this award, at this time when you're under such pressure. It's worth at least four times that. You can't buy this kind of PR."

"Eighty grand, Herman? That's pretty steep. Let's split the difference. Forty and we got a deal."

"George, I can get $50 grand from Howard Stone and he doesn't even have the problems you do."

"Stone? What's he ever done?"

"I agree with you and I know how you feel about your competition, but this is about our organization."

"$60 grand and that's it."

"Sold, George. I knew we could count on you. I can't think of anyone who deserves this more. Congratulations."

Then Potter added, "George, I think I'll come to the annual meeting and make the announcement there. Maybe it will take some pressure off."

"Excellent idea. Thanks much. I can use the help."

Simmons was elated not only about the award but that he had effectively blocked the league from approaching Stone, the chairman of Thompson Brakes' primary competitor, Lawson Industries. Lawson had been continually profitable and its success obsessed Simmons.

He returned to his meeting with Hawthorne and Salter, telling them the news.

"I won the Civic League award for humanitarianism," he said. "And most important, I beat out that son of a bitch, Howard Stone. Can you imagine the league even considering Stone?"

Hawthorne and Salter both slapped Simmons on the back, shook his hand and offered their congratulations.

"You deserve it," said Hawthorne. "It would've been an insult not just to you, but to the business community to honor Stone. Congratulations."

"Absolutely," said Salter. "Congratulations. This is really good news."

"Yes, thanks fellows," replied Simmons. "I appreciate that. Now, let's get to our business."

Indicating urgency, he had called the two executives to his home that night to get an assessment of the asbestos situation.

Simmons turned to Salter, ordering him to take "whatever measures necessary to control critics at the annual meeting."

"I don't give a damn what Kaufman says. I don't want anyone making a fool of me. I don't want them playing to the press. Get them out of there if they start."

While Salter agreed, even he was perplexed on how to accomplish this mission. But he did not express his misgivings.

Then Hawthorne outlined the legal status of the lawsuit. A new judge would be assigned to the case. The study indicating little, if any, correlation between asbestos exposure and cancer should help. Outside counsel was preparing an answer to the suit and creating a list of cancer experts who would testify for the company.

"I think we're in pretty good shape," said Hawthorne. "We can drag this out for years, if necessary."

Hawthorne also reported that Angie Ferguson had turned down the company's offer. "She did not buy it even though we were prepared to be very generous," said Hawthorne. "She would've had more money than she ever dreamed of in her lifetime. But she said no. Beats the hell out of me why. Judy Robertson reported the Ferguson woman said it was a matter of principle. Maybe she doesn't understand, principle doesn't buy any bread. We'll keep this thing in the courts for years and she'll never see any money. Let her eat principle."

Simmons frowned. He had hoped for an out-of-court settlement to end the controversy.

"Stupid broad," the chairman replied. "Maybe I should go see her. You know, the power of the chairman's office."

"I think it would be a waste of time and I don't think you should be personally involved," said Hawthorne.

"Suppose you're right, but it pisses me off."

Hawthorne then suggested that the plan might have failed even if Angie Ferguson had accepted the deal.

"Her lawyers probably would have found out anyway and might even have demanded their fees if she had settled," he said. "That's one of the problems I thought about when we discussed it."

Simmons angrily confronted Hawthorne.

"Why the fuck didn't you say anything?"

Hawthorne, shaken, tried to cover over his mistake.

"There were other issues I really don't think we should get into now," he said. "Anyway, it's over."

Turning back to the court suit and the asbestos-cancer study, Simmons complimented Hawthorne on his work, adding that he was particularly impressed with his discussions with Collins on the research study.

"Maybe you fucked up on the Ferguson broad but this was nice work, Al, getting Collins to see it our way. Put the son of a bitch on our vendor blacklist. He should never have put us in that position. He's out from now on, got it?"

"Done," said Hawthorne.

Salter had no idea what Simmons and Hawthorne were talking about and he did not ask. He knew better.

In his progress report, Salter said his department was "looking into certain things" and it would be "premature" to bother Simmons with the details.

"Do whatever it takes. Don't even bother checking with me. If you think it'll help, do it. This issue is very important to Thompson Brakes. Lots of pressure is building from the shareholders and the directors.

"As of now, I think I have the board under control. The directors don't want to act because it would imply guilt and their asses are on the line as well. So I'm safe for now. But you never know, so cover all the bases."

"We are," Salter assured him.

Simmons then launched into a tirade over the *Blade's* plans to print the series on the company's employees.

"I don't understand the media," Simmons said. "I don't understand, for instance, why when we issue press releases, they just don't print them as they get them? They change them. Put anything in they want. I keep asking Kaufman why we even bother with all that work and he gives me that bullshit about freedom of the press. You ask me, they have a little too much freedom. Then I tell him I'll withdraw my advertising and he tells me that will make things worse. It will make the story bigger. A big company threatening a paper.

"So I have to sit by while they print goddamn lies about me and the company. It makes me so fucking mad after all I've done for the community. This award proves it."

Simmons paused, straightened his tie and then told the two of his meeting with Harrison.

"I made that son of a bitch sweat," said Simmons. "Twelve million in advertising talks, believe me. Harrison better act, if he knows what's good for him and his rag."

Simmons ended the meeting, walked the two to the door and headed to his library.

For the next hour, he worked, making notes on the speech he would deliver the night of the award ceremony. Then he telephoned Kaufman to inform him of the award. Kaufman answered the phone while in bed with Sue Merriman.

"Tim, I won the Humanitarian Award. You're among the first to know. I'm really honored and happy."

"Congratulations."

"Thanks, I want you to start thinking about a speech. A real barn-burner. I want to tell them the past is behind us, the future ahead. I made some notes before calling you. Do you have a notebook handy?"

Telling Simmons to hold on, Kaufman covered the mouthpiece of the telephone and told Merriman, "I wish you could hear what's coming up next. Can't wait to brief you."

"Tim, like I said, I want to make the point that the future is in front of us. We must face it. We have no choice." He stopped, asking, "Got that?"

"Uh-huh."

"We haven't given the future sufficient importance because we don't seem to understand that the past is gone; we can't do anything about it. So let's move ahead. That is the kind of theme I want to create. Do you understand?"

"George, sounds good," Kaufman replied, trying to keep from laughing with Merriman. He held the phone away from his ear so she could hear some of what Simmons said.

"We can't be afraid of the future. We must face it with courage. We simply haven't given the future sufficient importance as we conduct our daily lives." Simmons repeated himself. "We are too preoccupied with our daily lives, living from minute to minute. We can't afford that anymore. This world moves too fast. Today is tomorrow's yesterday. Boy, I like that. Did you get that down, Tim?"

"Yes. Today is yesterday's tomorrow. Very good." He reversed the wording purposely, knowing Simmons would not notice.

"And yesterday does not mean anything to us when we face tomorrow. America – the great country of ours – must begin to understand that. Because, if we don't, the very survival of this country is at stake. How's that? You may have to edit those thoughts and maybe add a line here or there, but I think we're on our way. What do you think?"

"No question about it, George," said Kaufman. "That's a hell of a thought. Makes you visionary, statesmanlike. We'll get to editing right away, and you'll have a copy within the next few days."

"Get on it right away. I think I have something here. I want them to talk about this speech. A thinker. I know we have some time, but start right away. We'll go through many drafts before we're done. This is a happy day for me."

"I understand, George. I'll start right away on the project."

After ending the conversation, Simmons reflected briefly that Kaufman did not seem very enthusiastic.

Simmons walked into the basement of his home where he'd had a small auditorium built. There was a stage with a curtain, a podium with a built-in air conditioning unit and a public address system.

He stepped up onto the stage and pushed a button at the podium that opened the curtains. He pushed another button which turned on the air conditioning unit designed to keep him cool when speaking. Then he turned on the PA system.

Looking out, he said, "I want to thank the Detroit Civic League, its board, members and the entire community for this very wonderful award."

He stopped, pushed another button and the basement filled with applause.

Smiling, Simmons continued, "I know there were many candidates, so I'm especially honored that I was the victor."

He pushed the applause button again.

He was about to continue his acceptance speech when the cellular phone in a leather pouch on his belt rang. He let it ring. He was not going to be interrupted.

THIRTY-FOUR

Kaufman and Merriman laughed uproariously at the irony of Simmons calling while they were in bed and at the hypocrisy of Simmons winning the league's award, the city's top honor.

"The past is behind us, the future ahead," she mimicked sarcastically. "Wow, let's hear more."

They both reveled in their ridicule of Simmons for a few minutes.

"Mr. Speechwriter, get right on it. Let's make this dumb ass a statesman."

Kaufman added, "Be more fitting if they gave it to some doctor or nurse who is putting his or her life on the line helping the poor in Africa or some place like that. But that wouldn't sell any tickets."

Kaufman explained to her that through the years, Simmons had received almost every community award available.

"I bet all those awards cost him a few million bucks," Kaufman said. "He has plaques all over his office walls."

In the morning, Kaufman asked her not to write anything about their discoveries.

"Don't do anything until you hear from me. And be careful. Incidentally, when does the series start and what's it called?"

"First installment is today. It's labeled 'Working with Death in the Air.' "

"Wonderful. That's objectivity." They both laughed and went their separate ways to work.

The timing was terrible. The annual meeting was scheduled for 10 a.m.

Kaufman headed to his office first and then to the auditorium, which was starting to fill up. Usually, the total attendance was about 100, including company attorneys, bankers, employees and supporter-friends of the chairman. Shareholders traditionally numbered only about 25. Kaufman expected about twice that number given the controversies and his prediction proved accurate.

The directors sat at a head table with a spot for Simmons in the center. When Simmons entered, Kaufman could see anxiety in his face.

Simmons shook a few hands in the audience and then took his place on the stage. He called the meeting to order, concluding the business part of the meeting quickly since it involved only the reelection of three directors.

He read the speech, but stumbled often. He was very insecure, anticipating a shareholder attack.

"That is my report. Thank you very much. Since we are having a special board meeting following this meeting, I can take only a few questions. I'm sorry, but I hope you understand. I really like the Q & A the best."

"Mr. Simmons, how in the world can you account for the $35 million loss? Don't you have any controls?"

Simmons fumbled through his briefing book. "As we have said," he read, looking down, "it was a one-time loss and it's behind us. We expect better things ahead."

"I didn't ask you that," the shareholder replied. "Do you have financial controls and why did they fail?"

Simmons stammered, "We have controls...these issues are very complex...I'm not sure we can discuss it with you today. But again, it's behind us. Let's give another shareholder a chance."

"Why are you getting a $300,000 bonus when the company did so poorly?"

A director sitting next to Simmons offered to answer the question. "I think I should address that since the board votes on salaries and bonuses. Mr. Simmons has no vote on that. We need to remain competitive. We need to pay competitive bonuses and salaries to attract and retain good people. And this is in keeping with what's going on in the industry."

"But he did not perform," the shareholder retorted to the director.

"We set some goals at the beginning of the year. Mr. Simmons attained those goals, the one-time loss – a one-time loss, I emphasize – notwithstanding."

The shareholders grumbled among themselves, obviously dissatisfied with the answer.

"Mr. Simmons," a woman said from the back of the room. "My name is Angie Ferguson. My husband, Paul, is dying of cancer."

A murmur ran through the room as heads turned to look at her. Simmons' hands started to shake; he turned a little white as the blood flowed from his face. He looked at Salter, who did not move.

Steven Marks, thought Kaufman. He admired the masterstroke. Kaufman had wondered why so many reporters attended the shareholders' meeting which generally did not attract much news coverage.

He must have alerted them, Kaufman thought.

"As you know, he and many of his friends worked in the plants for years, breathing in asbestos dust. Many died of mesothelioma and other cancers and my husband will die soon," Angie Ferguson said.

"Why do you refuse to help us with some financial assistance? I'm here to appeal to you. My husband could not come. He's getting worse and is too sick. Please, Mr. Simmons, I beg you to help us."

Angie Ferguson spoke softly and effectively. The audience was very quiet and the room was filled with tension. While Simmons wrestled with how to handle the question from Angie Ferguson, the directors sat stonefaced.

"Yes...I understand...," Simmons tried, glancing down at his briefing book, but there was no script relating to an appearance by a woman who would be a widow in a few months.

"This is a picture of my husband," she said, holding up a photograph. "My husband now weighs 170 pounds. Mr. Simmons, he was 220 pounds when he was healthy. I am told he will probably lose another 20 or 30 pounds before he dies.

"Mr. Simmons, I invite you and the directors to visit us to see for yourselves what this disease does. Watch my husband try to walk across the room, hunched over in pain. He sleeps sitting up because he can't stretch out without pain."

"We have talked about this many times," Simmons continued. "Yes, I know how you feel…and I'm sorry…yes, sorry…but…"

Simmons, recalling the standard reply, added, "There's no proof of a correlation between…"

Angie Ferguson cut him off in mid-sentence. "That's just not true," she said in almost a whisper. "You know that's not true. I hope you and the other directors can live with yourselves."

Suddenly, Simmons, not recognizing the insensitivity of his question, asked, "Are you a shareholder?"

She replied softly, "No, Mr. Simmons. My husband is a laborer not eligible for stock options nor were we ever able to buy any stock. I'm only a woman who is losing her husband. Mr. Simmons, do you know how my husband will die?" When her question went unanswered for a few seconds, she said, "Let me tell you. His chest will fill with fluid, making it impossible for his lungs to expand. In short, he will suffocate to death."

When she finished, she picked up her purse and, with the picture of her husband in her hand, walked to the podium. She reached up and placed the photo on the podium in front of a dumbfounded Simmons. She then walked out, followed by several reporters.

In the audience, Herman Porter, president of the Detroit Civic League, decided against announcing at this meeting that Simmons would receive the organization's Humanitarian Award, despite the fact that, like Marks, Porter had alerted reporters, indicating he would make an "important" statement at the annual meeting.

However, under the circumstances, he decided it would be inappropriate and counterproductive to make the award public at the meeting. He felt it would seem callous immediately after the impassioned plea from Angie Ferguson.

He left the auditorium. In the hall, a reporter from a local radio station whom Porter had notified stopped him for an interview.

"Are you still planning to give the award to George Simmons?"

"Of course, Mr. Simmons is a fine, outstanding citizen of the community."

"Why didn't you announce the award as you said you would? You called us, you know."

"Yes, I'm sorry. Mr. Simmons, you heard, was pressed for time with all the business and the special board meeting. We'll do it with a press release."

"You didn't change your mind, did you, because of Mrs. Ferguson?"

"Of course not."

"How does your organization feel about the asbestos issue and Thompson Brakes' responsibilities?"

"Well, you know I'm not an expert on that issue, but Mr. Simmons is an honest man and I believe him when he says there is no proof that asbestos caused this cancer. I feel sorry for the woman who just left but remember, if they pay her, the company is saying, in effect, it's guilty and it would have to pay others.

"That would set a terrible precedent, could cost millions of dollars as well as jobs and cause the stock to drop. All this because of a controversy created by the media. I'm not blaming you, personally. I should say some of the media."

"So you believe that Thompson Brakes has no responsibility at all for the deaths that have occurred?"

"I think I've answered all your questions. Thank you very much."

After Angie Ferguson left the meeting, one shareholder spoke up. "While we all sympathize with this woman, I must agree with the chairman and medical experts who say there's no relationship between the issue of asbestos exposure and cancer. The corporation also has no liability in this matter. Mr. Simmons, I also want to indicate that while we're going through hard times, we enjoyed good ones as well. You made us a lot of money and we should not forget that. I am confident you will display your fine leadership again."

A plant, Kaufman thought, and a little obvious. But better than nothing.

Simmons, smiling after the endorsement, recovered slightly and decided to adjourn the meeting.

"Thank you for your words of encouragement. I appreciate that. Now, I'm sorry, as I said, we have another meeting. Thank you all for coming."

That's drama, Kaufman told himself, and Merriman will kick herself for missing this one. She was tied up on the series on asbestos, so the *Blade* had sent another reporter.

Simmons and the directors hurried out through a side-door exit and the shareholders talked for minutes among themselves.

Kaufman headed back to his office, walking through tension-filled halls. Word had spread quickly about the appearance of Angie Ferguson, but even before her plea at the annual meeting, headquarters employees were displaying anxieties and unhappiness. Morale dropped dramatically as the asbestos story was building in the community. He expected nothing less, understood the atmosphere, but it created a very unpleasant environment.

Kaufman now knew the truth and, as he had told Sue Merriman and many of his other colleagues, the test of character comes when the pressure is on.

He made the decision that he could not live with himself as a PR professional under the circumstances and it was time for him to act. He considered the financial ramifications of putting his job on the line, but concluded he would live; he would survive.

He remembered what a neighbor had told him years earlier. "The salary, benefits and bonuses are the noose around your neck," the neighbor said, explaining how those in corporate life compromise their principles for financial security.

Well, Kaufman said proudly to himself, I am about to remove that noose.

He sketched out a game plan on his computer.

1. Contact "A" at institute.
2. See "B" next regarding negotiations.
3. Discuss discoveries with Salter.
4. Finally, see chairman.

"A" referred to Collins at the Research Institute and "B" was Steve Marks at the local union. He was vague on his computer in case some hacker – intentionally or accidentally – got into his computer. He purposely identified Salter and Simmons since that would imply appropriate corporate business. Maybe I'm a little paranoid, he thought, but better safe than sorry.

It was time to take some risks. He would discover in his upcoming meetings how good he was at bluffing. He was not terribly confident; he always lost at poker, but there was more at stake this time.

As he worked on his computer, the fax machine in his office turned on. He watched it as one sheet of paper dropped into a receiving basket next to the machine.

He walked over and read the paper. It was an editorial cartoon out of *The New Yorker*. An executive behind a desk was telling his visitor in an office marked "Public Relations": "We're interested in words, not deeds."

At the bottom, in handwriting, was a brief note. "Couldn't resist. Sue."

He smiled and walked back to his desk to continue planning. I guess it's better to laugh than cry, he thought.

He called Collins' office and asked for an immediate meeting, telling the secretary to inform her boss the subject was of the utmost urgency. Even if Collins were suspicious, Kaufman's instincts told him Collins would never call Simmons or anyone else at the company to report that Kaufman had asked for a meeting.

He received a return telephone call within a half hour and the secretary said that Mr. Collins would see him later that afternoon. The speed of the return call, Kaufman thought, was a good sign. It indicated he was scared or, at the very least, anxious to know why Kaufman wanted to see him. Whatever the reason, Kaufman was very pleased with Collins' prompt action.

As he sat in Collins' office, Kaufman tried hard to appear tough. He kept what was almost a frown on his face.

"Mr. Collins, thank you for seeing me," he began. "As you know, we are having somewhat of a crisis at Thompson Brakes."

"Yes, I know and I hope my report helped."

"Well, that's what I wanted to talk to you about. It did and it didn't."

He paused purposely to create more anxiety in Collins. He tried to read Collins and thought he spotted uncertainty.

"The report that we released to the press certainly was helpful overall to the company," Kaufman continued. "But the one that was leaked undermined, as I am sure you can imagine, our credibility."

Collins' mouth twitched a bit. He was not a man at ease.

"Yes, I can understand that, but I don't know anything about it."

Kaufman waited a few seconds, staring Collins in his eyes.

"That's what I'm here about," Kaufman said. He was purposely playing the tension for its optimum value.

"Yes?"

"Yes, the leaked report."

Kaufman still did not indicate what he wanted from Collins.

"Yes, I said I know nothing about that."

Taking what he knew was a big risk, he charged, "I heard what you said. But, Mr. Collins, I think you do."

If Kaufman was wrong in calling Collins a liar, he should throw him out of the office. But if, as he assumed, he was right, Collins would adopt other strategies.

Collins tried to show anger and indicate he was insulted, but he was not a good actor.

"I resent that, Mr. Kaufman," Collins said, but without any feeling. "I don't know what you mean."

Kaufman played the moment smoothly. He was forceful and confident.

"You see, Mr. Collins, I think I know what's going on in this case. All those involved tried to cover their tracks. But they made some mistakes. Professionally, the *Blade* took a risk printing the story on the leaked report, but I also know the reporter. And I feel she had the goods."

"So what do you want?"

That, of course, was an entirely inappropriate question if, as Collins said, he did not know anything about the leaked asbestos study. Kaufman knew he had Collins.

"I'm not sure why you would ask me that if you know nothing about this controversy," Kaufman said. "But I'll give you the benefit of the doubt."

Collins was becoming more and more fidgety, moving restlessly in his chair.

"Let me explain and please don't interrupt," Kaufman said. "Some very disconcerting things are happening at Thompson Brakes. Along with the leaked report we are talking about, Sue Merriman was attacked by a man warning her to quit writing about asbestos. He could've raped her, killed her, but he did nothing. So it's very clear that the attack was intended as intimidation.

"I have further information, which I can't disclose to you, that there may be a connection between the company and the suicide of Judge Faulkner.

I'm sure you've heard about his death. I don't know yet what else is going on, but I don't like the implications at all."

Collins volunteered, "This is all very interesting and, indeed, tragic, but what do you want from me?"

Kaufman replied slowly, "I'm coming to that."

He paused again, letting Collins sweat some more.

"I don't like the scenario, Mr. Collins, as I said. I don't like being the PR man for a company that lies, cheats and threatens people. I don't like being what might be called an accessory, even though I'm not involved directly. So I've decided to take some action, but I need your help and cooperation. No one will ever know you told me anything. I swear that to you. I need to know who at Thompson Brakes forced you to change the study."

Collins' face turned white. He picked up a pencil and played with it.

"I don't know what you're talking about, Kaufman. Now get the hell out of here."

Kaufman did not move. He sat quietly, sternly staring at Collins.

"I'm sorry, Mr. Collins. I don't believe you. I think I know what happened, but I need confirmation. As I said, no one will ever know."

"I said no," Collins answered more angrily than before.

Kaufman was unmoved, even smiling a little bit.

"Mr. Collins, here are your choices. You either just confirm that Thompson Brakes applied the pressure for a new report and tell me who it was or..." he paused, "or I'll leak it anonymously as an unnamed source to the press that you changed it at the request of Thompson Brakes. You know that I can do that, given my job and contacts. They'll use the information because I have credibility and I'm an official of the company. The PR man, no less. I must be telling the truth. You and your company would be ruined.

"But if you confirm what I want to know, I will not use your name or that of your Institute and we can both go our respective ways. You can continue to conduct research for Thompson Brakes and others."

Kaufman knew he could not and would not leak the information without confirmation from Collins, but he was betting that Collins was not sophisticated in media strategies.

Neither knew, of course, that although Collins had succumbed to the pressure and did exactly what Thompson Brakes wanted, he would never again work for the company.

"Not much of a choice, is it?" Collins stammered.

"No and frankly, that's the way I wanted it."

Collins played with the pencil, accidentally breaking it.

"Well?" asked Kaufman.

"You're right," Collins said. "Hawthorne demanded it of me. Mr. Kaufman, I had no choice. I have a family, a business…"

Kaufman stood up, indicating he was leaving.

"I'm not going to judge you. What you do is your business. You have to live with that. But you have my word that no one will ever know, at least not from me."

"I appreciate that. Thank you and I'm very sorry."

Kaufman left the office and, in the parking lot, indulged himself in a suppressed "whooppeee," adding, "Damn, Kaufman, you're good."

THIRTY-FIVE

At home, Kaufman poured himself a drink and reflected on his discovery. His meeting with Collins represented a turning point. A couple more breaks and he could face Simmons with his ultimatum. He was getting anxious while trying to control his optimism. Things could still go wrong.

As he studied his strategy, he thought about an observation made by the former General Motors executive John DeLorean. In his biography, *On A Clear Day You Can See General Motors*, written by J. Patrick Wright, DeLorean said, "I found myself questioning a much bigger picture, the morality of the whole GM system. It seemed to me there was (and is) a cancerous amorality about the system. The undue emphasis on profits and cost control without a wider concern for the effects of GM's business on its many publics seemed too often capable of bringing together, in the corporation, men of sound, personal morality and responsibility who as a group reached business decisions which were irresponsible and of questionable morality."

Kaufman believed that Wright probably wrote the concept for DeLorean, given the latter's checkered career, and DeLorean signed off. The observation was all too true, Kaufman knew, not just at GM – he had never worked there – but of the corporate culture generally.

Kaufman also learned important lessons from John Dean of Watergate fame during the Nixon presidency, who confided in his book, *Blind Ambition*, how he lost his moral compass because of the dynamics of power.

Dean described how he was totally seduced by the trappings of power in the White House. To reject ideas and recommendations that crossed the lines of morality, ethics or the law required tremendous self-confidence and a willingness to lose that power. And, Kaufman remembered, Dean explained that one is compromised the very first time one doesn't protest illegal, immoral or unethical behavior.

He slept well that night, confident that he would succeed in his goal.

When Kaufman reached his office, the first call he made was to Steve Marks to ask for a meeting. Marks was suspicious and hesitant to meet with Thompson Brakes' PR man. Was this a new corporate strategy? If so, what did Kaufman want? But he agreed to a meeting later in the day, primarily because he thought he sensed a tone in Kaufman's voice that was "different." He could not explain it, but his instincts – and he believed he had good instincts – told him a meeting with Kaufman would not be strategically risky.

"Well, what brings you to the camp of the enemy, Mr. Kaufman?" Marks began.

"By the time we're through, I hope to convince you that I'm here to help."

"That's nice to hear but hard to accept."

"I understand perfectly. I'm going to ask for your strictest confidence and then ask you to help me to help you. Please give me a few minutes."

Kaufman told Marks everything. He described the attack on Sue Merriman, stated that he had information that the published research by the Ann Arbor Research Institute was a bogus study and he confided to Marks that he was working "in other areas that will blow the top off this thing for Thompson Brakes."

Marks, still very suspicious, asked the obvious. "Why are you telling me all of this?"

"Mr. Marks, I'm a PR man. My job is to make my clients look good. I have no problem with that as long as I'm not being used to lie, cheat and, in this case, cause people hardship. I don't like my role very much right now. I have an opportunity to stand up for my profession and, even more important for my personal beliefs.

"As pompous as this may sound, let's just say I don't like what I see and I want to do something about it."

Marks was impressed by Kaufman's sincerity, but was still skeptical.

"You mean you guys in PR have standards?" he teased.

"Not many, but some. Maybe like some union officers," Kaufman added sarcastically.

"Touché," Marks replied. "So what do you want from me?"

"Do you have anything else, something solid, that will help me? Some kind of evidence?"

"You want me to turn over evidence to the spokesperson for Thompson Brakes?"

"I'm asking you to trust me. I can't tell you what I'm going to do but, believe me, it'll be in the interests of Paul Ferguson, the survivors of the other victims and, politically, the union."

Marks pondered Kaufman's unusual request and then excused himself.

"I'll be back in about ten minutes. Have a cup of coffee."

Marks left the office to meet with a couple of subordinates. Kaufman kept himself busy reading union literature on a coffee table next to Marks' desk.

Marks returned in about 45 minutes.

"Sorry, but you've got to admit this is a strange turn of events. I needed to talk with some of my staff."

"No problem."

Marks threw a cassette tape into Kaufman's lap.

"We'll take a chance. I've several copies of it so if you're here as what I might call a spy, nothing much lost, except the surprise element. If you're not on the up-and-up, I'm sure your attorneys will begin preparing some defenses. But I'll accept that risk. If you're legit, it'll help you and, hopefully, as you said, us – all of us."

"What is it?"

"Play it and it'll speak for itself."

"Thanks. If it's good, combined with what I got, I think you'll have your victory and a celebration in a week's time."

"I hope you're right. We'll see."

They shook hands as they parted.

"Steve," Kaufman said, using the union official's first name, "this meeting never happened."

Marks gave him a thumbs up sign.

Kaufman played the tape in his car. He was disgusted at the coldheartedness of Robertson's – Thompson Brakes' – bribe and the cynicism. But he was not surprised. He should have expected an effort to tempt the Ferguson family with financial inducements.

His disgust quickly gave way to utter glee at the evidence he had collected. His case was almost complete. He needed to make one more telephone call before taking his case directly to Thompson Brakes' power elite.

He called a crime reporter he knew from his days at the *Blade*.

"Do me a favor," Kaufman asked. "Call some of your contacts and ask them about the reputation of a retired cop, Lou Salter. I don't need details. Just good cop, bad cop. It's important. Next time, drinks are on me. I'll be in my office the rest of the day."

Kaufman was happier than he had been in years. He was singing and whistling as he drove. He was so happy that many of his colleagues, as he walked to his office, commented on his mood.

"Was last night *the* night?" one asked.

"Looks like Timmy finally got lucky," another smirked.

Kaufman waved good-naturedly. He checked with Merriman and left a message on her answering machine. While waiting for the call from the police reporter, he kept himself busy with odds and ends.

He did a little writing on non-deadline assignments and returned calls from reporters asking for comment on class action lawsuits being filed by shareholders who claimed that the company was guilty of misleading investors and, indeed, of fraud in not alerting the financial community to the write-off.

To each call, he reiterated the statement he always gave when asked about lawsuits: "We have not yet been served with the legal papers and thus are unable to comment."

Several suits, in fact, were being filed by shareholders around the country, seeking damages totaling $50 million. He reported the news inquiries to Hawthorne's office along with the statement he was giving reporters. He predicted that more suits might be forthcoming.

Finally, late in the afternoon, the call he wanted came in.

"So?"

"Bad cop. Very bad. Beats suspects. Wiretaps. Does whatever he thinks he needs to do. What's this about?"

"Really can't say. Nothing major. Thanks much. As I promised, drinks are on me. I appreciate the favor."

He stayed in the office late that night. He ordered maintenance to send him several empty boxes. He packaged them with his belongings, stored and camouflaged them in his office as well as he could.

Tomorrow, he would participate in the biggest poker game of his life.

THIRTY-SIX

When she arrived at his apartment, Sue Merriman could not help but notice his good mood. She had never seen him so happy.

"What's up, Kaufman?"

"I wish I could tell you, Sue, my love. But I've got to play this one out myself. We're gonna win and we're gonna win big."

He swirled her around the apartment, kissing her again and again.

"How about off the record?"

"Nope, not even off the record. Got to go it alone."

Her mood darkened because she felt he did not trust her.

"Sue, it has nothing to do with trust. I trust you implicitly despite your credentials as a journalist," he said, trying to inject some humor. "This is something I need to do for me and I need to do it alone."

She relented but was not happy. They went to bed and when they awoke the next morning, she was still sulking.

"You sure?" she asked one more time.

"Yup," he said. He showered, shaved and dressed in a hurry. He was just about to leave when the telephone rang.

"Is this Tim Kaufman?"

"Yes, how can I help you?"

"This is Bob Redman from the *Detroit Herald*. As you know, I've been covering some aspects of the Thompson Brakes story for awhile. I have to ask you some questions."

"Why don't you call me at the office?"

"The story is more about you than Thompson Brakes. It's about your relationship with a reporter, Sue Merriman, and a potential conflict of interest. I have pictures..."

Kaufman interjected. "I don't discuss my personal life with anyone. That's none of your business or anyone else's."

"I understand," said Redman, "but sources have given me pictures of the two of you and they maintain that because of your relationship, you have leaked information – false information – to her on the company. They claim you have stirred the controversy over the issue of asbestos and cancer."

"I've one statement," Kaufman said. "It's this. I've done my job professionally and ethically. That's it. I don't care who talked to you."

"You don't want to say anything else?"

"That's right."

"How do you feel about the leaked photos? Feel betrayed?"

"You have all I'm going to say."

"Are you going to quit?"

"I'll deal with it. As I said, I have nothing more to say."

"You must be angry, pissed. You must feel something, no?"

"I think we're done. I appreciate your call."

"Do you have Sue Merriman's phone number?"

"Hold on."

Kaufman covered the mouthpiece of the telephone and quickly briefed Merriman on the essence of the call from her competition. She was scared and did not want to talk to Redman.

"Might as well," Kaufman urged. "He'll get you sooner or later."

Kaufman handed her the telephone.

"Hello, this is Sue Merriman."

Redman was somewhat surprised at hearing Merriman answer. "I assume Mr. Kaufman told you about the nature of my call.

"Well, I've some pictures that show you and Mr. Kaufman in bars, holding hands, kissing..."

When she heard Redman's description, she felt like hanging up.

"My sources tell me that your boyfriend has been feeding you information, bad information on the company because of your relationship," Redman said.

"That's not true..." She stopped when she heard Redman's computer clicking as he was typing. Her voice was quivering slightly.

"What's not true...your relationship or that he is feeding you information?"

"Let me think." She stopped. This doesn't sound good, she thought. Finally, she begged for time. "Let me call you right back. I just got out of the shower. Give me ten minutes."

"Sure, but I'm on deadline."

I've used that dozens of times myself, she thought.

She tried to regain her confidence; Kaufman was not fazed. "Not so easy to be under the gun, is it?"

"Tim, stop it. What do we do? What do we say? I can't lie. I can't confirm it. Help me."

"I've already admitted our relationship. But do what's in your best interests. I've made my decision, which I'll tell you about later. You do what's best for you. But it's pretty hard to deny since I've talked with him and he has pictures, from Salter, I assume. In this case, he was pretty thorough."

Merriman paced the floor. She thought about Redman's potential story. She thought about her job. She reflected on being in the news rather than covering it and how she would be judged by others in the newsroom.

"I'm not even sure what that is right now. What's in my best interests?"

"If you want my view, put all this behind you. Acknowledge our relationship. Tell him very emphatically it did not compromise you. Then, to use a cliché, let the chips fall. But I know it's easy for me to say and harder for you to do. I'll support whatever you do. I'm sorry, but I've got to go. I'll check with you later."

He asked her if she still had Salter's business card. She ruffled through her purse and showed it to him. He grabbed it out of her hand. "Need it for a few hours. Thanks."

As he shut the door, he felt bad for her but, for now, he needed to concentrate on Thompson Brakes, specifically Lou Salter and then George C. Simmons, Jr.

She regained her composure and called Redman, telling him, "Yes, we have a relationship. No, he never fed me bad information...he never fed me any information. It was just like Carville and Matalin, you know the two political presidential advisors who got married. When they were going with each other..."

She stopped, recognizing how defensive she sounded.

"I don't know how you got the pictures."

"I'm not going to tell you."

"I don't expect you to."

"But don't you think this is a conflict of interest...at least an appearance of a conflict?"

"We are professionals. We do our jobs ethically. Neither of us has anything to be ashamed of."

"How do you think your editors will take this?"

"Ask them. I have to go."

"Do you own stock in Lawson, you know, Thompson Brakes' competitor?"

"I resent the question and I don't understand the point."

"An ethical issue has been raised about you. You cover business so I think this question is relevant, especially given your relationship with Tim Kaufman."

"Even if I did – and I don't – it would not influence me."

"That's what politicians say about PAC contributions and other favors they receive. But we journalists don't really believe them, do we?"

"I'm in no mood for a debate with you. I gave you my answer. If you think there's a story here, write whatever you want. I have to go."

She reluctantly acknowledged to herself that she was a story, a damn good story.

"You're only doing the piece because you get a chance to take a shot at the competition," Merriman said. "You wouldn't write it if the *Herald* were involved."

"Can't deny that I like sticking it to the competition. Can't deny your other point either. As an institution, we don't do very well when it comes to our own weaknesses. But as a media critic once observed, freedom of the press belongs to those who own the printing presses. All that aside, you can't deny that this is a good story, can you?"

Redman continued, "I'm going to do this piece for the *Herald*, but I'm going to develop it for one of the journalism reviews. It's an interesting angle. Probably happens more than we know, but this time you guys got caught. May cause you some problems. But I can't worry, as you know, about the consequences to you. I'm sorry. But it's a good one and you know, if I don't write it, someone else will. Good luck."

"Why don't you find out why they leaked the pictures?" she volunteered, immediately recognizing she was raising the issue of motivation Kaufman always posed.

Redman never heard her question; he had already hung up.

THIRTY-SEVEN

Kaufman worked on tempering his ebullient mood. In the next two meetings, the most important of his career – of his life – he would have to be tough, very tough.

When he arrived at work, he called the maintenance department, asking the supervisor to send someone to his office with a dolly. When the man arrived, he gave him $20 and told him to take the boxes in his office to his car. Then he telephoned Salter's office.

"Tell him I need to see him and I need to see him now. As soon as possible. It's very urgent."

Salter's secretary was shocked at the tone, replying somewhat sarcastically, "Well, I'll see what I can do."

"You do that," Kaufman retorted.

He had never enjoyed such freedom. He had power and he knew it. He liked it. He was euphoric.

His phone rang. "In a half hour, Mr. Kaufman," Salter's secretary said.

"I'll be there."

Kaufman walked into Salter's office with a hard look on his face. The poker pot was big.

"What's the urgency, Kaufman? Need my help on a press release?"

"You're a slime ball, Salter," Kaufman replied, surprised by his own choice of words. If Salter was offended, he did not show it.

"I know how you work. I checked you out. You've brought your gestapo tactics to Thompson Brakes. Well, I don't give a shit what orders Simmons gave you, if you ever so much as have Sue Merriman touched again, I'm going to blow you out of the water. Your face will be on every front page in the country and it won't look good."

Salter hardly reacted. He sat with a smirk on his face.

"Did I touch a nerve?" He opened a desk drawer and took out a large envelope. "Before we start making all kinds of charges, I'd be careful if I were you."

Salter opened the envelope and threw about 20 pictures toward Kaufman. Kaufman glanced at them. They were pictures of him and Merriman at the Splendid Cafe, walking streets holding hands, kissing on the steps of their respective homes.

"You're a slime ball, as I said. Too bad you wasted all this undercover work. They aren't going to do you any good. You see for blackmail to work, you need leverage. You haven't got any. So show them to whomever you like. I know you already leaked them to the *Herald*. I couldn't care less."

Kaufman did not tell Salter that after one more meeting, he would be a former Thompson Brakes employee.

"You recognize this, Salter?" Kaufman asked, showing him the business card with Merriman's name on it. "It's from the shirt pocket of the goon you hired. You use some very bright people, Salter. I understand now what you meant by helping with PR. Did you really think that you could intimidate the entire paper even if Merriman decided to back off? You're one bright fellow."

Salter was still unmoved. "That card doesn't mean shit," he said.

Kaufman continued, "How did you know that Stern's son was named Bobby?"

"What are you talking about?"

"In the meeting with Simmons, you said Faulkner fiddled with Stern's son, Bobby. How did you know the kid's name?"

"I think I read it in the paper."

"It wasn't in the paper. The cops didn't release the name because the boy is a minor."

For the first time, Salter's face turned grim.

"You see, I think you bribed Stern. You promised to pay him off after he serves his time and somehow he convinced his son to make the charges. He probably intimidated his son, given that he beat his mother. The kid must have been scared to death of his old man."

"You can't prove that."

"You're right, but I can leak it, which is just as effective in this case, if not more effective. As the official spokesperson for the company, they'll believe me. And I think you'll agree that a call to the cops would lead to an investigation."

Salter denied all of Kaufman's charges, stating, "You're way off base."

Kaufman leaned across Salter's desk and, in the most intimidating voice he could muster, said, "Leave her alone. Leave us alone. If you're thinking of getting both of us, I've left a paper trail with some people, not just about you, but others in the company, including Simmons, which would destroy this place. So be forewarned. Have a good day."

Kaufman walked out with almost a spring in his step. He was pleased with his performance and thought he had been convincing. He was confident that neither Merriman nor he had anything to worry about from Salter.

One more to go. Rather than call, he stopped by Simmons' office and told Susan Gray that he needed a meeting with the chairman as soon as possible, preferably later that day.

"Tell him I said I can't wait. It's very important, Susan."

THIRTY-EIGHT

When Sue Merriman arrived at the office, her voice mail message told her to see the *Blade*'s managing editor, Joseph Brennan. It was urgent.

She had expected the message since she was confident that Redman would call Brennan after talking with her and Kaufman. But she delayed a meeting with Brennan, wanting to read the *Herald* first.

Maybe I'll dodge a bullet, she said to herself. Maybe the news hole was small.

But she was wrong. When the *Herald* arrived at her desk, she turned to the business section and, to her disappointment, read:

Reporter's Involvement with Thompson Brakes Exec
Raises Ethical Issues for Media

> Detroit, Michigan – The reporter covering the controversial issue of whether exposure to asbestos caused cancer among the employees of Thompson Brakes, Inc. has acknowledged that she was romantically involved with the company's public relations spokesperson.
>
> In an interview with the *Detroit Herald*, Susan K. Merriman, one of the *Detroit Blade*'s top investigative reporters, admitted a romantic relationship but stated she and Tim Kaufman, Thompson Brakes' vice president of corporate communications, continued to do their jobs professionally and ethically.

She denied that he fed her information on the asbestos issue to make the company look bad or help her professionally. "We are both professionals," she said. "We did our jobs ethically. Neither of us has anything to be ashamed of."

Kaufman made a similar statement to the *Herald*, stating, "I have done my job professionally and ethically."

Sources leaked pictures showing Merriman and Kaufman holding hands and kissing in various places in Detroit. They maintained that Kaufman was the one who made public false information about the asbestos issue to Merriman.

Blade Managing Editor Joseph Brennan said he was unaware of the relationship and would have to study the matter before making any comment. However, he added he would be "very concerned" if the charges proved to be true. He added that "Sue Merriman is an exceptional reporter, one who is highly-talented and I have full confidence in her."

Thompson Brakes officials did not return the *Herald*'s phone calls. Media and public relations experts around the country and at journalism schools were critical of the relationship.

"Certainly, reporters must not only avoid real conflicts of interest but also the appearance of conflicts," said Gary Waterman, a professor of journalism. "She certainly is entitled to a personal, private life, but she should have disqualified herself from covering the story."

Owen Longsworth, president of Longsworth Public Relations, Inc., one of the nation's top PR firms, had a similar reaction. "Mr. Kaufman should not have put himself in that kind of situation," said Longsworth. "We have enough problems with our image in PR without creating new ones. Such behavior is inexcusable whether he did his job ethically or not."

Waterman and Longsworth said if Merriman and Kaufman were their employees, they would fire both from their respective jobs.

Merriman glanced at the rest of the story, which ran another five inches.

Redman quoted more "experts" who basically shared the views of Waterman and Longsworth. None defended Kaufman or her.

When she turned the page to read the continuation, she saw a picture of Kaufman and herself kissing in front of the Splendid Cafe. Merriman, shaken, called Brennan, who ordered her to his office.

She walked over to Brennan's office, knocked and entered, closing the door behind her. She held the *Herald* with the story in her hand. Brennan pointed to the paper. "I've already read it, Sue. I'm surprised at you. You never mentioned anything..."

"I'm sorry, Joe, I didn't think. Whatever the reason, it's over. And I want to make this easier for you. I'm resigning."

She noticed that Brennan did not protest her offer to resign.

"You're an excellent reporter and you had a fantastic future," said Brennan, "but under the circumstances, I'm going to have to accept your resignation. We're taking enough of a beating about the story itself, let alone this. Sue, I can't tell you how sorry I am."

"Joe, I appreciate your comments. I'm sorry, too. But there is more to this than Tim Kaufman. It's ironic that I am resigning and being held accountable for a personal relationship even though I did nothing wrong. I did my job professionally. But I was hailed for the story on Faulkner, which I know now was false and literally killed a man. I'm having doubts about the business, Joe. And that's not good for me, for you or the *Blade*."

Brennan, a veteran, had heard her complaint before; he had his reservations as well. He had spent more than 25 years in the news business and was respected, not just by the media, but generally by those he had covered and his staff.

"We have our weaknesses," he admitted. "We make mistakes. We err. But the media remain the bulwark of society."

Merriman pensively replied, "I know, but I agree with Bernard Kalb, who told a group of journalists that the sentinel of democracy may have gone AWOL. He added that while he worries about today's media scenario, he worries even more about what it will look like in ten years. I tend to agree. We make mistakes but we don't do much about them. We err but become defensive about accountability. We use sources, like I did on Faulkner, without worrying about truth, whatever that is.

"Joe, you know as well as I do that the cops and prosecutors use us regularly to leak information when they can't get indictments.

"And we use the information not because of a so-called public service but because if we don't, the competition will. Look what happened in the Clinton-Lewinsky intern sex scandal case and to Richard Jewell, the suspect in the bombing at the Atlanta Olympics. At least Jewell got his day in court because he was so high profile. Most people who have their reputations ruined unfairly by us never have the chance to set the record straight. You know, Joe, we might be spreading some asbestos dust of our own and the resulting cancer we cause might be just as deadly, if not more so, than mesothelioma. Not only are we, in effect, killing those we cover with our superficiality, but society is breathing in our asbestos dust, and that sure does no one any good.

"Joe, we take corporate America on for covering up when they screw up and screw up badly. But tell me, when has any media institution ever stood up and said something like this, 'The story we ran was wrong ... all of it ... it was based on false information, bad premises and we deeply regret its publication.' You know it happens frequently, but we act just like Thompson Brakes and other corporations. Nothing separates us from them except that we have power and no accountability and that, in a sense, makes it worse.

"At least I understand why corporations like Thompson Brakes act the way they do. They want to protect profits and, while that's obscene, at least I understand. But we in the media stonewall for no reason other than our arrogance."

Brennan did not argue with her. Indeed, he shared many of her concerns. "But the answer is not to run," he said. "The answer is to try and improve the system."

"I hope you're successful. But the next time you preach ethics, read the local papers and then watch the evening news along with shows like *Hard Copy*, *A Current Affair* and even the so-called responsible shows like *Dateline* and *Prime Time Live*. This infotainment should make your stomach turn.

"And once the mass media snowball rolls down, it's tough, if not impossible, to push it back uphill.

"The fiasco over NBC's staging an explosion of the GM pickup truck is only the tip of the iceberg. You and I know these kinds of ethical violations happen all the time. Misquotes, errors, distortions, but there are no apologies. We in the media make a big deal that NBC apologized. NBC apologized because GM is powerful and GM had $2 million to spend on an investigation. And let's not forget that GE, a GM supplier, owns NBC.

"No one has apologized to Judge Faulkner's family or to the many other Faulkners who are stung by the media every day.

"The special interests know our weaknesses and use us. Consider how we cover Washington. Liberals make the most outrageous charges against conservative appointees and vice versa. We don't care if it's true or not. Joe, we don't print the truth; we print he said, she said.

"We complain about candidates being so negative in campaigns but the few who deal with issues get no coverage. Then, hypocritically, we ourselves blame the media on the editorial pages. It's ridiculous."

Suddenly, he asked, almost in anguish, "You're not becoming a turncoat like many others and going into PR?"

She laughed, "You've got to be kidding. No, I'm not ready to help corporations, government, the legal system hide their dirty little secrets from the Merrimans and the Brennans. Not yet, anyway."

He got up from behind his desk and held out his hand. She shook it. Then he walked closer to her and gave her a hug.

"I'm not disagreeing with you, Sue," he said quietly. "I'm still hoping that we do more good than harm. If some are hurt in the process, maybe that's the price we pay in a democracy. That's inevitable."

"Perhaps, but that's playing a little loose with other people's lives. Right now, being somewhat of a victim, I don't like it very much. It's much easier when my name appears at the top of the story instead of in it."

"Sue, I wish you well," he said. "Maybe when this blows over, you can come back in a little while. I know I would like that."

Momentarily, her eyes filled with tears.

"Thanks. Maybe when this blows over. Right now, I need time to think about my future – professional and personal. I need time to think this through."

Before leaving, she volunteered, "Joe, when they call you about me, say and do whatever you have to. Don't worry, I'll understand. It really doesn't matter to me."

"Thanks, Sue. That helps." Then he paid her the ultimate compliment in journalism: "You're one helluva reporter."

THIRTY-NINE

Beaming and confident given the evidence he had uncovered, Tim Kaufman prepared for his meeting with George C.L. Simmons, Jr.

But first he walked into the office of Ruth Sanderson in the PR department. He told her he was resigning and to prepare a release that stated he left to "pursue other business interests."

"Ruth, remember we talked about what we would do when we knew the truth? Well, I know it. So the time has come."

"Want to unload?"

"No, because that would put pressure on you. But we've talked so many times about whether we – you and I and our colleagues in PR – are doing the right thing and we comforted ourselves by concluding that as long as we didn't actually know if we're representing less than moral people, we were okay.

"Maybe that's a rationalization, I don't know. But now, when I know what I know, I feel compromised, dirty. You and I've talked about helping corporations who pollute the waters, destroy the lives of people over 50 who are suddenly fired, discriminate against minorities and all that. We talked about investor relations when I asked your help in announcing the $35 million loss.

"It occurred to me that all the segments on *60 Minutes* are the same. Mike Wallace and cohorts uncover wrongdoing and then they interview everyone who covers up. They even cover up when a life is at stake, like the wrong suspect being sent to death row. But the story is always the same and it's guys like us who help develop cover-up strategy. I've had enough, especially now that, in this case, I have the evidence."

"But you left the media for similar reasons, so what now?"

"I'm not saying the media are right. Lots of problems there, too, and in the law and medicine as well. Look at what they call seeking the truth in the O.J. trial. They coach witnesses, hide others – do whatever they have to do to win. It's a travesty. Doctors cover-up not only their own mistakes but those of their colleagues. They call it, I believe, professional courtesy.

"But enough. I need to do what I need to do. You have a family and need to work. I understand that. Corporations understand that. They work on you to trade ethics for stock options.

"Being single, I have a little freedom. I'm not preaching. Maybe if I had the pressure of having to support a family, I'd continue rationalizing. I don't know. I can't speculate about the what ifs. From here, I'm going to Simmons' office and do something all of us have dreamed about. Briefly, I have the opportunity to bite the hand that feeds – fed – me. It's going to be a unique, wonderful experience to say what I want to say – and do."

Kaufman concluded by recommending that she also draft a release stating the company was setting up a multimillion-dollar fund for the families of those Thompson Brakes employees who died of cancer. "Leave the amount open for now," he added.

Then he alerted her to possible news inquiries on his relationship with Merriman.

"You may also get some questions from the media about whether I'm personally involved with Sue Merriman," said Kaufman. "You can say that I am and that I did nothing unethical or unprofessional. If they ask you whether it represents at least a perception of a conflict of interest, feel free to say it was. Acknowledge it because it was.

"First time and probably the last you'll be able to answer totally honestly without preparing a Q & A. And the company will like your candor. Take my word for it. Again, good luck and thanks for all the help."

Sanderson was confused but did not push him to explain any of the issues he mentioned, particularly the last one. She recognized that he was not about to elaborate.

He shook her hand and left to attend his last meeting at Thompson Brakes, Inc.

Simmons looked peeved at being pressured into a meeting.

"Haven't got much time, Tim. What is it?"

Kaufman decided to get right to the point.

"George, I want you to establish a $40 million fund for Mrs. Ferguson and the others."

He stopped. He wanted his words to sink it.

"What the hell are you talking about?"

"I want you to establish this fund," Kaufman repeated. "It's the right thing to do. It's fair, it's just, they deserve it. Thompson Brakes screwed up. So let's try to do something right."

Kaufman was playing him, setting him up a little, toying with him.

"You're crazy. Get the fuck out of here before I fire your ass."

Kaufman did not move. He smiled at Simmons, who started to appear not only puzzled, but concerned.

"Hear me out, George," Kaufman said quietly. "See this business card with Sue Merriman's name written on it? It's Salters. She ripped it out of a shirt pocket of a son of a bitch who attacked her in a parking garage. As he roughed her up, he told her to lay off the asbestos issue. I'm sure you agree with me that Salter hired the bastard. Unfortunately, he forgot to tell him not to carry his business card.

"I also have good information that Salter bribed that guy Stern to make the charges that Judge Faulkner molested his son. Another nice corporate touch."

Kaufman lied about having evidence, but he thought he carried out the bluff well. "This, George," said Kaufman, holding the tape Steve Marks gave him, "is a tape of a meeting between Judy Robertson and Angie Ferguson in which she tries, on behalf of Thompson Brakes, to pressure Angie Ferguson into accepting a deal. George, you shouldn't send amateurs on these missions."

Kaufman was enjoying himself. He was on a power binge.

"I have good information that your sycophant Hawthorne forced Collins to change the research institute's report. Another amateur job. I'm sure there were other Hawthorne fuckups that would not make the company look very good. George, you need some professionals around here. Think what would happen with Hawthorne on a witness stand in court."

"That information is protected by client-lawyer privilege, Kaufman."

"Unfortunately, your lawyer doesn't know the law. Other than that, he's competent. There is no lawyer-client privilege when criminal activities are involved and, further, in Hawthorne's case, his legal obligation is to the corporation – not to you. Claiming lawyer-client privilege in a medical research report will hardly hold up.

"By the way, as I indicated, I don't expect Hawthorne to understand or comprehend any of this. He's probably the dumbest son of a bitch I know in that high a position. But that's your problem."

Simmons remembered Hawthorne assuring him of client-lawyer privilege. He regretted not double-checking Hawthorne's opinion. He turned his anger on Kaufman.

"Kaufman, who the hell do you think you are? Don't you know who you're talking to? I'll have your ass. I've been waiting for the right moment and this is it. I know you've been screwing that broad from the *Blade* and I was going to fire you anyway."

"George, you were always one who knew how to put things delicately. I know Salter took pictures of me and Sue Merriman. To put your mind at ease, we have a relationship and, no, I never told any stories out of school. I don't give a damn whether you believe that or not. Salter has already leaked those pictures to the press. Thus, they are of no use to him, you or the company. Another bonehead play.

"Let's get back to the issue we're talking about. If all this evidence I've got ended up in the press from an 'informed source,' George, you and the company would be in the papers for months. There might even be a criminal investigation with all I've got. And, frankly, I think the board would be a little upset, not at what you did, but at what your actions did to the stock."

Simmons was contemptuous. "I don't like you coming into my office..."

Kaufman finished his sentence, "...and blackmailing you? You must admit, I do it better than your henchmen."

Simmons spoke firmly. "If all that happened, it happened without my knowledge."

Kaufman shook his head. "Well, I don't quite believe that but even if you gave no direct orders, as the chief executive you set the moral tone of the organization. You don't have to give orders; your subordinates know what they can get away with. I think your phrase was 'just do it.'

"They know they have your approval to do anything to get the job done – anything. You don't care how it's done. You take the results – good results – whether the means are immoral, unethical or even illegal. And the board doesn't give a damn either as long as the financial results are good. It'll act, but only when things get out of hand, which means the stock nosedives.

"It's just like Watergate. It really didn't matter whether Nixon ordered the break-in and other dirty tricks. All the Nixonites knew he wouldn't protest their tactics."

Kaufman suddenly realized he was wasting his time with a lecture on morality to the chairman. He probably did not understand a word, Kaufman concluded. He decided to get back to the issue at hand.

"Here's the way I see it, George. I'm really doing you a favor. Listen carefully. If you establish the fund, the board will reward you. They can't fire you because it implies guilt. They can fire you and may fire you if you don't do anything and the bad publicity continues. It's not that they don't sympathize with you because they run companies that do the same thing, but they have to watch out for their own asses.

"If you accept my proposal, and I'm confident you will, the Civic League will love you. It will look like a grand gesture because that board is made up of people like you. The league would rather honor you with the fund than without it. Some people might even picket the dinner if you continue on your present course. That would embarrass the league tremendously.

"What's more, you can write to your shareholders that you did it to save them years of legal fees for the likes of the Hawthornes out there. You can say that it wasn't an admission of guilt. And I think the stock will jump because my proposal is much less than what Wall Street thinks this may ultimately cost you. You'll be out of the media and you might even get an editorial or two commending you. And you probably can get some tax benefits as well.

"George, don't you see, I'm helping you. You may have to swallow your pride a little bit, but you're a pragmatist. Even Steve Marks may say something nice about you. I think the union will accept this because they know they may lose in court or at least be tied up in legal battles for years."

Kaufman sat back and let it sink in.

"If I do this," Simmons said, "how do I know I can trust you? What if you go public in a press conference or something like that?"

"You really don't know that you can trust me, but I'm a pragmatist as well. More importantly, I'm a bit of a coward. I don't want to go public because I know what our society does to whistle-blowers. People who act on conscience, who have the courage to speak out at their own expense, become pariahs, outcasts. I don't want to be one of them. I'm not a hero and I want future employment somewhere.

"It's people like you, Salter and Hawthorne that we honor. I know enough to maintain my cover. I don't like being a leper and I have no problem surrendering any credit I might get.

"But remember, George, it doesn't really matter whether you believe you can trust me. Frankly, I don't really think you have a choice."

Simmons, desperately trying to control his anger, suggested that Kaufman might leak the information anonymously.

"It's a possibility and it's tempting," Kaufman replied. "You'll have to trust me, George, on that one. I just want to get this behind me. My involvement may not have caused mesothelioma, but it may have contributed to some cancer in ethics."

"What the hell are you talking about?"

"Never mind, George. Let's wrap this up. You have my word and I'll keep it."

Kaufman got up and, in conclusion, said, "I would like to read about your generosity within a week. Take a few days, George, get your ducks in a row, and I think this is going to work out very well for you. I really believe this is a very easy decision and I know you'll make the right one. If I don't read about your story within a week, you'll read about mine and you'll read about mine for a long time. Here's my ID badge."

He walked out of the office and used the public telephone in the lobby to call Sue Merriman.

"She no longer works here," the switchboard operator said.

"What do you mean?"

"I really don't know. I was told she left earlier in the day."

Kaufman was upset by what he heard, distressed about the possible consequences of the Redman story and worried about the reaction of the *Blade*'s management.

Then he called Steve Marks.

"Don't do anything for a week. Simmons is going to establish a fund but it won't be $90 million. My guess, between $30 and $40 million and I think you should take it. But that's your decision. Be patient for a few days. Thanks for your help."

"Can you tell me how, why and so on?"

"Steve, don't ask. You don't want to know. You don't need to know. I'm not going to tell you anyway. Let's just say with a little prodding, he saw the light. Thanks again."

"If you're right, I guess we should thank you. A week, huh?"

"Yup, see you around."

He left the Thompson Brakes office building elated. Then it occurred to him that he had successfully used with Collins, Salter and Simmons the very tactic – the threat of a leak – that he considered reprehensible.

If you can't beat them – and you can't – he said to himself, you might as well join them.

Kaufman walked to the parking lot and, for the first time in years, felt like a totally free man. The corporate noose around his neck, which his neighbor had so clearly and aptly described to him, had finally been removed.

FORTY

Simmons was furious when Kaufman left his office. Never in his career had he been pushed so hard. He felt trapped with his back against the wall and he did not like the feeling.

That fucking bastard, who does he think he is? Simmons growled to himself.

Not only was he angry at finding himself on the defensive, but he did not like losing to Kaufman. It was one thing to compromise with his directors, other CEOs, or with executive officers of his company, but to be forced into what he considered a surrender to a subordinate like Kaufman was almost too much for him psychologically.

As he was processing Kaufman's ultimatum, he took solace in the fact that no one would ever know that he was being blackmailed into creating the special fund. That is, if he could trust Kaufman. He thought he could because what Kaufman said about his reluctance to be a whistle-blower made sense. Thus, Simmons concluded he could surrender to Kaufman's pressure without public exposure.

When he finally calmed down, Simmons recognized that Kaufman was basically right in his evaluation. He sat at his desk scribbling notes on how to best implement a "Kaufman plan," a plan he knew he would have to pursue. He recognized he had no choice.

For the next hour, he made a list of possible solutions, all the time concerned about saving face. Saving face was very important to him.

When he concluded his planning, he called Susan Gray and asked her to set up an emergency directors' meeting.

"Susan, tell them it needs to be held within a week in our boardroom and that it's important," he said. "Take a poll among the directors on the best date and then set it. Emphasize to all of them that they should do all that is possible to accommodate whatever date we decide on."

Then he called Judy Robertson in the human resources department, asking her to come to his office to discuss how many Thompson Brakes employees would be eligible for assistance under the contemplated special fund.

"I need you to conduct a study on who might qualify for assistance," Simmons told Robertson when she arrived. "Include survivors as well. I need good numbers – potential cost and how long such a plan would be in place."

"How long?"

"Yes, use some actuarial tables to see how long we might have to pay you know, how long they might live. I want to see what it will cost us, not only in the short term but long term as well. Do you understand?"

"I think so, but some of it might be just a guess."

"Make it your best one. This is important."

Simmons assumed that most of the victims would be over 60 or even older and, if the contracts were properly written, the company might be able to keep its financial obligations to a minimum.

"One other thing," he continued. "I want you to work up a plan for downsizing the company by about 500 people. The exact number should equal a savings of between $30 and $40 million over five years. It's time we got rid of some deadwood. We have to placate our investors as well. We haven't done anything for them throughout this controversy."

Robertson was startled by both requests, asking Simmons if he had any specific areas of the company in mind for the cutbacks.

"No, but I want you to target those with more than 20 years here," he instructed. "Those are the high salaries."

"Mr. Simmons, that might subject us to potential age discrimination suits," she offered quietly and meekly.

"Do you think I'm an idiot? I know that and I expect you to develop a plan that includes some younger people. Camouflage it. But just do it."

Robertson, frightened, apologized. "Of course. I'm sorry. We'll get it done." She grabbed her legal pad and some papers, dropping a few on the floor. She picked them up and hurriedly left Simmons' office.

Dumb broad, he muttered to himself.

Then he called Hawthorne and asked him to draft an agreement to establish a $35 million fund, but to include very limited rights for survivors.

"I want the least financial obligation, Al," said Simmons. "I think if we do this, the union will withdraw its suit. The union will cave in because they'll believe they won. So let's make the most of it. Got it?"

Hawthorne, somewhat surprised, quickly offered, "We'll squeeze them by the balls. You got it. George, I think you're doing the right thing."

"Thanks, Al. I think we are as well. Get this ready ASAP. I'm calling an emergency board meeting."

Almost fully recovered from his confrontation with Kaufman, Simmons set the fund at $35 million, believing that Kaufman expected him to reduce the $40 million and that he would not return to demand the other $5 million. For the first time in weeks, he believed he could put the asbestos-cancer issue behind him and, equally important, satisfy angry shareholders with a layoff plan.

Maybe Kaufman, the bastard, did do me a favor, he thought.

Then he called Rodney Kramer, the head of the law firm Kramer, Wilkinson and Thomas, which served as outside counsel. He wanted some independent advice.

"What if and, Rod, this is hypothetical, I – I mean, the company – was backed into a corner and had to make restitution on the asbestos issue? Is there any way out?" he asked.

"I would need to do some research but..."

Simmons quickly stressed, "This is hypothetical."

"I understand," Kramer replied, "but one thing you might consider is declaring bankruptcy. Other companies have done that in situations like this one. But I don't know if this course of action would be available to you since the company is charged with an intentional tort."

"You mean, they-win-the-battle-but-we-can't-pay kind of scenario and we win the war? We would indicate that we'd like to help but can't financially? Ain't our fault, sorry fellows. I sort of like that."

"Yes, that's basically it but I would need to check on the intentional tort charge – whether you could declare bankruptcy and get around any payments."

Simmons liked the prospect of neutralizing Kaufman. The more he thought about the possibility of outwitting Kaufman, the more he warmed to the idea. But suddenly, he realized that bankruptcy would reflect on his management ability – or more accurately, the lack of his ability. It would be an admission of failure – a very public one.

"Forget it, Rod," he said. "We are a sound company with a good future. Anything else?"

Kramer was puzzled by Simmons' sudden change of heart. "I think your asbestos suppliers are liable," Kramer offered. "I'm sure of that. Did you ever have conversations or correspondence with them over the danger of this stuff?"

"Is this privileged?"

"Absolutely."

"Of course we did, but we knew it would cost us big."

"Then, why not sue them and make them liable as well? If we lose the pending suit, at least they'll share some of the financial burden."

Simmons was elated. Transferring some of the burden, guilt, responsibility to a third party, those that supplied him with asbestos, was logical and politically very beneficial.

"Could we do that even if the suit were dropped against us?"

"Of course. One has nothing to do with the other."

"I like that. Prepare the brief and call me when it's ready. Rod, this is a priority. Make it for as many millions as you think makes sense. Got it?"

"I'll start as soon as we hang up."

Simmons gloated over his plan. If he saved $20 million from the layoffs and got his asbestos suppliers to agree to contribute even $10 to 15 million in out-of-court settlements, the financial pressure on Thompson Brakes would be eased dramatically. We might even break even, he thought, or make a buck or two.

He immediately called Robert B. Iverson, chairman of Iverson, Inc., a long-time supplier of asbestos to Thompson Brakes. There were other suppliers as well, but Simmons called Iverson because his company was the largest and he wanted to test his plan.

"Bob, I'm not going to fuck around," he told Iverson. "You know what we've been going through. You read the papers. I'm thinking about voluntarily establishing a fund for the cancer victims, but we're having hard financial times here.

"So, here's the situation. I want $25 million from your company because you have liability as a supplier. I'm going to ask for money from the others as well. If not, we're going to sue. That's it."

"You're kidding of course, George, right?"

But Simmons, demanding $25 million for negotiating purposes, could tell that Iverson's heart was not in his protest. Iverson had expected such a demand from Simmons for some time.

"Don't fuck with me, Bob. You know better. No, I'm not kidding. We had talked about the dangers of asbestos and you guys did absolutely nothing to help us protect and warn employees."

"George, we've had a good business relationship for a long time," Iverson countered. "We've also been a good, loyal and dependable supplier and now you make this unbelievable demand. If we give you money, think of the precedents I'd be setting."

"Screw the precedents. Frankly, I'm tired of hearing that word. That's legal horseshit, Bob. Talk to your lawyers. They'll tell you the score, that you're on the losing end. Mine are preparing legal documents. I don't want to have to use them. Get back to me within a week with an offer – a good offer. I don't have time to play around."

Then he added, "Bob, I'm not threatening you, but you know what we have in the files."

Iverson understood the implications to his company if sensitive documents became public. At the same time, Simmons was hoping that Glen Johnston, whom he had fired for leaks of documents that should have been destroyed, may have overlooked others he could use against Iverson. He hoped that Johnston had not been thorough; he might need some of the documentation to pressure Iverson and other suppliers. Considering the irony, he could not help but smile. Regardless, he was reassured that he would win because Iverson and other suppliers, of course, did not know that the files had been purged.

"Bob, I want to get out of the papers and believe me, you don't want to get in," he said, threatening Iverson as Kaufman had threatened him.

Simmons, pleased with his conversation, was confident that Iverson would share in the financial obligations and if Iverson did, the others would follow with some contributions.

Simmons was feeling jubilant when Susan Gray told him the board meeting would be in five days. So that he would not forget, he immediately went into the adjacent boardroom to check that his chair was higher than the others. He gave it a couple of spins up.

Then he made a list of reports he would need for his briefing book. This would be one of the most important meetings he had ever held with his directors.

A few days later, Robertson reported to him that at a maximum, about 200 employees might be eligible for benefits, and that assumed all had asbestos-related cancer or might contract the disease.

With survivors, the total population that might be in line for some kind of benefits would be less than a thousand, including spouses and children.

The total cost over a 15-year period – a time frame calculated on the best estimates of life insurance experts – would be about $20-35 million, depending on the life spans of the victims and their younger survivors, particularly children.

Actually, not as bad as I thought, Simmons told himself, and he also assumed the total would be much less considering the restrictions Hawthorne would draft and which, he believed, the union would accept.

Then he reviewed the downsizing plan developed by Robertson, which identified 460 employees, most of them Thompson Brakes veterans. Total savings, Robertson projected, would be $31 million over the five-year period Simmons had stipulated.

Following his review, he called Ruth Sanderson, instructing her to draft a press release announcing the voluntary establishment of a $35 million fund and downsizing of the work force.

"Remember, stress the fact that we're creating the fund voluntarily. We have no moral or legal obligation," Simmons said. "And you work on this alone, no one else, Ruth.

"This is extremely confidential," he added. "Touch base with Al. He has my proxy. You do well on this, Ruth, and it could mean big things for you at Thompson Brakes. I should tell you that Tim Kaufman has resigned."

Sanderson was somewhat shocked, not at the news about Kaufman, but at all that had happened in a very short period.

"I understand, Mr. Simmons," she replied. "I'll get right on it. I think the press release should lead with the fund and end with the downsizing. Don't you agree?"

"No question. The downsizing is a message to the investor community," he said. "We'll emphasize that in the shareholder stuff. Get on it."

Sanderson quickly tried to sort out all the developments and also how she would handle the press release. She had to admit to being flattered by the call from Simmons and the implied promise of a possible promotion, especially in light of Kaufman's resignation.

She sat smiling at her desk. Assistant VP has a certain nice ring to it, she thought, not considering how premature her conjectures might be.

She put her ambitions on hold and went to work on the press release as Simmons studied his plans for the directors' meeting.

Simmons knew that the meeting would be crucial, a real test of his leadership, his control of the board and, ultimately, it would affect his future. He would have to make a convincing argument to retain support of the majority of the board and survive. He would never spend more time studying for a board meeting than this one.

For the next few days, Simmons reviewed reports and figures like a college senior preparing for major final examinations. He was not going to flunk this crucial test. Also, to assure himself of some board support, before the meeting, he called and briefed his allies on the board.

He pushed Robertson for all kinds of information on employee demographics. He put immense pressure on Hawthorne to develop the most restrictive agreement. He made calls to various departments to obtain supporting documentation.

Then he called the city's premier public relations firm and awarded the company a special contract to prepare him for the board. He wanted a complete Q & A for the meeting and advice on going public with the announcement. He was not about to trust Sanderson at this juncture in the Thompson Brakes crisis, not knowing her capabilities or loyalties.

Moreover, he felt more secure with outside counsel, given all the internal politics he would have to worry about in briefing Sanderson. He also did not know how much information Kaufman had shared with her.

The day of the board meeting, Simmons was as agitated as he had been at the annual meeting. He walked around the table shaking hands and making small talk. He was doing his best to display confidence.

He walked to his seat at the head of the conference table and explained why he had called this special meeting.

"As you all know, we have had considerable public discussion in recent weeks regarding two major issues," he began. "The one-time loss and the asbestos issue."

He looked down at his briefing book and read to himself, "Avoid the words *problems*, *crisis*, *controversy*."

He spent a few minutes rehashing the two issues and then outlined his ideas to create the fund and implement a layoff program.

"I think both of these programs will help us," he offered. "Investors will support the downsizing, the community will like our fund offer and, most important, this will all be behind us."

After a brief pause, one of the directors, Richard Cousins, not necessarily a Simmons ally, spoke up.

"Won't the $35 million fund imply guilt?" Cousins asked.

Simmons calmly turned the pages of his briefing book, looked down and replied, "Not at all. We will say that we're doing the right thing. We'll say we still believe that asbestos exposure did not cause any health problems, but the continuing debate is costing all sides time and money."

Simmons was proud of how he handled the implied criticism.

"I think George is right," said James Moran, one of Simmons' supporters. "It's time to move on. The lawyers are the only ones making out. Let's get on with it."

Cousins was not so easily convinced, asking Simmons, "What about the downsizing and age discrimination?"

Simmons, pleased that he was prepared, said, "If you look at the demographic breakdown in your briefing books, you'll see we included a small percentage of younger employees. We can make a case that we did not target a certain age group."

"But most are between 50 and 60, right?" Cousins asked.

"Yes, but again, I think we can handle that publicly, especially if we announce the asbestos settlement."

The board debated the two proposals for about an hour but Simmons was able to infer from the discussion that he would win board approval.

And win he did. He felt relieved and was almost thankful that Kaufman had forced the issue.

After the board's decision was made public, Simmons read the *Blade*, and, for the first time in months, enjoyed the news coverage on his company.

The reaction from Steve Marks to the $35 million fund was subdued but supportive overall.

"We'll have to study the offer," said Marks, emphasizing that he considered Thompson Brakes' decision a proposal, still subject to negotiation. "But it certainly is a step in the right direction in assuming some obligation for the tragedy they caused. We commend the company for stepping up to its responsibility and finally recognizing its culpability."

But he added he was concerned about the downsizing which included members of his union. "We are deeply disturbed about the company's plans to lay off almost 500 people, most of whom are older employees. We are saddened that the company would target these loyal employees, who have devoted their careers to Thompson Brakes. That's another issue we'll look at very carefully."

Marks said he had ordered the union's attorneys to study the downsizing and decide if there were any grounds for age discrimination suits.

Overall, Simmons was pleased with the coverage and with himself, and relieved that the major crisis appeared to be finally over. While he did not want to admit it, he understood that he was indebted to Tim Kaufman.

Thank God no one would ever know.

At about the same time, Kaufman was reading the *Detroit Blade*'s story on Thompson Brakes' announcement in a diner just south of Michigan's Mackinac Bridge. He was heading for a vacation in Michigan's Upper Peninsula.

The story in the outstate edition of the *Blade* was the banner in the paper. In addition there was a sidebar on Simmons and his history of making contributions to the community. An editorial commended the Thompson Brakes chairman for his "compassion and leadership."

A little overdone, Kaufman thought, but then he did not know how Bob Harrison, the *Blade* publisher, when pressured by Simmons, decided to placate the Thompson Brakes chairman.

Then a headline on a short story, highlighted within a box, caught his eye. It read:

Award-Winning Reporter
Resigns from the Blade

The *Detroit Blade* has announced the resignation of Susan K. Merriman, an award-winning investigative reporter, effective immediately.

Joseph Brennan, the paper's managing editor, said that Merriman resigned after reports that she had a personal relationship with Tim Kaufman, vice president of corporate communications at Thompson Brakes, Inc.

"Ms. Merriman was assigned to cover charges that Thompson Brakes was aware that its employees were at risk in contracting cancer from exposure to asbestos, but that the company did not inform employees or offer them any protection," said Brennan.

"She resigned because her relationship with Mr. Kaufman, the spokesperson for the company, gives the appearance of a conflict of interest. We accept her resignation with regret. Her work at the *Blade* was outstanding and we stand by every word she wrote at the *Blade*, including her stories on the Thompson Brakes asbestos crisis. However, we agree that journalists must avoid not only actual conflicts of interest, but also the mere appearance of potential conflicts. We express our gratitude to her for her contributions and wish her well in whatever she plans to do in the future."

Kaufman felt sorry for Merriman, but he knew that the *Blade* had to write a story about Merriman, given the coverage in the *Herald*. Under the circumstances, he thought they handled her "resignation" well.

He turned his attention back to the main story, reading the quotes from his successor, Ruth Sanderson.

"We are a responsible company," she said. "We have always been a company which tries to do the right thing and we are pleased to do so again. This does not imply any guilt on the part of Thompson Brakes. We did this entirely on our own. There was no pressure from anyone."

Kaufman could not help but smile; exactly what he would have said.

I guess they had a noose her size in stock, he thought.

EPILOGUE

George C.L. Simmons, Jr.: After the Board approved establishing a $35 million fund for cancer victims and for survivors of employees who died of the disease, he received a raise from the board. At the next shareholders' meeting, one of the directors commended the chairman for his "outstanding leadership on a very sensitive issue. George Simmons handled this issue with business acumen and compassion for the employees."

In the news story about the fund, the company also reported that Glen Johnston, former vice president of environment and health, had resigned to "pursue other business interests." Sources who wished to remain anonymous were quoted in the paper stating that Johnston had misled management on the history of the asbestos issue, that management had never really understood the full extent of the problem.

Simmons received the Civic League's award and the *Blade* published this story on page one as well.

A year later, however, Simmons unexpectedly announced his intention to retire. The financial performance of the company continued to flounder and sources reported that the chairman had been forced to resign. "Thompson Brakes never recovered from the financial and PR disaster of the asbestos controversy," they were quoted as saying.

At the time of Simmons' resignation, the company's stock traded at 13-1/4, about a third of the value of the stock five years earlier and half of its book value, making it a candidate for a takeover. The pressure was intense on the board to make a change, and the directors acted accordingly. The day Simmons resigned, the stock rose 2-1/2 points.

Thompson Brakes also reported that it settled investor class action lawsuits, which charged the company with misleading investors, out of court for $16 million. The company said the settlements were not an implication of guilt. Instead, Thompson Brakes said it wanted to avoid protracted litigation with "corresponding legal costs that could total millions of dollars."

In the company's proxy statement, Thompson Brakes said that Simmons would continue to serve "as a consultant" to the company and receive $500,000 a year for five years. Including his stock, stock options and bonuses, Simmons left Thompson Brakes with an $18 million package.

Alfred Hawthorne: Like Simmons, he was rewarded with a raise and also was promoted. Before his resignation, Simmons gave his legal counsel the additional title of executive vice president and commended him for his "sophisticated legal insights, which helped bring the asbestos issue to such a successful conclusion."

But with Simmons' resignation, Hawthorne's future at Thompson Brakes was in doubt and he sought other employment. He received several offers for senior positions in legal departments at other major corporations, ultimately joining a prestigious law firm.

Louis Salter: He continued as vice president of security but, in a reorganization, was assigned to report to the legal department Hawthorne would leave. Salter did not like that – he hated lawyers – but given the circumstances, he accepted the reassignment as gracefully as possible.

Judy Robertson: A few days after she completed the employee cutback plan for Simmons, she was informed, in the written notice she helped draft for the employees affected by the "downsizing," that she was part of the layoff. She was devastated by the news, ultimately needing counseling. During her therapy, she remained unemployed while searching for a management position in a corporate human resource department.

John Barrister: After serving as acting vice president of environment and health for several months, he was elected vice president by the board of directors.

Steve Marks: He was elected a vice president at the union's national office in Washington, D.C. He would become a major power in union politics.

Sue Merriman: She continued to feel guilty over her role in the suicide of Judge Faulkner. She never fully recovered emotionally or psychologically. She agreed with much of what Kaufman had said about the media and became disenchanted with journalism. After resigning from the *Blade*, she enrolled in the graduate school at Ohio State University where she studied philosophy while working as a manager in a bookstore. While she liked Kaufman very much, against his protestations, she broke off the relationship, stating she needed to start over.

Tim Kaufman: He was unemployed for several months before deciding to seek a job as a university journalism instructor in Michigan's Upper Peninsula. He shared some of Joseph Brennan's idealism and hoped to "make a difference with young students." He wanted to "get out of the rat race" and he had always enjoyed Michigan's U.P.

Angie Ferguson: Eight months after Dr. Sobel's diagnosis, Paul Ferguson died. Under the conditions of the Thompson Brakes fund, she would receive payments of about $1,000 a month for eight years. With a part-time job to supplement the $12,000 annual compensation, she worked hard to make ends meet, but she managed. Ferguson's funeral was attended by Angie, the Ferguson children, other family members, widows of Thompson Brakes employees who had suffered similar fates and Steve Marks. No one from Thompson Brakes' management attended the funeral.

ABOUT THE AUTHOR

Berl Falbaum has a diversified background in communications, having served in executive positions in the media, politics and business. He also has taught journalism and public relations at Wayne State and Oakland Universities in Michigan since 1968.

He began his career as a reporter for The Detroit News *and served as chief of its City-County Bureau before resigning to become administrative aide to Michigan's lieutenant governor.*

His four-year career in politics was followed by 15 years in executive positions in three major corporations where he handled a variety of communication responsibilities, including media relations, strategic planning, investor relations and speechwriting.

In 1989, he founded his own public relations company, Falbaum & Associates.

Falbaum has spoken and written extensively on the media and the coverage of public affairs, and he is the author of Just for Fun, The Anchor, Leo & Friends *and* The Definitive Guide to Organizational Backstabbing.

He and his wife, Phyllis, live in West Bloomfield, Michigan. They have two daughters, Julie and Amy.